GRAND, DEATH, AUTO

BOOK #14 IN THE KIKI LOWENSTEIN MYSTERY SERIES

JOANNA CAMPBELL SLAN

spot on publishing

Joanna Campbell Slan

Spot On Publishing

9307 SE Olympus Street

Hobe Sound FL 33455 / USA

http://www.SpotOnPublishing.org

http://www.JoannaSlan.com

Revised 09/03/2020

Covers: http://www.WickedSmartDesigns.com

Grand, Death, Auto: Book #14 in the Kiki Lowenstein Mystery Series by Joanna Campbell Slan. – 1st ed.

ISBN: 978-1697173277

CONTENTS

1

"There's a cop in our kitchen," said my daughter, Anya. I noticed with surprise that she was wearing a pink sweater over her favorite floral dress. That dress had been in the dirty clothes hamper last night, but she wanted to wear it today, so she'd gotten up early to wash and dry it. The fact she'd taken responsibility for the chore herself brought a smile to my face. My oldest child was growing up. In fact, her birthday was three months away. She would be turning fourteen.

The years had flown by!

"Oh, a cop in the kitchen? The one I married?" I winked at Anya over the head of her youngest brother, Ty. My five-month-old has three adorable wispy curls of brown hair on his otherwise bald pate. Wearing a fresh diaper and a dusting of baby powder, he was ready for his breakfast bowl of warm rice cereal topped with chopped bananas. Ty is still nursing at night, but he's been eagerly exploring real food for a week or so.

"Nope." Anya rolled her eyes at my joke. "That cop doesn't ring the doorbell. Not anymore, at least. He has his own key. Or did you notice?"

"I did."

A lot has changed in our lives since Detective Chad Detweiler made his first appearance. Notably there have been births, deaths, weddings, and funerals. Plus investigations. Can't forget those.

There's also been my daughter's journey into the teenage years, and all the emotional ups and downs. Most of the time, she's a miniature adult, but once in a while, she's just a tall toddler. In the filtered light of the upstairs hallway, Anya's features were hard to make out, although her platinum blonde hair picked up the sunbeams and glowed like a halo.

"Come here, sweetie." I motioned with my free hand. Anya backed up to me. While I jiggled Ty on one hip, I grabbed the tag sticking up in the back of her sweater and smoothed it down. "A strange cop is in the kitchen? What else is new?"

I tried to sound unconcerned. Being married to a police detective is new to me. The presence in my home of men and women carrying firearms takes a bit of getting used to, and I'm not quite there ... yet. Anya's late father was a real estate developer. If you'd have asked me, I would have told you that real estate developers don't carry guns. I was wrong. Dead wrong.

"This new guy is a cop from Illinois. One I haven't seen before." In the six months since Detweiler and I've been married, my daughter has become rather blasé about LEOs (Law Enforcement Officers) showing up at our house. Most of them show up at dinnertime because Bronwyn Macavity, aka "Brawny", our Scot nanny, is a fabulous cook whose reputation has become legend in the St. Louis County Police Department.

"Right. I wonder who it is. I guess we'll find out soon enough. Erik? Honey, come on. If you don't hurry, you'll be late to school." I opened the door to my middle child's room. Erik's back was to me, and I could tell he was trying to buckle his leather belt. He'd gotten it for his sixth birthday. The new addition to his wardrobe has caused all sorts of problems. The dexterity it demands often leaves Erik frustrated. He needs a head start when nature calls. After two accidents, I wanted to toss the belt in the trash, but my son loves his new fashion accessory.

"Ta-da." Erik twirled around to show off his achievement. For a little guy, threading a belt through all the loops and buckling it is a major victory. Anya and I both cheered for the kid. "Bravo! Way to go! High five, buddy."

While I carried Ty down the stairs, Anya took Erik's hand. Soon he would be too grown up for holding onto his sister. I hoped that Erik and Anya would remain close as the years rolled along.

At the foot of the stairs, the sweet fragrance of petunias and freshly mowed grass drifted toward us. So did the strident male voices. I'm getting used to police business being conducted under my roof, but the tone of the conversation told me this visit was different. Anya, Erik, and I hesitated before walking into the kitchen.

"I'm only asking—" the visitor began.

"No. She's not a cop, and you can't guarantee—"

Yes, there was a problem, but it could wait. I needed to feed my kids breakfast and get them off to school. "Go on," I said as I gave Anya a tiny push forward. She led Erik into the kitchen and I followed to the sound of chairs being scooted back from the table.

Our visitor jumped to his feet, as did my husband. The stranger had the squat body of an MMA fighter, eyes the color of wet shale, and a face shaped like a busted up shoebox. This cop had seen his share of rough times. He gave me a once-over, studying me from head to toe, while I did the same to him. I took particular note of his Illinois State Police baseball cap. Because we live across the river in a suburb of St. Louis, Missouri, my curiosity was piqued.

My husband made the introductions. "Honey? This is an old classmate, Detective Randall Schultz. He's retired from the Illinois State Police."

I stepped forward to say, "I'm Kiki, and this is Ty, our youngest."

"Call me Schultz," our guest said while staring at the baby and extending his hand to me. His shake was firm but not unkind.

Detweiler continued the introductions, "Schultz this is my daughter, Anya. My son, Erik—"

"Gina's kid?" Schultz's jaw dropped. "I heard rumors. Geez. I didn't believe them."

"Yes, well ..." Detweiler's tone was evasive.

But Schultz was far too astonished. He rambled on, "Man, that's low. Really low. And then she took off?"

Detweiler made a swift slice-across-the-neck gesture with his index finger, a warning for our visitor to shut up. It took Schultz a minute, but he finally caught on that talking about Gina, Detweiler's deceased first wife, was not appropriate. Especially in front of Erik, her mixed-race son, the boy she'd begged us to adopt in a letter from the grave.

Still, Schultz couldn't help himself. He kept staring at our oldest son.

I couldn't blame the man. There's that famous tune in *Sesame Street* where the announcer asks which item doesn't belong in the set. Our family could have been featured on that *Sesame Street* segment. Anya is as pale as an iceberg. I'm blonde with blue eyes. Detweiler has dark blond hair and green eyes. Ty has green eyes and sandy brown hair. Erik is mixed race. His skin is the color of a Starbucks' caramel macchiato, and his curls are red.

Schultz rocked on his heels as he worked through the logistics. Since Gina was a striking redhead with alabaster skin, it's easy to figure out that Gina got pregnant while cheating on Detweiler. Erik is the result of her illicit relationship with a black cop, a man who'd been a mentor and instructor to both Detweiler and Schultz.

"That's just hard to credit," Schultz said while staring at Erik.

At that precise moment, the *clomp-clomp-clomp* of shoes interrupted the visit. Usually Brawny doesn't make much noise. This morning I was glad for the interruption when she came down the hall that separated our kitchen from the laundry room and garage. Right behind the nanny was our harlequin Great Dane, Gracie.

My husband had a twinkle in his eye as the nanny and the dog approached. I could tell he was laughing at Schultz's astonished reaction. But my husband didn't forget his manners. He said, "Brawny? This is Detective Randall Schultz, retired. An old friend of mine. Schultz, this is our nanny, Bronwyn Macavity. Bronwyn served in the SRR, the Special Reconnaissance Regiment. That's a British special forces unit."

"You don't say." The retired detective offered our nanny his hand. She responded with a strong shake. Schultz went from staring at Erik to staring at Brawny. Or maybe he was intrigued by her outfit. She wore a plaid skirt fastened with a gold pin, a white blouse, knee socks, and brogues. A sporran, the traditional fur-covered pouch that hangs from the belt, was part of her ensemble.

"And this is our dog, Gracie." Detweiler looked down at our black-and-white giant with her sweet floppy ears. "Gracie, shake."

The big dog obediently offered her paw.

Once Schultz recovered from the multitude of surprises, I could see him trying to figure out how a detective managed to afford such highly skilled live-in help. The answer was none of his business.

Brawny nodded at the men. In her thick Scotch accent, she said, "Excuse me, gentlemen. Kiki? I was thinking I'd treat the bairns to breakfast at McDonald's. Is that all right with ye?"

I hesitated, because I don't like the kids eating fast food, but a gleam in Brawny's eyes suggested she knew best. At forty-two, Brawny is technically middle-aged, but she has the youthful build of an athlete. She works out every morning with my husband. Their friendly competition has been a boon to Detweiler, as she's pushed him into terrific shape. There's nothing soft and fuzzy about Bronwyn Macavity, except when she looks at our children. Then her whole demeanor changes and her eyes become suffused with love. No doubt about it, she would lay down her life for my babies. On this particular morning, she'd heard enough of Detweiler's conversation with our guest to surmise that the situation in the kitchen wasn't appropriate for my kids.

With that unerring instinct all children have, Anya realized she could press her advantage. She looked from Brawny to me and back to Brawny and said, "Coffee?"

That's another food choice I don't like my kids to make. But today it wasn't a battle worth fighting.

"Yes, sweetheart. This morning you can have coffee," I said.

"McDonald's!" Erik whooped with joy.

"McDonald's." Anya shrugged.

"'Tis a rare treat. However, today's a good day for it." Brawny sealed the deal.

Detweiler chimed in, "Kids? Do you have everything you need for school?"

Of course, they did.

I gave Anya a kiss and leaned down to plant a smooch on Erik's forehead. "You two be good for Brawny."

"We will," Anya and Erik said in one voice.

"Why don't I take the young master?" Brawny opened her arms to Ty. "The weather's balmy. He'll enjoy the ride."

I handed off my baby.

"We'll be back." With that, Brawny marched our crew down the hallway to the garage.

I stood in the kitchen, staring after them, with my heart in my throat. I love my kids so much. Gracie left Detweiler's side and trotted over to me. She sat down at my feet and leaned her whole body against my legs. That was her way of offering comfort. I absent-mindedly reached down and fondled her ears.

It took me a minute to tear myself away from the empty hallway.

"Kiki?" Detweiler called to me. "Honey? Brawny made a batch of cinnamon rolls. They're still warm. Can I pour you a cup of coffee? We saved a seat for you."

That was his way of asking me to join him and Detective Schultz.

2

"You're aware, I take it, of the rash of teen suicides we've had in Jarvis Township?" Schultz started talking as soon as I sat down. He didn't even wait for Detweiler to fill my mug with steaming hazelnut coffee.

"Who isn't?" I poured fresh cream into my coffee and added two spoons of sugar. Every night the news led off with another horror story. So far, seven kids had taken their own lives. One at a time. Seven different methodologies. Two others had tried to commit suicide but had been unsuccessful. That didn't include one girl who was in the hospital in a coma.

"Yes, the suicides have been well-publicized," Schultz said. He sipped his coffee and looked me in the eyes. "As you might imagine, the state police are doing everything possible to track down what's behind all this. They've even brought me out of retirement as a consultant to help them figure it out."

His phrasing seemed odd. I repeated his words, "What's behind this?"

"Uh-huh."

"I don't understand. According to the news, this is one of

those unfortunate situations where kids copy each other. Like lemmings follow each other off of a cliff."

"That's an urban myth," my husband explained. "They don't do that, honey."

"Oh."

Schultz nodded at me slowly. "I know what you mean. In most instances, that's exactly what happens. The kids influence each other. But I believe there's something else happening in Jarvis Township. Something more ... organized and targeted."

"You're thinking these kids were killed?" I blurted without censoring myself.

"No," he hurried to say. "Well, maybe not. We can't tell. I'm worried that someone's working behind the scenes. Manipulating these kids. Encouraging them."

"W-w-what?" I stuttered. "Encouraging teens to hurt themselves on purpose?"

"Yes." Schultz winced. "You might have seen the news about that girl who talked a boy into killing himself. There was also that woman who pretended to be a teen and told her daughter's classmate she was better off dead. So then the classmate committed suicide. I'm worried there's someone evil out there who knows these kids well enough to manipulate them."

Surely, there'd been a mistake.

"But those situations you just described were one-offs. Oddities. You're talking about a whole bunch of kids killing themselves over at Jarvis Township High School."

"Right. But the analysts have studied other communities with high suicide rates among teens. None of them come close to this. This is the worst sort of anomaly you can imagine, and it's happening in a school with only 325 students!"

I reached for one of the cinnamon rolls. The numbers tumbled around in my head. Seven suicides and ten attempts in a student body of 325. That seemed like a lot of carnage to me.

Schultz must have read my mind. "It's bad. When experts ran the numbers, they were stunned. Especially given that this is a sparsely populated rural township. In addition, the rate of self-harm has gone up exponentially."

"I doubt that there's any one person behind this. Social media has been weaponized," Detweiler said. "Kids get confused by online influencers. What the influencers present an idealized version of life. When teens compare that ideal to their own lives, they panic. One thing leads to another. It doesn't take much to push a sensitive kid over the edge."

"Whether it's one person or two or a group, we need to figure out what's driving this." Schultz grabbed a cinnamon roll and tore it to pieces.

"I think these kids are being encouraged to take their own lives. I don't know how. I don't know who. I don't know why or when," our guest said. "But I don't think these problems are happening in a vacuum."

"What do the parents say?" Detweiler got up. He came back with the coffee pot and refilled all our cups. As my husband sat down, I pushed the pitcher of cream toward our visitor. Detweiler continued, "I assume you've interviewed friends, classmates, siblings, and neighbors."

The detective's spoon clanked against his mug as he mixed several spoons of sugar into his drink. "Of course. Nobody reports seeing or hearing any suspicious interactions. In fact, it's really weird. Those close to the victims tell us that in the weeks leading up to the attempts, these kids had never been happier. Ever. That's one of the reasons parents are so distraught. These suicide attempts seem to come out of nowhere. The families are totally blindsided."

"Seven kids?" I repeated.

"Might even be nine. Could be ten. Or eleven. We're not sure. Two more teens have died in separate suspicious car crashes. No weather complications, no speeding, no unfamiliar stretches of highway, no treacherous roads, nada. There have also been a rash of accidents. Self-harm incidents. One case of alcohol poisoning. Another kid locked himself in the garage with the car running. Luckily, his mom found him in time."

This was a lot worse than the media had reported.

"And you're sure this isn't of those copycat thingies? I've read about suicide epidemics among young people," I said.

Schultz shook his head. "I don't think so. We hired a psychiatrist to conduct forensic examinations of the personal belongings of three of the victims. He's believes these deaths were triggered."

"How can he make a judgment call like that?" I asked. "Today there are so many ways that kids can have a secret online life. They could have used the family computer. Or gone to an Internet cafe. Or bought a throw-away phone."

Schultz studied me. "All I know is that we've lost seven kids. Maybe even more. All in four weeks. We have a problem over in Illinois. And that's why I'm here. I heard through the grapevine that Chad Detweiler's new wife ..."

I bristled at that adjective "new." Schultz made it sound like I was an appliance brought in to replace an older model. Yes, my husband had been married twice before. Erik's mother Gina had been Detweiler's first wife, his high school sweetheart, and she'd cheated on him. Then he married Brenda, who became a drug addict. Nothing like that was going to happen again. No way. I resented the fact Schultz made it sound like I was one in an ongoing parade. I didn't like it, and I wasn't going to stand for it.

"His current, his only, and his last wife." I folded my arms over my chest. A hint of a smile flitted across my husband's face.

"Uh, right." Schultz was flummoxed. He hadn't counted on me standing up for myself. "No offense meant."

I didn't respond with the expected, "None taken." Instead, I gave him an icy stare. To my astonishment, he burst into laughter.

"I'd heard you are a pistol. No pun intended. Good for you. That's why I'm here. The cops on your side of the river sing your praises. They say you've got moxie. You aren't afraid of anything. Nothing gets past you. I'm hoping that's true because I need your help. Unofficially, of course."

"Okay. I'm listening."

"I've heard you're pretty good with arts and crafts. Is that right? The art teacher at Jarvis Township High School will be going on maternity leave next week. I was hoping you could take her place as an observer until school's out. That's less than three weeks away. You won't be in any danger. You would have to apply for the job, filling out all the paperwork, but I can assure you that if you apply, you'll be hired. You would be paid like any other substitute teacher. Do you know enough to keep the students busy for two weeks more or less?"

"That's easy—" I started to say, but my husband interrupted.

"I've already told Schultz the answer was no. Absolutely no." Detweiler reached over and took my hand.

That steamed my coffee. After years of being treated like a doormat in my marriage with my late husband, George Lowenstein, I was not about to let my current husband boss me around. On the other hand, I wanted to make an informed decision. There had to be a balance.

"Excuse us a minute please, Schultz." Looking at my husband, I stood up and tilted my head toward the hallway.

Detweiler got to his feet reluctantly. I don't often get mad at him, but when I do, it's a doozy. My husband marched dutifully behind me as I led the way to his office. Once I closed the door, he threw up both hands in a gesture of surrender. "Honey—"

"Don't you 'honey' me." I sounded like a character in a TV sitcom.

He closed his eyes and heaved a world-weary sigh. "Sorry. I know better. The second the words were out of my mouth, I realized how you would take them. I screwed up. Please forgive me."

His apology took the fight right out of me. I didn't protest when he tried to hug me. He whispered, "I was being overly protective. I've got a bad feeling about what's happening, and I don't want you in the middle of it."

I relaxed into him. I love the feel of his body. The way he held me close made every cell inside me sparkle with joy.

He sighed and added, "The logistics would be a nightmare."

He had a point. With three kids, I couldn't walk out the door on the spur of the moment. Since Ty was born, I've gained a whole new respect for Napoleon. He moved entire armies across great distances. Getting three kids across town is challenging enough for me and I have a nanny!

And I almost told Schultz, "I'll do it!" What was I thinking?

Maybe I was trying to escape. As much as I love having a brood of three, there are days when I feel totally drained.. Worst of all, I don't like to share how I feel. To admit that motherhood isn't always the most fun job in the world would somehow diminish me. I work with moms all day long in my scrapbooking and craft store, Time in a Bottle. My clientele, scrapbookers and crafters, are fabulous mothers who are dedicated to their kids. Yesterday, I helped a young mom put together an album memorializing her stillborn child. How could I ever tell her that I wasn't looking forward to going home because my nanny had the night off? I couldn't.

As this rattled through my head and I realized I wasn't really angry with Detweiler. Sure, he'd overstepped his boundaries. The bigger problem was that I needed a break from my family, and the police officer in the kitchen had offered me a way to get one.

"You're right, of course. The logistics alone make helping

Schultz impossible." I kissed Detweiler. Not a passionate kiss, but a quick, "I love you."

"I promise not to speak for you again," Detweiler said. "You're an adult. You're capable of making your own decisions." He hugged me and let me go.

"Yup." I took his hand. Together we walked back into the kitchen.

Detweiler pulled my chair out for me. Schultz had a hopeful expression in his eyes. That faded when I said, "Please accept my regrets. You're dealing with a tragic situation, but I can't help you. The logistics are impossible. We have two kids who are looking forward to their summer vacation. I'm still breastfeeding our baby. I have a business to run." The weight of my responsibilities came tumbling down all around me. "My presence would be a distraction at best."

Schultz's entire demeanor changed. Sitting there with drooping shoulders, he toyed with the spoon he'd used to stir his coffee. The utensil left a brown liquid splotch on his paper napkin. He said, "It was a long shot, but I had to give it a try."

I excused myself to get ready for work. Not long after, my husband showed his friend the door.

As I DROVE to Time in a Bottle, I thought about Schultz's request. Over the years, I'd met many people who've lost loved ones to suicide. Even though I know that suicide is an act of desperation by a person who is in incredible psychological pain, a voice inside me screams, "That's so selfish!" The pain that suicide victims inflict on those they leave behind is horrific.

How were the parents of the young suicide victims in Illinois handling their grief? If they were like the surviving family members I'd met, their souls had been torn into confetti-sized pieces and scattered. Their guilt was tremendous. One mother who visited my store kept repeating, "If only I had called her thirty minutes earlier!" Surviving family members seemed doomed to keep asking themselves over and over again, "What if?"

With these gloomy thoughts in my head, I pulled into my usual parking space a half an hour before the store opened. Gracie sat next to me in the passenger seat. She has been coming to Time in a Bottle ever since I adopted her. Most of the day, she snoozes in the back room.

Two of my coworkers had arrived before me. They were kind enough to put on a pot of Kaldi's coffee. Kaldi's is a local chain. Although that's part of their appeal, I love their coffee because it's fabulous. Truly it is.

The back room was empty when I walked in. That could only mean that my coworkers were busy out on the sales floor. After hanging my purse on a hook and putting Gracie in her doggie playpen, I picked up her water bowl, washed the Pyrex glass container with dish soap, rinsed, and refilled it. Simple tasks create a soothing rhythm, a familiar pattern that can be calming. After I set the bowl in her doggy playpen, I poured my third cup of coffee for the day. Dosing it liberally with cream and Stevia, I reviewed what Schultz had told us.

I pulled a chair over to the table we use for our breaks and wondered: What would I do if Anya's middle school had an epidemic of suicides? Would I try to help track down the cause? Or would I have said no, like I did this morning? Had I made the right decision? Should I have agreed to help Schultz? I was so caught up in arguing with myself that I didn't notice my friend and second-in-command, Clancy Whitehead, until she waved a hand in my face.

"Kiki? Hello? Where are you? I've been talking to you for five minutes. Anybody home? Here's the detail sheet from yesterday's sales." She took the chair next to mine and handed me the register tape.

I shook my head the way a dog does after a bath. "Sorry."

"Spill it." Clancy's eyes drilled into me. My pal is a Jackie Kennedy look-alike who dresses with a classic flair. In my imagination, Jackie Kennedy must have had a touch of OCD, because Clancy certainly does. She goes through hand sanitizer the way an allergy sufferer goes through tissues. Clancy asked, "What's going on in that curly-haired head of yours?"

"Just a lot on my mind," I said. "That's all."

"Good morning, Kiki," said Laurel Wilkins Riley as she walked in from the sales floor. Laurel is my third-in-command. I'd forgotten she was coming in early to take an inventory of our paper selection. Laurel is drop-dead gorgeous, and she's three months pregnant. She's a terrific salesperson and my customers love her.

Realizing that Clancy was staring at me, Laurel asked, "What's up?"

"Nothing," I lied.

"Something. And she's not telling us." Clancy frowned at me.

"When I have something to tell you, I will. How's that?" I smiled at my two dear friends.

"Sounds fair to me," said Laurel.

Clancy only grunted.

3

---

*T*he store was busy all day. I ate half a tuna fish salad sandwich and a bag of baked chips while on my feet, waiting on customers. Grabbing a bite here and there is not my preferred way to eat. However, Laurel had to leave early for a doctor's appointment. Clancy was busy in the back, placing orders for new merchandise. Margit Eichen, the other full-time worker, had the day off.

We were missing our part-timers. Rebekkah Goldfader, daughter of the store's founder, was taking her finals at Washington University. My sister Catherine has a new full-time job working at a day care facility.

The responsibility fell to me to greet guests, work with them, help them make their selections, and ring up their purchases.

At three twenty, I loaded Gracie in the car and went to pick up Erik and Anya. Today was a big day, and I knew they would be excited. We were going to visit Sheila and Robbie Holmes, the kids' grandparents. Sheila is the mother of my late first husband, George Lowenstein. Robbie is Detweiler's boss and the chief of the St. Louis County Police Department, although he's recently taken time off. Sheila suffers from alcohol addiction.

Robbie forced her to get treatment in Palm Springs, California. That was six months ago. Sheila recently "graduated" from a halfway house. This would be our family's first visit with them since she completed her treatment program.

Sheila is the reason that I was driving to CALA, the Charles and Anne Lindbergh Academy, where Erik and Anya are enrolled. Generations of Lowensteins have gone there. CALA is a swanky private school that's more than a century old. The central building sits on nearly 100 acres of wooded land. With its grandiose white columns and brick facade, the place almost screams, "Old money!"

When Anya turned five, Sheila insisted that her granddaughter attend the school as a legacy student. Sheila even offered to pay the thirty-grand yearly tuition. I would have been nuts to turn her down because CALA has a terrific academic program. When Detweiler and I adopted Erik, we figured that he would have to attend a local public school—no big deal. But having kids at two schools with two different schedules would have made coordinating school vacations and daily transportation a nightmare. I told Sheila what was happening.

She pitched a fit in the headmaster's office and bullied him into accepting Erik Detweiler as a legacy student as well. When Sheila wants something, nothing stands in her way. Especially if that roadblock takes the form of a hapless authority figure citing senseless rules.

Even the students realize CALA is prestigious. Like her schoolmates, Anya doesn't walk as much as swagger to our car, doing her best to prove that she's totally independent when, of course, she's anything but. She's already looking forward to getting her driver's license. The thought of her behind the wheel of a car makes me woozy. What people call St. Louis is really a sprawling bi-state area, spread out over Missouri and Illinois. Our metropolis encompasses 8,458 square miles. The various municipalities are situated on hills and terraces overlooking the Mississippi River. In the spring, we can have hail the size of baseballs. In the summer, we have heavy rains and flooding. In the winter, we get treacherous black ice, ice storms, sleet, and snow. As a result, the highways going back and forth from Illinois (Land of Lincoln) to Missouri (Gateway to the West) are eternally under construction. None of this is conducive to safe driving, particularly for beginners.

I tell myself that I'll worry about that when the time comes. Not today. That's my mantra: Not today.

Currently, I share school pickup duty with Brawny. Although carpool chops up my work day, I enjoy having this "alone time" with my children. Before Erik came along, Anya and I used to have our best conversations in the car. Erik's arrival has changed that, somewhat. So has the addition of Baby Ty. The intimate conversations that Anya and I used to enjoy have dried up like puddles in the sun. With the addition of two more children, I'm more distracted than ever, and life happens at a faster pace. I really, really, really try to make time to be alone with Anya, but that's happening less and less frequently. Even when we plan our mother and daughter time well in advance, a crisis inevitably occurs. Take the other evening for example. Anya and I had written "movie night" on the calendar in purple ink. We'd picked a girlie theme, settled in her room with popcorn and soft drinks, and closed the door. All was well until we heard a scream from the bathroom down the hall.

Detweiler was in trouble. Big, brown trouble. He'd been bathing Ty in the sink on the bathroom counter when the baby grunted, grimaced, and groaned. Those were warning signs from the top end of the naked infant. The bottom end expelled a geyser of hot poop. The smelly mess covered one entire wall of the bathroom. It also dripped down onto the floor. Detweiler had no choice but to keep holding a smelly baby and scream for help. When I got there, the poor man was gagging and trying not to puke.

As interruptions go, that was a real show stopper. The clean-up took so long that movie night had to be canceled.

Despite fewer opportunities to be alone with Anya, I do my best to notice the offhand comments she weaves into larger conversations. These are casual remarks. Flippant, and oh-so-easy to overlook.

Other mothers have told me that their teens do this, too. The kids float trial balloons and act like they don't care when the sad truth is the message should have been written on a billboard in huge letters. Being a vigilant parent takes a lot of energy. Admittedly, with three busy kids and a business, I'm chronically tired. I hope that an abundance of love will make up for my deficits. That's the one thing I have in a never-ending supply, my love for my family.

I have to pay a lot of attention to Erik, too, even though he's only six. He's bright enough to understand things that go over the heads of his peers. He's also insecure. That makes sense because his mother and stepfather died fairly recently. This peculiar combination of intelligence and neediness means that he listens very carefully to our conversations and internalizes what he hears. He's also incredibly clingy. Anya doesn't complain, but I know there are times when she wishes she had me all to herself . . . with one exception.

Anya doesn't mind sharing me with Gracie. I often call Gracie my favorite mistake. When I rescued her, the last thing I needed was a 130-pound mouth to feed. But Gracie has been a saving grace. She's my kids' best friend, a protector of the first order, and a never-ending supplier of sloppy affection. Because she comes to work with me, Gracie rides along during carpool. Erik shares the back seat with the big dog. That makes Gracie instantly available for much needed after-school cuddling.

All in all, Erik's transition to CALA has gone well. One reason is that his teacher, Maggie Earhart, is a longtime friend of mine. She knows Erik's backstory, and she's sympathetic to his losses. Maggie's naturally an empathetic person, and she's especially tuned into our little boy.

Anya had already climbed in and buckled up when Maggie surprised me by walking Erik to the car. Typically, she uses the time after school to get her classroom ready for the next day. After helping Erik climb into the back seat, Maggie came around to the driver's side to say hi.

Maggie has a sturdiness about her. That solid quality is part of her personality. It's underscored by her no-frills wardrobe. I don't think I've ever seen her in anything soft, flowing, or floral. I rolled down the car window to talk. "Hey, Maggie. Haven't seen you in a while. How're you doing?"

"I'm fine and Erik's doing well, too." She thumped her knuckles against the car door as a signal I could drive away but I had another agenda.

"A quick word," I said. "You've heard about the problems they're having at Jarvis Township High School, right?"

"Uh-huh," she said. "We had a meeting today. Administration has warned us to be vigilant. *Things* like that are contagious, for lack of a better word." She'd said "things" instead of "suicides" with a nod toward Erik. I understood she was trying to protect my child. I appreciated her thoughtfulness, but I also was confused.

I asked, "Contagious? What exactly do you mean by that?"

Maggie narrowed her eyes and stared hard at me. With a sigh of exasperation, she said, "That sort of problem can spread from Illinois to here."

It could spread? Was she warning me that CALA might have its own rash of suicides? With only five days left in the CALA school year? It didn't seem possible, and yet...

I whispered the word, "Really?"

She nodded. "Exactly. That's why they were warning us."

From the passenger seat, Anya followed our conversation intently. She spoke softly, "A couple of juniors were talking about it at lunch. They think suicide can be cool. Romantic even."

"Romantic?" I looked at Anya like she'd sprouted horns. I couldn't believe my ears. "Do they have any idea how ugly someone looks after ...?"

I caught myself in time.

Maggie's expression changed from smug to shocked.

I swallowed hard. This had to be a misunderstanding. My beautiful, vibrant daughter was telling us she thought suicide was romantic? No way!

"You need to nip that in the bud, Kiki," Maggie said quietly. She's always the first to tell you what to do. Today, I had a hard time appreciating that quality.

The car behind me tapped its horn with impatience. I needed to move.

"Thanks, Maggie," I said as I checked my side and rearview windows. When I knew it was safe, I pulled into the traffic heading away from the school.

After merging onto Highway 40, I used the rearview mirror and checked on Erik in the back seat. He was leaning against Gracie with his eyes shut. A silver strand of drool dripped from his mouth. This seemed like the perfect time for a teaching moment with Anya. I hoped so.

"So, tell me more, honey. I would like to hear what your friends are saying about the problems at Jarvis Township High School."

As often happens when I bring up a thorny subject, Anya became fascinated by the passing scenery. "Just the usual stuff."

"Indulge me. I'm out of the loop. What is the usual stuff?"

"The cool kids think it's neat. Everybody's talking about it. Lynn Melon? She used to be on the golf team. She knows all about people committing suicide. I mean she knows everything! Her cousin up in Michigan had a best friend who committed suicide while Lynn was there on vacation. Lynn got to go with her cousin to the funeral. Lynn told everyone what happened. It was so neat. See, this girl liked this boy. But the boy was really popular, and he didn't pay any attention to her. So she killed herself. Then at the funeral, the popular boy threw himself on the coffin and cried his eyes out. They had to drag him away. Lynn said it was like a scene out of *Romeo and Juliet*. So romantic!"

I wanted to shriek, "Are you out of your mind?" But if I over-reacted, Anya would clam up. I proceeded cautiously by asking, "So you're convinced Lynn knows all about suicide. And what did your friends say? Did they think what happened was cool? Or romantic?"

I nearly choked over that last word.

"Yes," Anya said with a heartfelt sigh. "Lynn says that the dead girl left a note for the popular boy, telling him how much she loved him. After he read it, that's when he felt guilty. Just terrible. That's why he threw himself on the coffin. Everyone was watching when he did it. I think that's pretty cool. I mean, he ignored her and now he's sorry. Isn't that romantic?"

No, I wanted to yell, that is not at all romantic. Not even remotely. That poor boy will be messed up for life—and why? Because a girl liked him and he didn't like her back? Was that fair to him?

Instead of yelling, I considered carefully what I wanted to say. I wanted to be honest—and I didn't want to shut Anya down. I could *kind of* understand what my daughter was getting at. If I put myself in her thirteen-year-old head, I could imagine the drama of it all: the spurned girl, the popular boy, the tragic suicide, the poignant note, and the boy's subsequent very public remorse. Could you call that romantic? Maybe. Certainly there were definite *Romeo and Juliet* aspects to the story.

Anya shifted her position in the passenger seat. She was studying me and waiting for my response. I had to tread lightly. My goal was to keep the lines of communication open.

"I can certainly see why some people might call it romantic. All of us want to be loved desperately by another person. In that sense, yeah, there's a romantic element to what happened. But more accurately, I find it tragic. Absolutely tragic. To get a popular boy's attention, a girl kills herself? How does that work for her? She's not around to enjoy his attention, is she?"

Then I shut up. Silence can be a powerful tool.

"Hmmm." Anya went back to staring out the window. "I guess. I mean, that girl is gone, so even if he is madly in love with her *now*, what's the diff?"

"Right. It's not like the girl benefits from his guilt, does she? Anya, at the risk of sounding crass, you've seen dead animals. Roadkill? Little mice that our cats catch? That dead squirrel Gracie found in the backyard? You know how gross their bodies look. After you die, your body deteriorates. Is that romantic? I don't think so."

"Gross, Mom. Trust you to turn something romantic into something that makes me want to vomit."

"I thought we were having an honest conversation, honey. While I sound like a party-pooper, I'm just telling it to you straight."

With a shrug, Anya said, "Okay, I see what you mean."

"Honey, we're not talking Snow White here. That poor girl was not going to magically wake up, thanks to a kiss on the lips from that popular boy. After the funeral service, they closed the lid on that wooden box and lowered her into the ground."

"Moo-oom," Anya wailed.

"You know it's true. Remember your father's funeral? The casket was closed, but remember how we stood there in the sleet while they lowered it into the ground? Was that romantic? I think not. It was final and sad and not one bit pretty."

By then we'd arrived at Sheila and Robbie's house. In a perverse way, I hoped that Anya would bring up her strange view of romance to her grandmother. Sheila Lowenstein Holmes would set Anya straight. Sheila's good at straightening out people. Other people. It remained to be seen whether she had corrected her own course.

As I parked the car, I felt nervous. With one brief exception, we hadn't seen Sheila and Robbie for six months. That's how long she'd been receiving treatment for alcohol abuse. Robbie had chosen to stay near his wife while she was going through the program. They had missed a lot in six months, including the birth of Baby Ty. Of course, I'd sent photos, but that wasn't the same.

Before they'd left, we'd spent every Friday night celebrating Shabbat, the Jewish Sabbath, with Sheila and Robbie. This would be our first family get-together in six months. Brawny thoughtfully suggested that she bow out. I appreciated her sensitivity. In my mind, this was our chance to put our family back together. If all went as planned, this would be the first of many Friday nights when we would all be together again.

I wondered how my mother-in-law would look. Sheila has always prided herself on her appearance. She's naturally a regal woman whose white hair and denim-blue eyes are nothing short of arresting. However, alcoholism is not a pretty disease. Before Robbie took her to rehab in Palm Springs, California, she'd begun to look like a clownish version of herself. Even though booze was ruining her life, Sheila resisted the process of getting sober. She even went so far as to bribe a janitor to buy her vodka that she hid it in an empty Pine-Sol bottle. Fortu-

nately, the experts eventually wore her down. From Palm
Springs, she "graduated" to a halfway house in Texas. After a
month in Texas, her counselors felt she could continue her
recovery at home.

According to Robbie, rehab had definitely changed Sheila
for the better. She'd been using alcohol to run away from her
feelings and to drown her fear of being rejected. There'd been a
major breakthrough when she admitted to that she was scared
to death no one needed her anymore. Her own son, George, and
her first husband, Harry, were dead. I had remarried and had
Detweiler. Anya had both of us. Robbie had been self-sufficient
before he married Sheila. She didn't see any particular reason to
stay sober when being drunk was a lot more fun. It had taken
months of counseling, but the therapists finally managed to
drum it into her thick skull that her dependence on alcohol was
a problem and not a solution. Detweiler and I had flown to
Texas for a family counseling session. There we put all our
metaphorical cards on the table and explained that if she kept
drinking, we could no longer trust her with our children. So by
her own actions, she had precipitated the outcome that she was
most afraid of.

I'll never forget that awful meeting and how Sheila broke
down in sobs. Detweiler and I had agreed that no matter what
she did, we wouldn't back down. She knew we were serious—
and Anya means the world to Sheila. (She loves Erik, too, but
she's loved Anya longer.)

I wondered what this evening would be like. I had to believe
that Sheila had changed. A lot. Although I doubted that sobriety
had mellowed her acerbic personality.

All these thoughts were cluttering up my head while Anya
was still thinking about roadkill. She threw open her car door
and flounced out. "Mom, you are disgusting. Just plain gross."

To punctuate her point, she slammed the car door hard

before stalking off. Erik slowly blinked himself awake. I got out of the car. I opened the back passenger door and encouraged Erik to wake up. "Come on, sweetie. We're here at Gran's place. Let's get out of the car. Gracie is going to beat us to the door if we don't hurry."

Erik used the dog to push himself into an upright position. The befuddled kid looked around at his new surroundings and yawned. Gracie sat there patiently. She's such a good dog that she didn't jump over him to hop out, although she could have.

Erik took his time climbing out of the car. He can be pretty goofy when he's drowsy. I offered him my hand. As he took it, he raised solemn eyes to me and said, "My mama is in a box in the ground. She's dead."

And here I thought he hadn't heard me.

4

*M*y husband was waiting at the front door for us. Anya walked ahead, but Detweiler asked her to wait for Erik. The little boy let go of my hand and ran to his dad. Detweiler gave both kids a kiss and watched as they raced inside the house. Gracie jumped out and loped past me. The big dog disappeared inside the house, too.

My heart was in my mouth as I walked up to Detweiler. I was thinking about what Anya and Erik had said in the car. But I did my best to push those thoughts aside.

"What's happening?" I asked. "Status report?"

"Robbie and Sheila bought a new high chair for Ty," Detweiler said. "They practically fought with each other for the chance to hold the baby. Now they're cooing over Ty. It's a regular love-fest."

"How does Sheila look?" I knew that rehab had been rough for her in all sorts of ways.

"Pretty much like Sheila always looks," Detweiler said. "A little older. Tired. Come in and see for yourself."

That familiar push-pull of excitement and dread went to war inside me. What if she wasn't doing as well as the counselors had hoped? She and Robbie had only gotten home from Texas last week. Robbie had asked us to give her time to settle in before we came over. "The transition back to St. Louis will be tough on her," he'd said. "She'll have to face old triggers. Not to mention the problems she caused and the damage she's done."

That made sense. My mother-in-law had picked fights with members of Bellerive, the swanky country club she belonged to, as well as just about anyone else who wandered across her path. She'd also been arrested for driving under the influence, which meant that Robbie's coworkers and members of the LEO community knew about her problems. Although no one had come right out and said it, I had a hunch she'd gone to battle with several people in the CALA community. As an alumna and a donor, they didn't want to break ties with her, but people grimaced when her name was mentioned. Facing all those upset people would be a challenge for anyone, but it would particularly rankle Sheila because she had a naturally haughty demeanor.

"She's over the moon thrilled to see Ty," Detweiler said. "Robbie says she cried and cried because she missed being here when he was born."

Sheila hadn't been allowed outside contact for the first two weeks at Palm Springs. After that, her contact was limited. Only recently had she been allowed to Skype and talk with the children on the phone. Of course Ty couldn't carry on a conversation! All we could do was show him off.

Sheila and Robbie aren't really Ty's grandparents, or actually Erik's grandparents either, but early on Detweiler and I decided not to make that distinction. Anya, Erik, and Ty are siblings. They are our children, Detweiler's and mine. His parents are grandparents to Anya and Erik and Ty; Sheila and Robbie are grandparents to Anya and Erik and Ty. Detweiler's niece Emily Volker is my niece, too. Period. End of discussion.

To their credit, all the various family members have agreed with our logic. More importantly, I haven't noticed any sort of favoritism. No treating the "real" grandkids differently from the non-blood kin. For that I would be eternally grateful.

Of course, there is one exception to the no-favoritism rule. My mother has made it perfectly clear which of my children she favors. I try not to let it bother me, but that woman is a total hypocrite. I cringe with shame when she calls Erik "that black child." My sisters and I jump all over her when it happens, but Mom persists in making racially insensitive remarks. One of these days she's going to say something obnoxious in public and all holy heck will rain down upon her head. Until then, she's managed to insert her racist commentary into sneaky side remarks. Usually, listeners do a double take and assume they've heard her wrong.

They haven't.

I tell myself I love her. After all, she is my mother. But if you asked me to talk about the love I have for her, I'd be at a loss. The truth is I love her out of obligation, and that's a thin veneer that cracks and flakes easily.

On the other hand, I do love Sheila. She's a fabulous grand-mother when she's sober. She's a great source of parenting wisdom. She respects and loves me.

Facing her now was going to be tough. Before Robbie hand-cuffed her to the steering wheel and drove her to Palm Springs, she'd been incredibly angry with me. I'd told her she could no longer drive the kids around or be with them unless another adult was present. Not surprisingly, she hadn't understood my reasoning. Like most alcoholics, she had a zillion excuses for her bad behavior. In fact, she'd gone as far as to argue with me.

The little girl inside me had wanted to capitulate. After all, I'd grown up in a household with two alcoholic parents. I'd been trained to accept their warped view of the world.

But this wasn't about me, it was about my kids. In the face of Sheila's fury, I had stayed calm and stood my ground. I'd been firm but kind. "Sheila?" I'd said, "I realize this is hard for you to hear and harder still to accept, but you are not going to drive my kids anywhere or babysit them by yourself until you get help. Are we clear?"

That ultimatum meant that I was the first family member who occasioned Sheila's wrath. The second was Robbie when he called a halt to her drinking and driving by taking away her car keys. The third was Detweiler when he showed up at her house and told her in no uncertain terms that he was not going to allow her to get drunk in front of our kids ever again. I hoped that Sheila had come to see that our demands were not cruel. They were designed to protect our children--and her. I prayed that she had gotten over being angry with us.

Of course, that wasn't my only concern. I needed to speak with Sheila, Robbie, and Detweiler about Anya's comments on the ride over. All of us needed to be aware that my daughter might have gotten caught up in the twisted idea that suicide was romantic. We needed to present a united front. There couldn't be any daylight streaming through the chinks in our solidarity.

"Honey?" he said when I didn't automatically step into the house.

From our spot near the front door, I could hear the kids chatting happily with their grandparents. Erik was talking freely to Robbie. Anya and Sheila had a million things to catch up on. The kids were being showered with attention. That was fine. Sheila had been away a long time. If she wanted to spoil her grandkids now, she had earned the privilege.

This seemed to be a good time for me and my husband to slip away because no one would miss us.

"I need just a minute to talk with you," I said, leading Detweiler from the front door into Sheila's side yard. As quickly as possible, I filled my husband in on what had tran-spired in the car. I began with my conversation with Maggie about Jarvis Township and ended with Anya's comments about suicide, since that was a topic we needed to address ASAP.

"Romantic?" He rubbed the back of his neck. "Does Anya have any idea how bad a corpse smells? Did she realize that dead people void their bladder and bowels? Has she thought about what that poor girl looked like when the EMTs found her? She had to be a mess."

"I told Anya something similar. Maybe not so specific ..."

"How could she think that was romantic? That's ludicrous." Smacking his fist into an open palm, he paced the lawn. I've rarely seen him that agitated. Then again, this was Detweiler in protective mode. Of course, he was upset.

Grabbing him as he made the next circuit, I said, "Honey, calm down."

"I am calm."

"No, you aren't. You're pacing and smacking your fist into your palm. Those are not the actions of a calm man."

"Anya can't possibly be serious. I'm going to go in there and—"

"You will do nothing of the sort. She's already ticked off with me because I ruined her fantasy. She needs to have one of us that she can talk to. Give reality a while to sink in. She needs time to think this through."

Finally, he sighed. "Okay, Kiki. You make a good point. I can't believe she could be so naive. How crazy is that?"

I stared into his amazing Heineken-bottle green eyes. "It's not crazy. It's immature and childish. She's only thirteen!"

Detweiler rested his forehead against mine. "You're right. I should know better. I see it all the time. Kids think they are invincible. I've been called to the scene of enough car crashes to last me a lifetime. Anya is just being a normal teenager. Do you think she listened to you?"

"I don't know. She listened with her ears, but if you're asking if she accepted the truth of what I was saying, it's too early to tell. Erik did." I repeated what Erik had said.

Detweiler cursed under his breath and said, "At least Gracie and Ty are not trying to kick over their traces."

"Not yet," I agreed. "We have years before Ty becomes a teenager. Gracie, bless her heart, is Gracie. She puts the 'great' in Great Dane, doesn't she? Now, we better make our appearance or we'll have another problem to solve. Onward and upward. One step at a time."

We walked hand in hand. As my husband held the front door for me, I sniffed the air appreciatively, and said, "One meal at a time. Smells like Linnea made brisket."

Linnea Jackson has been the Lowensteins' maid for decades. Not only is she a fabulous cook, she is also incredibly loving toward my kids. Plus, Linnea's one of the few people who can get Sheila to get down off her high horse.

"She did make brisket. She also made a tater tot casserole, a salad, green beans, and two special desserts."

"I wonder if that means she's happy to have Sheila home."

His smile flickered. "Who knows? It's too early to tell. This hasn't been easy for anybody. Especially for Robbie."

"Wow. And how are Sheila and Robbie getting along?"

"Hard to say. I was here with her and Robbie for only ten minutes before you arrived. They spent most of that time arguing over where the new high chair should go."

"That's not quite the same as saying that Robbie and Sheila are fine, is it?"

"No, it's not. Time will tell. I have to give them props that they've made it this far. Sheila seems determined to rebuild her life. According to Robbie, she's the one who wanted to reinstate the Friday night family dinners. We know how much the kids mean to her. And how much you mean to her."

I swallowed hard at that. Sheila hadn't liked me at first. For eleven years, she and I'd had an uneasy truce. George Lowenstein's murder changed everything. After I tracked down my husband's killer, Shelia grudgingly came to respect me. We aren't exactly friends. We don't giggle together or share confidences. But I do love Sheila. I really do. I know how she grieved after she lost her husband and then her son. I've seen Sheila put Anya's needs before her own. I've witnessed Sheila growing into her role as the wife of the Chief of Police.

Yes, Sheila has a lot of good qualities. Despite our rocky beginning, I admire the fact that she's taken responsibility for her drinking and worked to change her ways. My father never did. He put booze first and his family second, and the alcohol killed him. My mother still drinks. She doesn't care about anyone but herself.

Was tonight too soon to tell Sheila about Anya's cockamamie idea that suicide could be romantic?

I decided it was. At the very least, I needed to let the evening unfold and see how my mother-in-law was doing. With that in mind, I followed Detweiler into her dining room.

5

*R*obbie Holmes didn't see us walk in because he was fussing with Ty's bib. However, Ty crowed with excitement when he saw his dad and me. Flapping his arms is Ty's newest trick, and he went to town when Detweiler and I came into the dining room. His grandfather got a gentle punch in the nose that alerted him we'd arrived.

"Kiki, you're a sight for sore eyes." Robbie opened his arms to hug me. He's a big man, but he's also surprisingly gentle. He whispered in my ear, "Thank you for all you've done. You've been terrific to Sheila while she was away."

It didn't seem like I'd done much. I'd sent her packets of photos and simple updates on what the kids were doing. A couple of homemade cards. A purse-sized scrapbook with photos of Ty. That's all.

"You're very welcome." I gave his upper arms a quick squeeze of appreciation.

"Where is Sheila?" I looked around for our hostess.

She heard my voice and came out of the kitchen. Her gait was halting and her eyes telegraphed an insecurity that I've never seen before. It was almost as if she was asking, "Can I come back? Am I forgiven? Or will you reject me and make me pay for being an alcoholic?"

My throat thickened with emotion. Sheila has never seemed so beaten down. She couldn't even hold her head up. This sense of shame was totally foreign to her. My heart hurt to see her brought so low.

Detweiler was right when he said she'd aged. There were more wrinkles around her eyes, and that sassy sparkle of hers had faded. I took two steps toward her, hesitating because she can be prickly. To my surprise, she nearly knocked me down as she rushed over to give me a hug. Whatever else had transpired during rehab, apparently she'd decided it was okay to love me. As I hugged her back, unexpected tears filled my eyes.

Sheila kept on hugging me. In fact, I quickly realized that she was clinging to me as if I were a lifeboat. The immensity of her emotion nearly swamped us both. I kept swallowing down the lump in my throat and trying to find the right words to welcome her back.

"Kiki, I am so glad to see you. Thank you for coming," she said but she didn't let go of me.

Who was this woman? I went from teary-eyed to shocked. Such unrestrained affection was new to me. Especially from Sheila.

Glancing over my mother-in-law's shoulders, I caught Anya's eyes. The look on my daughter's face said it all. She, too, was amazed by her grandmother's transformation. While I watched, Anya's expression changed. From amazement she went to pleading. My daughter was silently begging me to accept the changes in her grandmother rather than question them. I nodded that I understood.

As Sheila slowly turned loose of me, I did the mental gymnastics required to reorganize my thinking about her. Okay, she had changed. Maybe she had successfully defeated the demons that drove her to drink. For now, at least. There was nothing to do but enjoy this for as long as it lasted.

The surprises kept on coming. In honor of Sheila's return, Linnea had not only cooked a fine meal, she'd insisted on staying and serving all of us. Detweiler hadn't told me that the maid was waiting in the kitchen. Usually Linnea cooks the meals and leaves. When I realized she was still here, I hurried into the kitchen to give her a big hug.

"I've missed you," I told her.

"And I've missed you and the children, too," she responded. She pronounced "children" as "chill-run." I love her southern accent.

Linnea has to be older than Sheila, but not by much. She's thin as a rail with coffee-colored skin, pure white hair, and eyes that remind me of Hershey's Kisses. As always, she wore a black dress, a frilly white apron, and white orthopedic shoes. Linnea moves with the grace of a dancer, and I'd been told she can do a mean jitterbug.

Anya said from the other room, "Mom? I'm hungry. Is it time to light the candles? Gran, is it Shabbat yet?"

"Yes, darling, of course. Would you like to say the prayers?" Sheila handed over a box of matches. We bowed our heads as Anya said the centuries-old prayer in Hebrew. Erik pouted a little because he wanted to light the candles, too.

"Maybe next time," Sheila said, surprising me all over again. She'd been very cautious about affording Anya the privilege of lighting the candles. The very idea that she'd let a little boy handle fire in her home was proof she'd softened since being gone.

Linnea began bringing in the food. It was incredible. Just terrific. We piled our plates high. Dishes were passed around for seconds. Erik even ate thirds of the tater tot casserole. Linnea promised she would write down the recipe and share it with

Brawny. The *pièce de résistance* were the dessert selections. Linnea really outdid herself. She made banana cream pudding and a caramel ice cream sundae with pralines. Of course, I had one of each. My tummy was so full that I had to reach under the tablecloth and loosen my belt a notch.

I was tickled to hear that Linnea made tons of extra food for us to take home. I guess she hadn't gotten the memo that our new nanny was also a fantastic cook. Fine by me. I love Linnea's food, almost as much as I adore her. Sending us home with leftovers was her way of spoiling us. Who was I to complain?

After dinner, the big kids carried the plates to the kitchen. Ty watched and banged his spoon against the tray of his new high chair. When Erik and Anya had cleared most of the table, Sheila said, "Anya? Erik? I told you when you arrived that if you helped clean up after dinner, you could open the gifts we bought you. They're in the family room."

Anya and Erik raced away, coming back to show off an assortment of books and jigsaw puzzles. I worried that they would complain these gifts were too old-fashioned and low tech, but both kids happily skipped back into the family room to put their puzzles together.

"I don't know how long we have," Robbie said as Linnea poured him a cup of coffee, "so I want to talk quickly."

How long we have? What on earth? Everything had been perfect. Was that only an illusion?

Robbie continued, "As soon as school's out, Sheila and I would like to take the two older children to Disney World and then on a cruise."

I was stunned. Erik had grown up not far from Disneyland before he came to live with us. He'd been to the theme park too many times to count. But visiting a Disney property had been a longtime dream for Anya. She had only seen her friends' photos of Disney World and Disneyland. Year after year, she'd begged

6

*L*ater that night, while staring up at the ceiling and watching the shadows cast by passing cars, Detweiler and I snuggled in our bed. His arm was around me and my head was resting against his chest, making this was the perfect time to discuss Sheila and Robbie's proposal. Even before we started talking, I could sense that we were on the same page, a single sheet of paper full of mixed feelings.

All three children were asleep, but there are some subjects that provoke whispers even when everyone is off to dreamland. Having a drunk for a relative is one of them. My husband said, "Robbie kept repeating that a big reason Sheila got sober was because she wanted to be involved in Anya's life. She also cares about Erik, but not surprisingly, she's closer to Anya. Sheila told the counselors that she has a real fear that Anya has been turned off by her drunken antics. I think that's reasonable. I told him that Anya had been disappointed in her grandmother. I also assured him that we had encouraged Anya to think of alcoholism as a disease."

I nodded even though my head could barely move against Detweiler's chest. "Robbie told me the same thing when we were in

Texas for the family meeting with Sheila's counselor. I believe it. I really do. I'm just not sure that the two of them can handle both Erik and Anya. You know how clingy Erik can be. It's taken him nearly a year to feel confident enough to play at his schoolmates' houses. When he's hurt or upset, he still runs to Brawny, although Anya and I are close seconds. Maggie says he's doing wonderfully well, all things considered, but the structured environment of school is a big help in making him feel secure. He barely knows Sheila."

Detweiler kissed the top of my head. "True. But I am impressed by how far he's come. Especially recently. He's calling you 'Mama' and he's dropped the 'Kiki' part."

From the start, I hadn't pushed the child to think of me as his mother. That was a designation I was willing to earn, not demand. Gina would always be the person he thought of first as his mom. I was entirely okay with that. To his credit, the little guy decided I was "Mama Kiki," until the day he shortened my title to "Mama."

The first time he called me "Mama," I fought the urge to throw my arms around him and smother him with kisses. Instead I pretended it was nothing new. No big deal. The second time he called me "Mama," he looked straight at me and waited for my reaction. It was as if he wanted to see how I'd respond. Of course I was thrilled. Absolutely. But I didn't want him to think he'd made an irrevocable decision. So I gave him a quick hug and carried on. Since then, he's been calling me "Mama" most of the time.

"Erik barely knows Sheila." That was a fact. I wasn't saying anything that wasn't obvious. I added, "Which is, I guess, a good reason for him to go and spend time with her. But I worry that it'll be too much for him. On the other hand, if Anya goes without him, that'll sting, too. There's a part of me that wishes Robbie and Sheila hadn't made the offer. If we say no, and Anya finds out, that'll be another problem entirely. She's almost too old for Disney. This might be her best chance for going. Sure, she'll act like she's too cool for all that nonsense, but secretly she'll be thrilled."

"Robbie is eager to bond with Erik," Detweiler said, "and he wants to spend time with Anya, too. Robbie's kids have been really squirrely about letting him see his grandkids. They call on him whenever they want to use him as a babysitter, and they ignore him the rest of the time."

"That's mean."

"Yeah," Detweiler agreed. "You can say that again. They're just using him, and it stinks. His kids blame him for their mother's death, even though they know it's not his fault. His guilt gives them leverage."

"When did he tell you all this?"

"He grabbed me early this morning when I was on my way into work. We slipped out for coffee. He wanted the lowdown on what's been happening in the department, and he figured that I'd be perfectly honest with him. Which I was. He didn't share the idea of the cruise, just so you know. He didn't jump the gun and tell me before you. All he and I discussed was the department. It wouldn't have been appropriate for us to discuss police business over dinner. He hasn't told the mayor when he's coming back. Robbie wants to keep his decision under wraps for the time being."

"Does he trust Sheila's sobriety?" I asked. "Is he hesitant to go back because he doesn't think she'll stay sober?"

"I didn't ask him that point-blank, although I wondered. He seemed to realize what I was thinking. He told me that he still has four more weeks of paid vacation time that he wants to use before he officially goes back to work. This way he can help Sheila get settled."

"Prescott Gallaway is not going to give up his position as the temporary chief of police without a fight."

"True. That's another reason Robbie chose to use up his vacation days before going back. He wants to learn as much as he can about alliances that have formed while he was gone. He needs to see who's still loyal to him. Get a heads-up on folks who've already decided they would be better off backing Prescott."

"Gee whiz. Sounds like you're describing a military coup rather than a police chief returning to his job after a leave of absence."

Detweiler's chuckle was warm and his chest rumbled as he suppressed a laugh. "Sounds that way, because it is that way. Robbie's return will be more of a military coup or a political upset than a simple return to work."

"I don't envy you. I hate it when people choose sides. That always means that one side stands to win and the other will undoubtedly be cast as the losers."

"You've nailed it. I figure I have four weeks to go before I'm knee-deep in a pitched battle. When I think about what lies ahead for Robbie, watching two kids and a recovering alcoholic sounds like a real picnic, doesn't it?"

"Does that mean you're okay with letting Robbie and Sheila take the kids on a cruise?"

"No. I'm not sure how I feel about allowing Robbie and Sheila to take our kids. My first thought was, no way. Then I realized, why not? Until she started drinking, Sheila often took Anya for weekends, didn't she? Sometimes even longer? Robbie is the chief of police, and a grandfather many times over. Anya is old enough to care for Erik all by herself if necessary, and it won't be, will it? Even so, I'd like to research the cruise, the cruise line, and the programs for kids. If those don't pass muster, no reason to move to stage two."

46

"Stage two being?"

"If the ship and the ship's program are solid, can Robbie and Sheila handle two kids? Assuming that Sheila stays sober."

"Is there another stage?" I was fascinated by how his mind had broken down this problem.

"Stage three is, what will Robbie do if Sheila falls off the wagon? If that happens, how will he take care of the kids? What's the plan?"

The headlamps of a passing car illuminated a branch of the maple tree next to our house. The tender leaves danced in the flickering light. The slant of the lights elongated the foliage, turning the leaves into giant hands. Of course, it was an illusion. Was it the same with our human problems? Were we exaggerating certain concerns and minimizing others?

Maybe.

A light snore from Detweiler signaled he was asleep. His way of breaking down our problem made sense. If reports on the cruise came back negative, we could shut down Robbie and Sheila's request immediately. Saying no would be easy because we could blame the cruise programming.

If the cruise was well-reviewed for families, and if other parents and grandparents had good things to say, the situation would be more complex.

With that in mind, I drifted off to sleep.

---

7

*S*aturday was a busy day for our household. Anya had golf practice, Erik had soccer practice, and I needed to go clothes shopping for Ty. He'd outgrown most of the clothing we'd gotten as newborn gifts. I hate shopping. Period. Just hate it. I considered sending Brawny on the errand, but her taste and mine are not in sync when it comes to kids' clothes.

Brawny is a fan of British monarchy. As such, she eagerly follows the young royals through Google Alerts, Instagram posts, and magazine articles. Left to her own devices, Ty and Erik Detweiler both would be dressed exactly like young Prince George, full stop. More than once I'd heard my straight-laced nanny coo over the young prince's outfits. She'd even gone so far as to knit Erik a cardigan that exactly matched one modeled by young Prince George. Yes, the sweater was darling, and Erik wore it for his school picture, but the cardigan was also a bit OTT (Over The Top) for daily wear in St. Louis, Missouri. In fact, I thought that Detweiler was going bust out laughing the first time Erik made his "royal" appearance at the breakfast table.

I felt torn. I didn't want to discourage Brawny from making

8

While sitting around the dinner table that night, Detweiler reminded me that we'd promised to have Sunday brunch at his parents' farm. "That's tomorrow. Had you forgotten?"

"Yeah," I said. "I guess I did."

Brawny passed me a bowl of creamed spinach and said, "I told Thelma we would bring deviled eggs, pasta salad, spinach and strawberry salad, and cookies."

I fought the urge to groan.

Anya said, "Mimi has two new quarter horses. One's Bert and the other one's Ernie. Both are rescues. Isn't that great? I can't wait to see them! Emily and I are going to ride them on that trail that goes around the soybean fields. Maybe not tomorrow, but later, after Mimi teaches me more about horses."

After dinner while I rinsed off dishes in the sink, I tried to find an excuse to stay home. My alone time was in short supply, and I needed a couple of hours by myself. I was toying with how to say I wasn't going, when Detweiler appeared at my elbow and said, "Tomorrow is Dad's birthday. I bought him a gift from us, but he'd love a card from the kids."

Even though I was eager to avoid Thelma, I couldn't bring myself to disappoint her husband.

"The kids and I can make one." I smiled at my husband. Thanks to my scrapbook store, we always have cool art supplies at the house.

Anya stuck her head in the kitchen. She'd heard Detweiler. "I'll get out the paper and the stickers."

"Don't forget the markers," I called after her.

Ten minutes later we were gathered around the kitchen table. Erik and Anya were having a blast. Paper pieces were everywhere. Ty sat in his bouncy seat and chewed on the edge of one.

"How do you spell Mimi?" Erik asked.

"I'll help you with that," his sister assured him.

"Mimi and Pop said I can slide down the hay," Erik told me. "Not with a sled. Those are for snow. I have to use a cardboard box. Do we have one?"

"I'm pretty sure we do. There was a stack of them in the basement from when we moved. I'll go and look after I put away the leftovers." I transferred Brawny's mashed cauliflower with bacon and sour cream into plastic tubs. The mix had been delicious. My kids are the only children I know who absolutely love their vegetables. That is all Brawny's doing.

"Emily will be there," said Anya, referring to Detweiler's niece, Ginny and Jeff Volker's daughter.

"Both my sisters and their husbands will be coming," Detweiler said. This was for my benefit, a way of telling me that I wouldn't be alone with Thelma.

"I wish I had a horse. Emily says she'll teach me to ride Western." Anya's smile was huge. My daughter loves critters.

"Thelma has a new quilt pattern she wants to show me." Brawny looked up from her knitting. "She sent me photos.

9

The Kressigs must have arrived first because their beat-up gray Camry was at the far end of the drive that divided the grassy area between the barn and the house. Dark-haired Patty is thirty-five-year-old girly girl but she's tougher than she looks. Like me, her weight goes up and down. Her best feature is her pretty hazel eyes. She's the middle Detweiler child. Her husband, Paul, is probably two years her senior. He's the sort of guy who could have been handsome, but somehow missed the mark. He's a big man with meaty hands and a loose way of carrying himself. Patty does bookkeeping for a feed supply company. Paul bounces from job to job.

Ginny and Jeff Volker must have pulled in second, given the spot their new car occupied. At thirty-seven, Ginny's the oldest of the Detweiler siblings. She's tall and thin like my husband. Her fine, fly-away hair is strawberry blonde. She's a no-nonsense type of person who likes button-down shirts and Dockers. Maybe that's because she works with so many men in the parts department of a auto supply store. Her husband Jeff's round face makes him sort of goofy looking. He has dishwater blond hair that's graying at the temples. Jeff recently turned forty, and he works for Farm Bureau in their county office.

Detweiler pulled in behind the new Buick Trans Am, a fancy gold model with wire wheels. We knew the car had to belong to the Volkers because Jeff had been lusting for one since Christmas. My husband said, "I guess Jeff's having a mid-life crisis."

"I guess so," I responded.

The crunch of our tires brought Emily Volker barreling out of the farmhouse with the screen door clattering shut behind her. With colt-like legs and knobby knees, she raced to our car. Detweiler climbed out while I turned around and undid the buckles on Ty's car seat. Emily hopped from one foot to the other while my husband lifted Ty out. I opened my door and Gracie jumped over the console and onto the grass. I think she had to pee. Normally Emily would have made a beeline for the dog, but recently my niece has been telling me, "I want a baby brother, just like Anya and Erik have."

Emily must have decided a cousin was the next best thing to a new sibling because she was all over our baby. Jumping up and down, she chanted, "Can I hold him? Huh? Can I hold Ty?"

"Of course," said Detweiler. "Be sure to support his head. That's the heaviest part of a baby."

I stayed close to the girl while she jiggled Ty with an awkward expertise. "He's gotten so big! And heavy."

"That's what he's supposed to do," I said. "Ty has a very full agenda. Eat, sleep, poop, pee, and explore the world."

"How about if you give Ty back to his mommy and give your old uncle a hug?" Detweiler said.

I took Ty from Emily so she could greet her uncle properly.

"How are you, sweetie?" Detweiler asked, putting his arm around her shoulders. Soon she'd be taller than I.

"I'm fine." She shot her uncle a sunny smile that immediately faded. "But Uncle Paul isn't doing so good."

"Is he feeling poorly?" I asked.

"Not sick, if that's what you mean."

I relaxed a little. Although I couldn't protect Ty from every stray virus and bug, I did my best to avoid putting him in contact with sick people.

Emily rattled on, "Uncle Paul's just upset. Crying and everything. I've never heard a grown man carry on like that."

That last phrase came directly from her mother. I'd heard Ginny admonish her daughter for "carrying on" more than once.

"Crying?" Detweiler frowned. "That doesn't sound like Paul."

I wondered what sort of bad news we'd be hearing. Patty and Paul had a litany of problems with money. Paul had rampant bad judgment when it came to financial matters, and Patty had an envious streak that only made their situation worse. The senior Detweilers had already cosigned one loan to get the Kressigs out of hock. I wondered if Paul came to ask for their help again.

"Yeah, I've never seen a man cry like that."

"Over what?" Detweiler asked.

Emily didn't have time to answer because Brawny came down the lane in the Highlander. Seconds later, she parked and the car doors flew open. Anya and Erik raced toward Emily. Erik hugged her low and Anya hugged her high. The three scrambled around like a litter of happy puppies.

I turned and looked at the farmhouse. Detweiler, did too. I suspected we were thinking the same thing: *Where was everybody?* None of the rest of the Detweiler family had come out to greet us. That was odd. Really odd.

What was going on?

I figured we'd find out soon enough. "Kids? Everybody grab something. Erik? Will you get Ty's diaper bag? Emily? Gracie's food and her bowls are in the gray tote bag. Anya? Ask Brawny what she wants you to carry."

"Honey?" I turned to my husband as Brawny came over to where we stood. She was carrying a cooler full of food. She set it at our feet and asked, "Where is everyone?"

"Beats me," my husband said.

Emily pulled my daughter close and whispered in her ear. Anya's mouth fell open.

"Mom?" Anya said, "Emily says that Uncle Paul's brother, Luke, tried to kill himself. He's in the hospital!"

Even Brawny winced at the news.

That explained why the Detweiler clan was holed up inside the farmhouse.

"Will he be okay?" Detweiler asked the girl. Our niece ignored him as she peeked inside Gracie's tote bag. "Emily? I asked you a question. How is Luke doing?"

This time Emily paid attention. "Luke? He's not dead. Not yet. They don't know if he's okay or not. He's in a comma."

"Coma," Detweiler corrected her.

"Right. That means he's asleep and won't wake up. Maybe never."

I bit my lip in frustration. Unlike Anya, Emily has lived a sheltered life. Her grandparents and parents are, to my mind, overly protective.

While I wouldn't wish Anya's experiences on anyone, especially another child, I think the Volkers have gone too far. They have infantilized their daughter. Emily's blithe assessment of Luke's condition suggested that she had no idea how dire the situation might be. But Anya did. My daughter's face turned pale.

"Well," said Detweiler, "Let's go see what we're dealing with."

"Do you have any idea why Uncle Paul's brother would try to hurt himself?" Anya asked her cousin.

"Nah. Not really. I know that he was in this club. It reminded me of Hercules? We're studying Hercules in school. He had to divert a river so it would clean out horse stalls. I wish I could do that. I hate mucking out stalls. I have to, of course. Otherwise, I couldn't keep my horse, but if I could divert a river, I sure would. Except, I'm not sure how you divert a river. I mean, really? Do you pick it up and aim it like a garden hose? Or dig ditches? Or what?" Emily skipped toward the Detweiler farmhouse.

We walked like a line of ants. Each of us was carrying something. I was glad to be holding Ty because my sweet chubby baby provided a welcome distraction from Emily's sad news. I vaguely remembered Paul bragging about scouts coming to see Luke back when he was in his sophomore year. That must have been what? Two years ago? That would make Luke a senior now. I wondered if the boy would ever be able to play baseball again, much less compete for a spot on a major league team.

Detweiler ran ahead and held the back door open with his foot. Emily raced inside and dropped Gracie's bag on the kitchen counter. "Anya? Come see the new horses!" Anya set down what she was carrying and the girls hurried back outside.

"Wait for me! Wait, Anya! Wait!" Erik screamed in frustration as he realized he was being left behind. He was taking his demotion from only child to annoying little brother hard. Before I could distract him, the boy dissolved into howls of anger.

Fortunately, Brawny was there to save the day. She's been with Erik since his birth. Nobody knows him better. Even though I never asked to have a nanny, I thank my lucky stars for her all the time. Dealing with a screaming six-year-old is never fun, but today Erik's tantrum felt like more than I could handle.

"Easy, wee lad," Brawny said as she swung him up into her arms. "We'll go outside and see what the girls are on about. Shall we? You wanted to feed the chickens, didn't you? I brought a bag of bread crumbs. They're in the car. Let's go get them. Come on, Gracie. You can come, too."

My dog obediently trotted along behind them.

The Detweiler kitchen is smallish. After Brawny took Erik outside, we could hear a tense conversation being held in the living room. It seemed to be wrapping up. Meanwhile, my husband took food out of the cooler while I put Ty in his high chair, a handmade maple seat that had held several generations of Detweilers, including my husband.

Louis walked in. Like his son, the head of the Detweiler family is tall and lean with a full head of thick hair. Whereas Detweiler's wavy dark blond hair is short, Louis lets his grow to his collar. My husband's hair has sun-streaks, and his father has gray strands here and there. On both men, the color variation enhances their attractiveness. Louis clasped me in a warm embrace. "Kiki? How are you, girl?"

"Happy birthday," I told him. "Many, many more."

"Hey, Pop, happy birthday," Detweiler said as he hugged his dad.

"Thank you both kindly," Louis said. "How's that baby? Where are Anya and Erik? Did they go outside with Emily? Did Brawny come? Where's Gracie?"

"Anya and Emily are headed for the barn. Erik felt left behind so Brawny took him outside before he upset Ty," I explained. "Gracie went with them."

"Pop? What's going on with Paul?" Detweiler asked.

"You musta heard?" Louis rubbed his jaw the same way Detweiler does when he's upset. But he didn't get to say anything else because his wife joined us.

"Chad? Thank goodness you're here." Thelma rushed past me to grab her son. She gripped his shirt sleeves for dear life. My husband gave his mother a kiss.

"Mom?" Detweiler asked. "Don't you want to say hi to Kiki?"

"Sure." She stepped away from him and said, "How are you, honey?" But it didn't sound sincere.

I decided to take the high road.

"I'm fine, Thelma. How are you?" I purposefully injected as much warmth into my voice as possible. As my reward, I saw Louis's shoulders relax. He was watching his wife intently.

"We've had better days," Thelma said. "Gina, Jeff, and Paul are all here. But Paul's in some kind of a state. His brother Luke is in the hospital. He tried to kill himself."

"What condition is he in?" My husband asked.

"Not good," his father answered. "They can't say much more than that. Not yet. He might not come out of it, son."

I could hear Jeff and Ginny Volker talking to each other in the next room. Then Paul's voice drifted in. He was clearly on the phone, cajoling someone on the other end of the call. The ragged, torn edge of his voice told us he was beside himself with grief.

"I take it Paul and Patty aren't staying for dinner?" I was being selfish. I had counted on their presence to help me keep my distance from Thelma.

"No. Patty isn't even here," my mother-in-law said quickly. "Can you believe that? What a shame. She's missing her dad's birthday. She's at the hospital with Paul's parents, Mary Martha and Fred. They've been there since about ten last night. Patty's been a great comfort to Mary Martha. Paul stopped by on his way home. He's going there to grab a change of clothes for Patty. She volunteered to spend the night at Luke's bedside. That way Fred and Mary Martha can get a little rest. Paul would stay over night at the hospital, but he shouldn't take off work. He's got that new job."

One of many new jobs, I thought to myself. Paul was one of those "get rich quick" guys who always had a new scheme going. This year it was bitcoins. Until they bitcoined him in the butt. Goodness knows how much money Paul lost.

Louis explained, "There's no way of knowing how long Luke went without oxygen. Mary Martha saved him. She wondered why he hadn't come to breakfast. After pounding on his bedroom door and not getting an answer, she walked outside and around the house to his bedroom window. That's when she spotted him hanging from the closet door by his belt."

"She screamed for Fred to call 911," said Thelma.

"Then she ran to the back porch and grabbed one of Luke's baseball bats. Smashed in the bedroom window. Crawled over broken glass to get to her son. She's all cut up, mentally and physically. If she hadn't been so bullheaded, that boy would be dead for sure."

Thelma continued, "One of the doctors said that Luke will never walk or feed himself. Another thinks he'll be fine as long as he goes through physical therapy. Who knows?"

Louis jammed his hands in his pockets and grunted. "Doctors. Not worth the paper their licenses are printed on, if you ask me."

"Oh, wow." I couldn't think of anything else to say.

"But Ginny and Jeff are here?" Detweiler asked.

"They are in the living room with Paul," Louis said. "We're all shook up. One of Ginny's best friends taught Luke English last year. A girl named Tammy Calhoun. You remember her, don't you, Chad?"

"Yes, I do. What precipitated this? Why did Luke suddenly try to kill himself?" While Detweiler asked questions, I dug around in my backpack, brought out toys for Ty, and put them on the tray of his high chair.

"Nothing. Not one blessed thing. At least not that the Kressigs know about. And those yahoos at the high school? They don't know diddly, either." Louis pursed his lips like he wanted to spit. "No sir. One day the boy is doing great. Thinking about which offer to take. Practicing his pitches. It's all good. Next thing you know, two weeks from high school graduation, this happens."

Luke had hurt himself, I figured it had something to do with the rash of suicides at the high school."

Jeff usually lets Ginny do all the talking, but today he spoke up. "We've tried to keep this low-key because we don't want to upset Emily. The advisors at her middle school have warned us there's a copycat element to these suicides. The last thing we want to do is make a big deal over Luke's attempt."

Once again I thought about Anya and her classmates and their misguided belief that committing suicide was romantic. Detweiler's eyes caught mine, but we both stayed silent.

"How in tarnation do things like this get out of hand?" Louis pounded the table with the butt of his fork. "What are those kids thinking?"

"That's the point, Pop," Detweiler said. "They aren't thinking. Suicide is usually an impulsive act. A knee-jerk reaction to a problem or disappointment. Although I have to admit, these don't sound as spur-of-the-moment as most suicides usually are." Detweiler shook his head. "Ginny? What specifically did Patty tell you about Luke? Did this come out of the blue? Was there a precipitating disappointment? Maybe he broke up with a girl or had a disagreement with a baseball scout? I'm grasping at straws here."

Ginny studied a piece of meat on her fork. Slowly she answered, "According to Paul, this came as a total surprise. In fact, just last week Paul was telling us that Luke finally seemed to have found his way. You know, even though he's a good athlete, he's kind of been an outsider. He got teased a lot. But Luke had found a group of kids that he jelled with, and he was finally feeling accepted. Then—wham. This happened. None of this makes sense."

Jeff picked up where Ginny left off. "When we saw him last, Luke seemed happier than ever. He was talking about his new friends. That's what makes this even more baffling."

"Could it have been a problem at home? Something Luke didn't want to share with Paul? Or something the Kressigs didn't want to share with you?" Detweiler directed his question to Ginny and Jeff. Part of my husband's job is asking questions and eliciting information from people. He does it well.

Ginny and Jeff looked to each other for answers. Ginny turned away first. "Patty has always blabbed to me when they've had problems. She's incapable of keeping her mouth shut. If Paul thought his brother was having issues, Patty would have told me. That's one of the biggest stumbling blocks in their marriage. Instead of Patty trying to work things out with Paul, she runs her mouth."

Jeff chuckled. "Drives Paul nuts. That's another reason this took us by surprise. Patty's the first person to holler 'fire' in a crowded theater. But she didn't see this coming either."

"Could there be a problem among the siblings? Luke's the youngest, right?" Detweiler asked gently.

"Mary Martha wanted more, but she couldn't have them. She tried and tried," said Thelma. "There's Paul, John, and Luke. Paul's the oldest by ten years. There were plenty of miscarriages between, and a little girl named Mary Margaret who died before her seventh birthday. If Mary Martha could have had more kids, she would have. In fact, she would have gone on until she had all twelve apostles sitting around her dinner table. John and Luke are what they call Irish twins."

I cut a cooked carrot in half and popped it in my mouth. The secret of Thelma's pot roast is a jar of onions. Fresh onions don't lend the same sweet flavor to the mix. She also pours in the juice straight from the jar. Funny how one little modification to a recipe can make such a big difference in the taste. After I ate my piece of carrot, I said, "I've never heard of Irish twins."

Detweiler's mouth settled into a scowl. "Irish twins are siblings born eighteen months apart. That phrase is a back-of nerve. My brother's there in the hospital, and you're spreading rumors that he's gay?"

"How do you know he isn't?" Patty raised her voice. "I could be right. You don't know. You don't have any better ideas."

"My brother isn't gay! You don't know what you're talking about." Paul slammed his fist on the table. The silverware jumped and the water glasses shivered.

"What did *you* think was bothering him?" Detweiler kept his voice neutral as he addressed Paul.

"I think he got into the wrong crowd. I figured maybe he'd met kids who pretended to be his friends and then dumped him."

"Is there any way to find out?" I asked softly.

"Beats me," said Paul, throwing up his hands. "The Illinois State Police came and took Luke's computer. Their computer forensics guy seems to think he can look inside and figure out what might be in there."

"What do Luke's friends say?" I asked.

Paul made a "huh" sound and shook his head. "The state police sent an officer who spoke to six kids Luke hangs around with. They had nothing to offer."

"Nothing at all?" I continued. So this young man was upset enough that he wanted to commit suicide, but none of his friends noticed? Maybe Paul was right. Maybe those kids were only pretending to be Luke's friends. Some part of this story didn't add up.

"We've been told that the other kids thought Luke was fine," said Paul. "His teachers say they didn't notice any problems. But then this happens and they claim it came out of the blue!"

Patty sighed and stirred her coffee. She wore an air of defeat. "I guess we'll have to wait and see what Luke says when he wakes up."

"*If* he wakes up," her husband added. "We need to get going. My parents are waiting."

Thelma got up and fixed doggy bags so that Patty and Paul could take food to the older Kressigs. We gave the couple hugs, and they drove away.

I took Ty into one of the spare bedrooms upstairs and changed his diaper. Brawny had been keeping an eye on the farmhouse. When she saw the Kressigs leave, Brawny brought all the dirty plates and cutlery into the house and grabbed a garbage bag for the paper napkins and empty water bottles.

"If you'll give me Ty, I'll put down a blanket so he can crawl around next to the picnic bench," Brawny told me when I walked back into the kitchen. "Don't worry about him."

The absence of little ears gave us adults a chance to talk openly. Thelma took this as an opportunity to dramatize her emotions. After all, she had a captive audience. "I am so upset. This is just awful. Awful. My heart is broken. Mary Martha and I have been best friends for decades. That poor, poor woman."

Even though I was only a bystander to this tragedy, my inner alter-ego, Ms. Uber-Responsible, kept chanting, "Do something. Do something. Do something. You have the opportunity. You can help. Take the cops up on it."

"They've got nothing to go on," I mumbled to Detweiler when we stood side-by-side at his mother's sink and rinsed out pots.

"There's nothing we can do," my husband said.

Ginny overheard us. "I wish you could do something to help, Chad. We're scared to let Emily go to school. This problem seems to be getting worse by the day."

"Why not pull her out?" Thelma asked. "There are only two weeks left to go. You could homeschool. Then she'd be safe."

"Mom? I work forty-plus hours a week. How could I home-school her? Emily is already behind in her reading composition.

I've tried to work with her, but we wind up fighting. I get frustrated and she gets angry. I'm worried that she'll fall even further behind during the summer. Taking her out now would only make matters worse." Ginny gathered up a pile of dirty damask napkins. Thelma always uses cloth napkins inside the house.

Jeff came up behind Ginny and wrapped his arms around her waist. "Maybe we can hire a tutor to work with her over the summer. The whole Jarvis Township school district is stretched thin. No wonder they can't figure out why the students are killing themselves. Imagine! Everywhere else in the country, loners are taking up guns and shooting their peers. Here in Jarvis Township the loners go off quietly and commit suicide."

There was a reason that the school district had so few resources. School funding comes from property taxes. The value of farmland here in Jarvis Township had dropped steadily. Money for schools had diminished accordingly. Sure, the prices would pop back up every once in a while, but farmland didn't generate the sort of tax revenue that commercial real estate did. It was a crying shame, but given the way tax income was dispersed, the rich areas would always have better schools with more resources, and the poorer areas would continue to hunt and peck for basic necessities.

We were nearly done when Louis said, "Boys? There's a baseball game on. Care to join me in the sports lounge?"

Of course he meant the living room. But the men didn't get that far because a dusty black pickup truck pulled up in the driveway. The young man who climbed out looked remarkably like Paul Kressig, except that he really *was* handsome.

"That's John," said Ginny as if I couldn't tell.

John's hair was darker than Paul's, his build more athletic, and he had a dimple in his chin. Those differences were minor. If John looked like Paul, and Luke looked like John, the three Kressig boys could easily pass as triplets.

The Detweiler men greeted John as he came through the back door. The scowl on the newcomer's face scared me. My tummy twisted into a knot. Was he here to tell us that Luke had died?

"Chad? I don't know if you remember me—" John said.

"Of course I do." Detweiler shook the younger man's hand and introduced me.

"Sorry to meet you under such sad circumstances," I said.

"I just came from the hospital. Patty and Paul were walking in as I was going out. We had a quick discussion. All of us want to know what sort of action law enforcement can take, if any. Chad? My parents would like for you to come over to the house. I know this is Sunday, your family time, and your dad's birthday, but—"

"No problem."

Thelma pulled John toward the kitchen table. "We were just cleaning up after our meal. Tell me what I can get you to eat. Don't be shy. I know you're a growing boy. Your mama would skin me alive if she knew I let you go hungry."

"Mrs. Detweiler, there's nothing I'd like better, but I'm not hungry. My parents need me right now. I'm sure you can understand."

"John? I'd like to bring my wife along with us," Detweiler said.

"Why on earth?" snapped Thelma.

"Mom? I have my reasons." Detweiler's tone was cold. To soften the impact he added, "Mom? Could you make sure Anya learns how to act around a horse? She's been looking forward to you teaching her. Ginny, can you see if Brawny needs any help with Ty and Erik?"

"Of course, come on, Jeff." My sister-in-law took her husband by the hand.

Actually Brawny was more than capable of caring for all the

children, but Detweiler's instructions to his sister created a neat segue for us as we followed John to his dusty Toyota pickup. Thelma and Louis stood on the back stoop watching our departure. I climbed into the middle between the two men. When we were pulling out, I saw Thelma swat away Louis's hand like he was an oversized mosquito.

_T_he drive to the Kressigs' house wasn't long distance-wise, but it seemed to take forever as it always does when you're facing a difficult situation. John told us he was in an airport, coming home from Army Reserves training, when he'd seen the text message concerning his brother. "Even before that, I knew something was wrong with Luke. Just knew it."

"Why?" Detweiler asked. "Was he depressed? Or—"

"No!" John said. "Luke was happy for the first time in ages. He finally felt like he belonged at Jarvis Township High School. Those were his words: 'I'm finally fitting in. Just in time to graduate!'"

John continued, "After I went away for basic training, Luke felt lost. See, I used to make sure he was included when my friends and I went out. He's never found it easy to make friends, and when I left, he was on his own a lot. I don't think our folks have any idea how hard it can be for a teen to live out in the middle of nowhere."

I didn't say anything, but of course, my husband had been in the same predicament.

"Luke's always said he wants to move to the city," John explained. "He has always taken a lot of pride in how he dresses. The other kids were always teasing him about his clothes, but this year someone started a rumor that Luke is gay. He isn't. Trust me on that. He just cares about looking good."

We bumped along another half-paved country road. This one led to a tri-level in a dirty cream color with stone accents. Instead of a red barn, there was a gray structure that seemed on the verge of collapse, a hog shed, and a bright blue Harvestore silo for grain storage. A neat row of red-and-white striped petunias bordered the sidewalk to the house. A woman with matted down gray hair and puffy eyes opened the screen door for us. If she was surprised that my husband had brought me, she didn't show it.

Detweiler gave the woman a quick hug. "Mary Martha? This is my wife, Kiki."

I said hello to a woman wearing a faded lavender housedress. Her forearms were wrapped in gauze, and in a few places, blood had stained the white mesh. The extent of the bandages spoke to how desperate Mary Martha must have been to rescue her son. Would I have climbed through a broken window for one of my children? You bet I would have. Mary Martha shuffled into the house on swollen feet shoved inside dirty house slippers. As she gestured for us to sit down, a gold crucifix peeked out from the neckline of her dress. That cross was the only adornment for a woman who epitomized the word "tired."

"Fred?" she called. "Chad's here. With his wife."

A man stepped out of the shadowy hallway. He was thin as a twig and his face was covered with a skimpy beard. His threadbare work pants sagged around his waist. Fred Kressig shook our hands before using his chin to point us toward a sagging sofa that smelled faintly of dirty hair and stale popcorn. The only light in the room came from a large picture window and a console TV with the volume turned low. John dragged in a chair from the kitchen, while his parents took over a set of recliners. I tried to look around without being conspicuous. The Kressigs' decorating scheme centered on their faith. Over their TV was a mournful painting of Jesus. The Savior was kneeling in prayer with his hands resting on a rock. A walnut bookcase was chock full of tiny angels, statues in all shapes, sizes, and colors. On the wall behind the sofa was a huge picture of the Last Supper, painted on black velvet. I could practically feel the apostles to staring down at us.

Detweiler took my hand. "I'm so sorry to hear about Luke. He's in our prayers. I brought my wife along because I think she might be of assistance. Let me explain why. My wife has been asked to go undercover at the school and report back to law enforcement."

The Kressigs listened intently. When Detweiler finished, Mr. Kressig said to me, "You turned them down?" His rheumy eyes were hard to look at.

"Yes, sir, I did."

Detweiler jumped in to save me. "At the time, the logistics seemed impossible. We live an hour and a half from here in a suburb called Webster Groves. We both have full-time jobs. But the biggest hurdle was that our two oldest kids will get out of school in four days. We still can't make a commitment. As you can see, it's complicated."

"Then I don't even know why John was so fired up about talking to you. Sounds to me like there ain't much you can do to help." Fred shuffled his feet. He was wearing his work boots. A small chunk of mud flaked off and fell into the olive green shag carpeting.

Detweiler spread his hands wide and said, "It's possible that be "sent into" anything, but I swallowed my anger. We'd discuss his semantics later. Detweiler meant well. He was explaining that the situation was more dangerous for me than it might seem on the surface.

"What would you do with your children?" Louis asked. "Aren't Erik and Anya going to be out of school? Will you leave them with Brawny? Those are going to be awfully long days for Kiki."

"We can take care of them for you," Thelma said. She quit washing the dishes long enough to turn and stare at me. Obviously she was feeling left out.

"Son, she's right," Louis added. "If you think you could make a difference, we'd be willing to help out in any way we can."

"Yes, we know you would, and we appreciate it but there might be another option. Sheila and Robbie Holmes want to take Erik and Anya to Disney World and then on a kid friendly cruise."

Thelma went berserk.

"You can't do that! Sheila drinks!" Thelma shouted. "You can't let those kids go on a vacation with a drunk. That's irresponsible."

"Thelma, darling, calm down." Louis patted the air as he got out of his seat. Crossing the room to where his wife was standing, he slipped an arm around her shoulders. "Let our boy talk."

"Mom, can you listen a minute?" Detweiler's tone was a warning. "The kids would not be alone with Sheila on the cruise. Remember? Robbie's a grandfather many times over. He's also the Chief of Police! And there's more. We have good friends who'll be taking the same cruise. The Earharts. Their daughter is the same age as Anya, and Maggie Earhart is Erik's kindergarten teacher. Maggie and her husband have volunteered to keep an eye on our kids if the need arises. Not that I think Sheila will slip up. She's been in rehab for months. They have AA meetings on the boat. Besides, those kids are Sheila's motivation to stay sober. She wants to be a part of their lives."

"Isn't that fine and dandy?" Thelma snipped.

Louis nodded at his son. "Sounds like you've thought this through, Chad."

"We've discussed it, yes, but we haven't made a decision about the kids' vacation or Kiki's involvement. There's the drive back and forth from Webster Groves. Kiki will have to see that the store is covered. Like you said, Dad, it's asking a lot of Kiki."

"You could stay here," Louis spoke softly. "You could have the whole second floor. There's room for your nanny, too. That'd give us a chance to spend time with the little one. We've been hankering to do that. Thelma and I would love that. Wouldn't we, Thelma?"

Thelma looked to me. Her eyes glistened with unshed tears. "I want to be a part of Ty's life. He's our only blood kin besides Emily, and the only way the family name will live on. Every time I see Ty, he's grown so much."

The pain in her was evident, and her words were more like a plea than a statement. Suddenly, I saw her differently. Yes, she'd been a real harridan toward me lately, but I also noticed how tired and old she looked. Was she worried that life was passing her by? Emily was growing up. Although she wasn't as independent as Anya, surely Emily was showing signs of wanting to go her own way. Spending time with her friends would soon usurp any claims that her grandparents had on her. Of course, Ty was growing even faster than Emily. This might be Thelma's best chance to spend time with him while he was still small.

My emotions had been all over the map and fatigue caught up with me. "If we could stay here, it would help a lot," I said. "Thank you both for the offer. Honey? Are you ready to hit the trail? The kids have school tomorrow."

"I'll round up the crew," Detweiler said.

14

S heila called and woke me up Monday morning. "Thank you," she said in a husky voice. "I can't tell you what this means to me." We talked for a minute. She promised to send me information from the cruise line and a day-by-day schedule of their activities.

I couldn't wait to tell the kids, and Detweiler agreed, so we told them over breakfast. They screamed with joy. I've never seen two such vigorous happy dances. They were so excited that they couldn't finish their breakfast, but Brawny warned, "Eat or you're not going." That settled them down.

Over the next two days, Brawny and I prepared for the kids' vacation. She photocopied all of Erik and Anya's medical records, made a contact list, and printed out a "permission to treat" form for Robbie and Sheila to hang onto. I called Maggie and told her what we had decided. Then I put Maggie in touch with Sheila.

Brawny and I started a list of what we would need to take with us to the Detweiler farm. In the meantime, I still had a store to run and three kids to take care of, two of those children were nearly wild with excitement. Needless to say, we were crazy busy.

Late Wednesday morning, Detweiler and I met Detective Schultz and John Kressig at a diner off of Highway 40 in O'Fallon, Illinois. Schultz got there first. I wasn't surprised to see he'd picked out a booth in the back of the diner so he could face the door. John strolled in shortly after we arrived, and Detweiler made the introductions.

Of course, Schultz already knew a little about the logistics we'd put in place in order for me to take the temporary job as art teacher. He also knew about John's plan to step in for his brother and act as back-up for me. John and I agreed that I would treat him like any other student. Otherwise, we'd tip people off to the fact we were working together. My husband and I decided not to tell Schultz about Brawny.

"The fewer people who know what we're up to, the better," my husband said.

I agreed.

Despite all our preparations, I was nervous. The purpose of this meeting was to give me my official marching orders. As I sat across from Schultz and John Kressig, a sense of seriousness came over me. I was really going to do this thing. Really.

"How's your brother doing?" Schultz asked John.

"I stopped by the hospital this morning. The doctors think he'll make it."

I felt a weight lifted until John continued, "They don't know what kind of shape Luke'll be in, cognitively, but they're confident he'll pull through. We're looking at a lot of physical therapy but given the alternative, that's fine."

When the waitress came by, the men ordered coffee and I asked for an unsweetened iced tea.

"Your brother talking yet?" Schultz studied the young man.

"No. He's kind of groggy."

I ignored the point she was making. "Both sets of grandparents are going to have their wishes come true. They've been asking for one-on-one time with the kids, and we're making that happen."

"You are so full of it." Clancy looked at me and laughed. "What a load of malarkey. Come on. What's the real scoop?"

"That's it," I said, as I struggled to keep a straight face. Clancy could always see right through me.

Laurel studied me quietly. "All right. What do we need to do to help?"

The next few days were hectic and emotional. Every time I thought about saying goodbye to my babies for two weeks, I got teary-eyed.

John continued to make his daily reports to Detweiler. I listened in, but I'll admit I was preoccupied. The big kids were going bonkers with excitement about their vacation. Brawny drilled them on safety procedures. She and I set out their clothes, taking care that every piece worked with everything else before we put them in suitcases. When we weren't packing, there were end-of-the-year activities at CALA. An assembly. A parent's brunch. And in my copious spare time, I worked with Margit, Clancy, and Laurel to figure out how best they could cover my hours. Because Laurel is pregnant and diabetic, I worried about her, but she assured me that her mother, my old friend Mert Chambers, could also chip in if need be.

Although none of the women believed my story about taking a vacation, they left the matter alone.

I was grateful for that.

15

*A*ll too soon we said goodbye to Erik and Anya. Although I fought tears, the kids were so excited about their upcoming adventure that they didn't seem sad at all to be leaving. Detweiler and I stood on the curb of our driveway and waved as Robbie carefully backed the red Mazda SUV into the street. He'd rented the roomy vehicle for the drive to Florida. Sheila had mapped out a route that included sightseeing stops, history lessons, and comfort breaks. She'd gripped me hard when we hugged goodbye and whispered in my ear, "Trust me. I won't let anything happen to your babies."

Later I would learn that Robbie had said something similar to Detweiler. Clearly, he and Sheila knew we were concerned about letting our kids travel with them. To be extra careful, we'd briefed both Anya and Erik on what to do if there was a problem. Both kids owned a cell phone. Our numbers were programmed into their phones. We'd ordered and received plastic lanyards that allowed the phones to hang around their necks and keep their hands free. I'd written our cell phone numbers on the soles of their feet with a fine tip Sharpie pen and coated the skin with Liquid Bandage, a precaution that

Anya found ridiculous but I'd read about it in a woman's magazine. If the kids were somehow separated from their phones or knocked unconscious, the numbers on their feet would work like dog tags had for soldiers. Over and over again, we'd drilled them on how to contact us, how to find a trustworthy adult, and so on. Maggie and her husband had all of our emergency contacts. That way she could call Sheila, Robbie, Detweiler, Brawny, or me if there was a problem.

Our preparation had been exhaustive. Anya and Erik had grown irritated by our practice drills. "I'm as excited about no more drills as I am about our vacation," Anya had groused to me as we packed her bag.

"I get it. Really, I do. Does all this really seem so extraordinary when you consider all we've been through? With your father being murdered, me being kidnapped, and Erik's parents dying?"

My darling daughter smirked while I tucked a stack of clean undies into her suitcase. The air was scented with the strawberry shampoo she uses. "Maybe you should send us away with four-leaf clovers in our pockets and Lucky Charms cereal necklaces around our throats instead of scribbling on our feet."

"Maybe." I swallowed hard. Anya did have a point. From an outsider's viewpoint, we probably seemed totally over-the-top when it came to protecting her and her brother.

Taking a breath, I said, "You, Erik, and Ty are the most precious souls on earth to me, next to Detweiler. I'd do anything to keep all of you safe, no matter how silly or farfetched it sounds. Maybe I've put you in embarrassing situations. That's entirely possible. If so, please accept my apologies."

She neatly folded a navy-blue headband into quarters. Finding a space next to her toiletries bag, she squeezed the stretchy ribbon into the slot. After she finished, she turned to me and said, "Mom? You are one nickel short of a quarter, but I know you mean well."

That cracked up both of us, giving us a chance to reclaim our good humor. "Honey, you're probably right. Think of how we'll laugh about this in the future."

*a*fter a busy Saturday at my store, my husband, Brawny, and I packed up the Highlander. We'd decided to go to the farm early in the day Sunday to get ourselves organized for the week ahead. I rode with my husband in his unmarked police car. Brawny was right behind us with Ty in his car seat and Gracie in the passenger seat. Rebekkah Goldfader, daughter of my old boss, had moved into our house temporarily to cat sit. She promised to give Martin and Seymour all the loving and attention they demanded as their due. I knew the kitties and the house were in good hands. We'd also gotten a couple of short text messages from Sheila assuring us that the kids were doing fine. Anya sent us a photo of her and Erik at Ruby Falls outside of Chattanooga, Tennessee.

"John Kressig called while you were showing Rebekkah where you keep the kitty litter," Detweiler said as we merged into traffic on Highway 40. "He wants to meet us at the farm. He's been going through Luke's things. He might have a lead worth following up on."

Sure enough, when we pulled into the driveway of the Detweiler farm, a freshly washed black pickup truck was already parked there. John was sitting at the picnic table with a note-book open in front of him. The noise of our car engine caught John's attention, and he looked up at us with a face full of expectation. We climbed out of the police cruiser and stretched.

Thelma raced out to greet us, explaining that Louis had made a grocery run. We hugged her and thanked her again for having us.

"John? I told you to come on inside. I've got biscuits in the oven."

"Thank you kindly, ma'am, but I've already eaten."

Brawny pulled in with Ty and Gracie. The nanny opened the door on the Highlander and the big dog ran out to piddle. Brawny unhooked Ty from his car seat and walked over to where we stood. Thelma was insistent that John join us for breakfast.

"Are you sure? My biscuits are the best in the county." Thelma kept pestering John. It was actually getting embar-rassing.

"Mom?" Detweiler said, "John's here to make a report to me. Kiki needs to hear it too. As soon as we're done out here, Kiki and I will come inside and eat."

While Thelma pouted and pulled on John's arm, Detweiler leaned close to whisper in Brawny's ear, "Try to keep my mom out of this, would you? At least do your best? Maybe offer her Ty as a bribe?"

"Aye," Brawny said as she gave him a broad wink. "Thelma? Have you seen how much this bairn has grown? Come and look. You'll want to hold this rascal. But first he needs a diaper change. Will you show me where I'll be sleeping? Gracie? Here girl." With the baby in one arm, the nanny grabbed Gracie by the collar with the other and led the dog toward the house. Although the big harlequin looked back at my husband with love in her brown eyes, she trotted along like the good girl she is.

My husband and I joined John on the picnic bench. John's spicy cologne mixed with the aroma of freshly cut hay with a side order of hog manure. The country. Got to love it. Once we were comfortable, the young man showed us the spiral-bound notebook. "Glad to see both of you. I think I've got an idea where to begin."

Opening the notepad flat, he pointed to doodles that his brother had done in the margins of the 8½-by-11-inch pages. Mainly, the scribbles were senseless, although a few reminded me of the fish symbol used by Christians , except Luke's were fatter. There were also daisies. Lots and lots of daisies. And triangles. Interlocking triangles.

"I hung around the hospital until I got the chance to speak privately to one of Luke's nurses. Her name is Bethany. I asked her to tell me if Luke says anything that might help us—"

John's comment was interrupted by a phone call. He pulled his iPhone out of a back pocket of his jeans.

I eavesdropped while John spoke to the person on the other end of the line. Detweiler was quiet, too, listening in as much as possible. It quickly became apparent that the caller was Bethany. The happy expression on John's face suddenly dissolved as he said, "Yeah. I understand. Thanks. See ya." He hit the end call button and turned solemn eyes on us.

"My brother came around for a few minutes. I think he waited until I left because he didn't want to face me. He wasn't conscious long enough to say much." From a seated position, John kicked the dust with the toe of his boot. "I think Luke's embarrassed. Ashamed. He has to know what he's putting Ma and Dad through."

I could only imagine so I kept my mouth shut.

"Onward and upward." John flipped to another page where there was a printed grid. "This is my brother's class schedule. I cross-referenced his schedule with all the other students who've either tried to kill themselves or succeeded at suicide. All the victims are seniors, by the way. At the risk of sending us down a rabbit hole, I figured that Luke had to have something in common with the other ... victims." Pointing with his index finger, he drew our attention to three periods during the school day: Art, Physical Education, and Computer Studies.

"I'll share this with the LEOs working the case. They might be able to confirm that these are also the classes that other victims took." Detweiler used his phone to snap a picture of John's list and sent it off to Schultz.

"It's not much, but I thought it would help," John said. "I can't make heads or tails of Luke's doodles, but they don't look like anything I've ever seen him draw before."

Now that we were past the logistics and the mission seemed real, I got to worrying. Sure, I could teach the art class. No problem. Okay, I might not do a spectacular job but I'd muddle through. However, what if I taught the class, and one of my students *still* committed suicide? Could I live with myself? Or would I blame myself forever? My mouth filled with saliva. I concentrated on not getting sick. Was it too late to back out?

No, I couldn't back out.

And not because it was too late.

I couldn't back out because I'd blame myself forever if I bypassed a chance to help the Kressigs and the other parents at Jarvis Township High School. In my heart of hearts, I didn't feel like I had a choice.

What if one of my children was at risk? I'd pray for somebody to come and help. Anybody. Maybe I was putting too high a value on my talents. Yeah, that was entirely possible. But what if this was my chance to be the answer to someone's prayer? I would never know unless I took it.

ducked as best I could, but I wasn't fast enough and one small branch slapped me across the face. The pain brought tears to my eyes.

I was terrified. I knew I needed to stop my horse, but how? Should I try to slide off? When I looked down, the ground went rushing past. Rocks. Branches. Dead leaves. Bushes. A stretch of dirt. Gravel. Nothing I'd want to land on. I was trying to pull back on the reins when I realized we were headed straight for a tree.

Bert didn't seem to care.

"Stop! Stop! Whoa!" I yanked the reins as hard as I could, but Bert kicked his back legs out simultaneously, as if to tell me to stop it. Leaves kept whizzing by. All I could see was green, and then I realized we were headed straight for a low branch that forked like the letter Y. Bert was aiming me at the crouch of the Y.

"Nooooo," I shouted.

At the last moment, my horse dropped his head, did a nifty little side step, and jammed my shoulders between the two branches. Then he trotted out from under me. I was stuck in the tree with my legs dangling in the air.

But not for long. While Bert ran off, gravity pulled me down to earth. As I slid down, the tree bark tore all the skin off of the top of my arms. I hit the ground hard and rolled to my knees. Through the trees, I caught a glimpse of Bert's tail fluttering like a triumphant flag.

"Bert? I'm onto you and your tricks. If I catch you, you are dead meat!" I screamed. "I'm going to turn you into dog food! See if I don't!"

Of course, I wouldn't do any such thing. I've been known to carry spiders outside and let them go instead of squishing them.

But I sounded tough. Really I did.

18

———

he sound of hooves crashing through the trees caught my attention. I blinked hard and saw my husband coming to my rescue.

"How did you know?" I whined.

"Mom and Ernie showed up at the barn without you. She couldn't figure out where you'd gone. Then Bert came back without you. I jumped on Ernie and came to find you. Is anything broken?"

"Noooo."

"Can you stand up?"

"Yeah. I think so." Grabbing the trunk of the tree, I hauled myself to my feet.

"Wow. You are a hot mess." Detweiler's eyes were saucer-sized. "For such a short ride, you sure did a lot of damage. To yourself. Can you get up here? Or do I need to hop down?"

"I think I can manage if you give me a boost," I said. My husband extended a muscular arm and helped me haul myself up and into his saddle.

I wrapped my arms around him and gritted my teeth. I

wanted to horsewhip his mother. How could Thelma have finished her ride without me? She told her son that she was surprised I wasn't right behind her? Ha-ha-ha! Bert and I had raced past her! She didn't hear me screaming? Or had this been her plan all along?

I had to wonder.

Back at barn, Thelma said, "Don't you worry, Kiki. Bert's just fine," she told me. I stuck my head around the barn door and found Bert happily eating oats out of a pail.

Thelma smiled and said, "I had no idea Bert hated to be swatted. None. Thank goodness Emily and Anya didn't ride him."

"Yup" was the best I could manage. I couldn't look Detweiler in the eyes.

"I hope this incident hasn't put you off horses," Thelma said.

"Nope." That was a lie. I'd taken a silent vow never to go near a horse again. Ever. I'd had enough.

Detweiler whistled at my blood-covered upper arms. "Mom? I think I need to get Kiki cleaned up. Can you take care of Ernie?"

Of course she said yes.

About an hour later, Thelma called us all to lunch. My face looked like a badly planned crazy quilt thanks to the many scratches and welts. Brawny had cleaned and dressed the raw skin on my upper arms before wrapping it with gauze. Since there weren't any kids to keep track of, the nanny would be joining us at our meals. When Louis walked in and caught sight of my face, his eyes got as big as dessert plates. "Stars above. What on earth happened to you, young lady?"

Thelma squirmed in her seat. Detweiler studied the floor. Brawny focused all her attention on Ty. I decided not to give Thelma the satisfaction of knowing I was in pain. Instead I said,

"Louis? I overestimated my horsemanship skills. By a lot. I learned a valuable lesson."

What I learned was not to trust Thelma Detweiler.

_a_fter lunch, Brawny put Ty down for a nap. My husband gave me a quick overview of what to listen for when I got to Jarvis Township High School. We'd chosen to sit in the dining room and give his parents their space in the living room. Louis is a big sports fan, and he likes listening to the various commentators discuss teams and players. But Thelma wasn't interested in sitting with her husband. Instead, she kept coming into the dining room and grabbing odd pieces of glassware from the display cabinet. Her behavior made no sense at all.

After Detweiler finished, I went online and looked at the school website. I tried to memorize the names of teachers and administrators. Next, I reviewed the lesson plan that Mrs. Eowin had created. The art teacher had set aside the last two weeks of school as a time for her students to work on their portfolios. As far as I could tell, their portfolios were nothing more than scrapbooks filled with homework, photos, and lists of personal achievements over the course of the previous year. At the bottom of the typed instructions, the teacher had scribbled a handwritten note: _Most of the Seniors have finished their portfolios, so all you need is to keep them busy._

I tucked the lesson plan inside a manila folder I'd labeled for the purpose. There were a couple of other papers inside, including a copy of Luke's schedule, my class schedule, my FedEx tracking sheet for the package of supplies, and a form from the back of the school's rule book. I was putting the folder in my backpack when a familiar car pulled into the driveway. It was Clancy. I shouldn't have been surprised to see her. She actually lives in Illinois and the Detweiler farm isn't that far out of her way.

My friend had no more than opened her car door and taken one glance at me when her eyebrows shot up to her hairline. "What on earth happened to your face? Did somebody horsewhip you? I've never seen anything quite like that. It's a whole new look for you."

"Like it? I can arrange for you to sport similar markings. Kind of reminds me of Seal, the singer. He has those scars on his face. Of course, his are healed."

"Yes, that is rather a big difference. Yours looks fresh."

"It sure is." As we ambled over to the picnic table under the big trees in the Detweilers' back yard, I related my ill-fated adventure with Bert. "You should see my arms. They are all torn up. Brawny wrapped gauze around them. Think of hamburger run through a meat grinder, and you'll get the picture."

"Show me."

I rolled up the sleeves of my tee shirt and waited for the inevitable gasp that signaled Clancy's shock and dismay. Even though the gauze had done its job, wound discharge had leaked through making a mess. After Clancy's sharp inhale, I offered to I bring us both something to drink. Clancy requested an iced tea, and I wanted the same, plus a couple of Advils. "Be right back," I said.

On my return, Clancy sipped her cold drink while I downed the pills. "That certainly looked painful," she said cautiously.

"It is." I picked at a piece of rough wood on the picnic table. "Basically, I lost my first layer of skin to that tree."

"That's all you're taking for the pain? Advil?"

"Yup."

"You're a better girl than I am, Gunga Deanna."

That made us both laugh because she was referencing the famous Rudyard Kipling poem that both of us love.

"Everything is working out at the store. Mert and Laurel plan to switch off so Laurel doesn't tire herself out. Margit is bopping around. You know how she is."

"Thank you for making sure the place is running smoothly."

"You can thank me by telling me what's really going on."

I smiled. It hurt my face, but I still did it. "I will. Not now but soon, okay?"

"I guess it'll have to be."

Whipping out her pocketbook, Clancy carefully reapplied her lipstick even though she was going straight home. She's the most polished woman I've ever met. I don't think I've ever seen Clancy without her makeup during daylight. What a jarring sight she was with her sophisticated clothing in an oh-so-country setting complete with cows in the pasture. The pungent scent of pig manure mingled with her Chanel No. 5.

As I walked Clancy to her car, she said, "What's with Thelma? I saw her glaring at us from the kitchen window. Why didn't she come out and say hello?"

"Beats me. I'm beginning to think she's jealous of me. She thinks I've usurped her position in her son's life."

"Boy, oh boy. Lucky you."

"Yup. That's me. Lucky Kiki Lowenstein."

"Lowenstein-Detweiler."

I laughed. "Careful how you say that, partner. Them's fighting words to the other Mrs. Detweiler. Once again, thanks again for taking care of the store while I'm gone."

"No problem." Clancy is never very demonstrative, but she gave me a light peck on the cheek. "Be careful, Kiki. I don't know what you're up to, but you have a talent for putting yourself in harm's way. I couldn't stand it if something happened to you."

With that she hurriedly climbed in her car and drove away.

20

$\mathcal{I}$ had hoped for a relaxing evening since I was getting up early the next day and teaching my first classes. Thelma had a different agenda. She had noticed Brawny working on her computer and realized the nanny might be helping us.

"Why do you need to drag Brawny into this?" Thelma asked her son when we sat down to dinner. I fought the urge to roll my eyes. I was hungry. I'd already had a long day, I hurt all over, and I was really missing my kids. Thelma sensed my vulnerability and pounced. "Kiki? Is this your doing?"

"Mom?" My husband stared at his mother. "Please give it a rest."

I tried to concentrate on the delicious meal in the center of the dining room table. The smell of roasted chicken with onions, celery, and carrots perfumed the air. Heaven on earth. I couldn't wait to dig in.

"Brawny doesn't need to be involved," Thelma said.

Meanwhile Brawny was quietly feeding Ty his nightly meal of rice cereal. He was growing so fast that nursing wasn't enough for him.

"Yes, she does," my husband said while dishing out a gracious helping of his mother's excellent mashed potatoes. "Brawny has insights that might be helpful to us."

Brawny fought a smile.

"Even though you are welcome here, we don't really need you," Thelma addressed our nanny. "So if you want to take time off, Brawny, you certainly can."

"Mom? It's not your place to make decisions like that," my husband said. "Brawny is wonderful with Ty. She knows his routine."

"You don't trust your father and me to take care of our own grandchild?" Thelma's fork clattered to her plate. The shrill edge of her voice caused Ty to freeze in shock. His sweet little face was framed with wispy curls and a soggy Cheerio was stuck to his nose. I giggled at the sight of him.

"Hon, you're not being fair." Louis reached for his wife's hand, but Thelma drew hers away, angrily.

"I am too! I am sick and tired of being treated like a second-class citizen in my own home! Everybody knows everything but me. I'm an outsider!"

"That's not true, Mom, and you know it. You aren't an outsider. You're the heart of our family," Detweiler said, looking her in the eyes until she dropped her gaze.

"But Kiki," she muttered. That's all the further she got.

"But Kiki," my husband repeated, "Kiki was asked to participate in an investigation into the suicides at Jarvis Township High School. I'm trusting you to keep that a secret. Her life might be at risk. Seriously, don't you realize that knowing you're here with Ty gives us the courage to try to help? We have no idea what's going on at High Jarvis Township School beneath the surface. None. We don't know if one person is involved, six people, or none. That's the reason we were asked to help. The local law enforcement agencies are shorthanded, and Kiki has a unique background that gives her a valid reason for walking into that school and snooping around." Detweiler wiped his napkin across his face. "To tell you the truth, Mom, if Luke Kressig hadn't tried to kill himself, we probably wouldn't have gotten involved. Period. We turned Detective Schultz down the first time he asked. But seeing as how the Kressigs are family, we decided we couldn't sit on the sidelines. Don't make me second-guess my decision, Mom."

With a tiny huff of annoyance, Thelma added, "So you say."

Louis took his wife's hand. "Thelma, I think maybe you and I need to speak in private."

"Oh, no," she responded in a mocking tone. "Taking me to the woodshed, Louis? No way. I said my piece. My son has sassed me and put me in my place, and that's enough for one evening, thank you very much. Now. Who would like dessert?"

With that she got to her feet and stormed out of the room.

An uncomfortable silence followed. We sat around the table like pieces on a chessboard waiting to be moved. From the kitchen came the sounds of rattling dishes and slamming cabinet doors. Under his breath, Louis said, "I'll talk to her."

Marching into the dining room, Thelma carried a tray loaded with fat slices of pie. The plates jumped up from the tray as she set it down on the table with a thump.

"You can get up and get your own coffee," she announced with a challenge in her voice. Brawny and I rose in tandem. On our way into the kitchen, Brawny whispered to me, "That woman has a mean streak a mile wide."

I whispered back, "Don't I know it."

21

*T*he next morning, Detweiler woke me with a kiss and a question. "Ready for your first day of school, little girl? Got your backpack organized? That bright red slash on your face is bound to make a good impression. Kids love anything out of the ordinary. What are you planning to tell them about it?"

I yawned and snuggled closer to my husband. The bed was so comfy and the task ahead seemed gargantuan. My arms were raw, my butt was bruised, and my upper thighs were sore from riding Bert. I told Detweiler, "I'm going to say I was vacationing in the Caribbean when we were attacked by a boat full of pirates."

"Good one. Do you really think any of the students will believe you?" Detweiler's chuckle was low and sexy as he planted a kiss on my forehead.

"No worries at all about selling my story of kidnapping. One look at my swashbuckling face, and they'll know I was involved in crime on the high seas. Or the high trees, in my case." I blinked and sighed. "The pirate gig, I can sell. I'm worried they won't believe I'm a substitute teacher."

"I'm sure they'll fall for that. After all, you teach scrapbooking and papercrafts all the time."

"Yes, but this is all about finishing their senior portfolios. At least for one or two of the students, it will be."

"That's different how?"

He had a point. It wasn't really different. The art teacher might as well have written, "Pretend you're hosting these students at your store," because the activities were nothing foreign to me. Essentially, the kids were working on a scrapbook designed to document their school year.

And these poor kids had lived through a horrible, tragic year. I had two weeks with them. I vowed to make our time together enjoyable. That was the least I could do. I had tons of goodies to pass out. I'd packed up paper, stickers, embellishments, adhesives, and punches. Granted, I wasn't a highly trained LEO with all sorts of investigative skills, but I was better than that. Way better.

I was a scrapbooker.

Right. Like that would make a particle bit of difference to a serial killer.

This seemed like the perfect time to bury my head under the covers and sleep the day away. I might have done just that, except that I suffered from a full bladder and an equally pressing sense of responsibility. I groaned and rolled out of my warm bed. After taking care of nature's demands, I tiptoed into the guest bedroom where Ty was sound asleep in a crib. As usual, Brawny was already up. She was sitting in a rocking chair and quilting while my little guy slept. Gracie was snoozing at Brawny's feet, guarding my son.

I stared down at my sleeping baby. I'd give anything to protect my children. But was I up to the task I'd set for myself? Brawny read my mind. "You'll be fine. I know you will be."

"Thanks," I said. "I'm glad you're on my side."

"You know I am. I'm your biggest fan. Next to my mum, you're the most extraordinary woman I know."

Her confidence meant the world to me.

"Kiki?" Detweiler called out. "Are you watching the time?"

"Coming." I'd laid out my clothes the night before, so I hurried into our room, expressed some milk, and got dressed. My husband and I were eating a quick bowl of cereal when his mother came into the kitchen. Thelma was wearing a tired blue chenille housecoat and slippers. She gave me a sour look and asked her son, "Wouldn't you rather have a proper meal of hash browns and eggs?"

"Nope. Thanks, Mom. I've got to drop Kiki off at school." He punctuated his response with a kiss on the tip of my nose.

Thelma stared hard to me. "Are you dressed appropriately? Shouldn't you be wearing something more professional?"

I looked down at my black jeans, my freshly ironed pink-and-black-and-white striped button-down shirt, and my black ballet flats. "I'm dressed for action. Mrs. Eowin's supplies might be in tall cabinets. I might need to climb on stepladders."

"Mom, she looks great. She's going to teach art. Art teachers' clothes always get trashed. Seriously. Leave her alone."

"Okay." Thelma sneered as I stood up and hoisted my back-pack over one shoulder. "If you say so. Don't listen to me."

After I put my cereal bowl in the dishwasher, I did my best to ignore Thelma. While she banged around in the kitchen, Detweiler and I reviewed the safety procedures we'd put into place. I had my cell phone, a button that whooped like a siren, and a can of pepper spray in my backpack. Brawny had practiced simple but effective self-defense tips with me. She was a firm believer that you could use just about anything to do bodily harm to another person, if necessary. "Ye have a fantastic imagination, so use it to save yourself if the need arises. You can do this."

"I play tennis. Art's my first period class."

"Do you like it?"

"Yeah. Matter of fact, I love it. I'd like to be an artist one day. Not that it'll ever happen."

That seemed sad to me so I stopped and asked, "Why not?"

"My parents. You know how old people are. They're pains in the butt. They've got it in their heads that I'm going to be a lawyer or an accountant. Whatever. Something really boring. Like their lives are. Boring. Gross. I hope not. They are so lame."

"Yup. Parents can be pretty shortsighted." I chuckled to myself.

"How about your parents? Are they cool?"

I wondered how candid I should be. "My dad's dead." And before my new companion could share sympathy, I added, "My mom is a total loser. Just a horrible, miserable excuse for a person."

"I hear you. Mine drinks like it is going out of style. Seriously. She's totally sloshed by the time she falls into bed at night. Dad sleeps in another room. Man. I seriously do not want to be like them when I get old."

"I hear you," I repeated the phrase because I'd read somewhere that echoing was a good way to encourage the other person to keep talking. My new friend pointed to the plaque that indicated we'd arrived at Room 176. Extending my hand, I introduced myself. "I'm Kiki."

"I'm Tadd Lancer. The third. Can you believe it?"

That made me laugh. "I guess I can. At least the people in your family can count to three. I'm not sure my parents were ever sober long enough to get that far."

The teacher's desk was at the far end of the room, so I walked over and set my backpack on the floor.

22

"**M**rs. Eowin is out on maternity leave," Tadd explained as he pointed at the over-sized desk that must have been her home base.

"Uh-huh." I put my lunch bag on that desk and looked around. My FedEx tracking number assured me that my box of scrapbooking supplies had been delivered to this room. But I didn't see the box I'd packed.

"Can you imagine? It's Mrs. Eowin's third kid. And her husband is a mechanic. I wouldn't want to be the Eowins. No way." Tadd's eyes followed me, and his easygoing expression began to change. "I wonder who our sub is going to be. Probably some old goat. The last sub I had was for geometry, and she had hairs growing out of her chin. Her name was Mrs. Billy. Can you believe that?"

His report stopped me in my tracks. "Mrs. Billy? Like Billy Goat? You've got to be kidding!" That's when I spotted my box shoved into a corner behind a trash can. I moved the can to one side and dragged the box closer to the desk. "Um, do you know where the scissors are?"

Tadd frowned. "You aren't going to open that, are you? Mr. Rusk will, like seriously, get salty with you."

I gave Tadd a reassuring smile. "I'll take the blame if he gets upset."

"But what about the sub? What if it's Mrs. Billy again? She'll have a seizure. I wouldn't do it. She was, like, older than my granny and tougher than an old shoe."

At that moment, Sidney Rusk, dean of students, stumbled into the room. I recognized him from his photo on the school website. At barely five feet six, he wasn't much taller than I. His greasy hair was slicked back and flecked with huge snowflakes of dandruff. His Coke bottle glasses were smeared with dirty smudges. His white shirt sported yellow stains under the armpits. His tie had a big splotch in the center, and it hung awkwardly pointing to one side. The perforations in his wingtips were clotted with mud. One of his socks had fallen down to expose a thin, white ankle.

There are homeless people walking the streets of St. Louis who dress better than Sidney Rusk. I wouldn't want this guy to walk my dog much less teach my kids.

I extended my hand and introduced myself. "Hi, you're Mr. Rusk, aren't you? I'm Kiki Lowenstein-Detweiler."

"Ah. Mrs. Lowenstein-Detweiler. Wouldn't just Lowenstein or Detweiler do? No? I guess not. You women and your hyphen-ated names. A sign of the times, I guess. Why you can't content yourselves with one last name is beyond me. Pity the poor students. I see you found your box. Good. Glad you did. Next time please warn us when you ship a heavy package. I had to get the janitor, Mr. Craig, to carry it to the room. Wouldn't want to put my back out. I guess you didn't realize how much that box weighed, did you? What on earth did you pack in there? Hmm? Nothing contraband, I assume? No? All right."

Poor Tadd looked totally confused. He stuttered, "T-t-teacher? You're a teacher?"

Tadd thought I was a student! How embarrassing for him and how flattering to me. I wanted to explain that I wouldn't blab about what he'd said to me, but now wasn't the right time. Poor Tadd walked to a chair at the back of the room as twenty-one students filed in and took their seats, too.

As for the weight of the box, only a weasel would have a problem with that. I lift boxes that size all the time. Heck, I lift Erik and he's heavier than that box. Pretty nervy of Mr. Rusk to complain, especially given that I was donating $500 worth of scrapbooking supplies to this school.

The bell rang, and Mr. Rusk kept talking at me. I had tuned him out. Either he didn't notice the bright red stripe on my face or he didn't care. "You did get a copy of the school board's rules and guidelines, didn't you? Did you sign the sheet at the back of it? I need that. I need proof that you have read and agree to abide by our rules."

Schultz had mailed the rules and guidelines to me and I'd received them before I left Webster Groves. I dug around in my backpack and opened the manila folder. The signed sheet was there. When I handed it to Mr. Rusk, he almost seemed disappointed.

"I'm far too busy to introduce you around. I can do this class, but you're on your own for everything else. Be a good girl and introduce yourself. You can manage that, can't you?"

Be a good girl? What decade did this man live in? I made a mental note to ask Brawny to look into this man's background. He struck me as a bona fide creep.

"Students?" Mr. Rusk rapped his knuckles on a desk. "This is Mrs. Lowenstein-Detweiler, and she's taking Mrs. Eowin's place while your art teacher is on maternity leave. I expect you to be respectful of her or else. Give her your full attention."

With that, he walked out of the room.

None of the students were sitting up straight. They slumped in their seats. They fiddled with their phones. A few even chatted with each other while two openly snickered. If this was Jarvis Township High School's version of full attention, it forecast a rocky future for me, indeed.

In my high school, we would have been given detentions for such nonsense. We wouldn't have dared to keep talking while an administrator was speaking. No way! I knew that kids didn't act like this in my daughter's school because I frequently volunteered there. Suddenly, a cold sweat broke out on my forehead. I gasped for air like a goldfish who'd flopped out of its bowl.

What had I gotten myself into?

The only students who looked at me with any sort of interest seemed to be Tadd and John Kressig. But when John realized he was sticking out like the proverbial sore thumb, he slowly slid deeper into his seat. Despite his "I don't care" posture, his eyes sent me a warm message of gratitude. I shot him the faintest flicker of a smile.

A wave of fear washed over me. I'd never done this before. Or had I? Honestly, I'd taught how many classes? *Tons*. I could do this. Besides, it wasn't like I had to meet any academic standards. To be honest, I was a glorified babysitter. I couldn't blame the kids for not showing Mr. Rusk any respect. He brought that upon himself. What happened next was up to me.

"All right," I said, clapping my hands to get their attention. "Inside this classroom, you can call me Kiki. That'll be our little secret, all right?"

"What happened to your face?" asked a boy built like a fireplug.

"A horse and I disagreed about the height of a tree limb. He won."

Another young man, one who looked like he lifted weights,

spoke up. "I thought maybe you were into fencing or martial arts."

"Nope. I've only ever been good at two things in life: scrapbooking and getting pregnant."

Now I definitely had their attention! A few giggles bubbled up.

"Obviously, I am not going to teach you how to get pregnant. You can figure that out on your own. Trust me, it's easier than you think."

Now there was outright laughter.

"So that leaves us with scrapbooking. And you know what? I think you'll like scrapbooking. I want us to have fun. To make sure that happens, I brought along this big box of supplies. Anyone curious about what's inside?"

Hands flew up.

"Cool. Tadd? Would you help me by coming over here and opening this up? Do you have a car key? Scissors? After all, this is an art room. You gotta have scissors."

A slender girl in a faded pair of distressed jeans and a Hello Kitty tee shirt pointed to a tall pair of metal cabinets. "All the supplies are in here."

Another student piped up, "Yeah, we didn't use them. Mrs. Eowin was big into theory."

"Huh? You mean to tell me that you were taking art, but you didn't get to make art?" I couldn't believe what I was hearing.

"That's right," said a boy who'd been sitting so low in his seat that only his shoulders and head showed. "Lookie, lookie, but no touchie."

"Sheesh. That's no fun." I couldn't imagine sitting next to a cabinet full of supplies and not being able to use them.

"Mrs. Eowin wasn't into messes." This came from a beanpole boy in the far left corner.

"Wow," I said, falling back on my favorite all-purpose word.

"And she's having her third kid? That ought to be a panic. Okay, listen up. I am the queen of messes. Honest to gosh. I'm a personal hot mess, and I love making messes. Are you with me?"

There was a tepid chorus of, "Yes!"

"More importantly, I think you can make art out of anything. Absolutely anything, and I'll prove it to you." While I'd been talking, Tadd had retrieved a pair of scissors and opened the box. He'd also kindly set it on top of my desk. I reached in and held up two lunch bags. "Please pass these around. I'd like each of you to take six of the white and one of the brown."

Since Tadd was next to the box, he handed out the bags. John had wisely put himself at the back of the room, an ideal spot for observing the other students.

"During the course of the week, I want you to fill your brown bag with ephemera. Does anybody know what ephemera is?"

A studious-looking young lady with designer glasses raised her hand. "Typically ephemera is paper, and it refers to things expected to be useful for a short period of time, like tickets, receipts, bill stubs, flyers, reminders, and tags."

"Very good." I turned to the chalkboard, found a piece of chalk, and printed EPHEMERA on the board. To the right of it, I listed tickets, receipts, bill stubs, menus, coupons, flyers, reminders, tags, notes, shopping lists, packaging, postcards, greeting cards, packing slips, directions, invoices, some letters, direct mail, some instructions, and some notifications. Turning to the group, I explained, "Greeting cards and postcards you might argue aren't part of this list, but I like the list to be as broad as possible. Anything you can put in the bag will serve our purposes."

"How about a French fries bag?" asked a chubby boy with a crew cut.

"Sure. Please realize that the oil might spread and ruin other stuff, but certainly any food container would work."

"A cap from a bottle of beer?" asked a muscular boy in the back.

That got the class snickering.

"Yeah. Some people might not agree because the cap is metal, but I'm fine with it. Think of this like a treasure hunt. We're going to make trash journals. You see, as we move through life we create trash. That's exactly what archeologists find that helps them to understand a civilization. In fact, they call such sites 'middens,' and they have tons of historical value. Our lives are interesting, too. Ten years from now, you'll look back and laugh about what you were eating, watching, doing, buying, and caring about. Let me give you an example." From the box, I pulled out a page I'd made when Anya was born. I also retrieved a page from when Ty was born. I put them side-by-side on my desk. "Come and look at these."

The students gathered around me. I showed them how on Anya's page there was a label for a can of formula that was different from the formula for Ty. Not surprisingly, the baby pictures taken by the hospitals were different. The clarity of the photos had improved immensely. The forms with essential information had changed, too. On Anya's page was a paper band that had been taped around her ankle. On Ty's there was a Radio Frequency ID band. In envelopes, I'd stuffed the bills from the hospitals. I took those out so the kids could compare them. One girl giggled and said, "I didn't know that having a baby was so expensive."

"It certainly is," I agreed, "and I'm blessed because my children were born healthy. The bills for babies with problems are astronomical. How about if you copy down this list—" and I pointed to the blackboard "—and write it on your brown bag as a way to remember what to save. Anyone have any other ideas about ephemera we can look for?"

"Parking tickets," said the guy who looked like a weight lifter.

"Pay stubs," said a boy.

"Those cards that always fall out of magazines."

"Recipes. Especially the free ones you get from the grocery store."

"Permission slips."

"Newspaper clippings?" the girl with glasses asked, and I answered, "Sure, why not?"

"Fortune cookie fortunes," said the fireplug boy.

"Sticky notes," said another boy.

Actually the hour ended too quickly. The students and I had fun brainstorming what they'd put in their trash journals. A few minutes before the bell rang, I said, "We'll start on your trash journals tomorrow. However, I would like for you to collect ephemera all week. That'll give you a better idea of all the stuff that floats around you and gets ignored."

The bell rang and the students filed past me. The boy who wanted to keep a French fries bag paused long enough to tell me, "Best class I've ever had. Ever."

John Kressig was the last to leave. When no one could hear him, he said, "Way to go. They love you."

Yeah, maybe I could do this!

23

The next period was my teacher prep period. I found the teachers' lounge easily because it was four doors down from the art classroom. Tossing my backpack over one arm, I squared my shoulders and walked in, not knowing what to expect. Clancy had once told me that teacher prep was typically a hotbed of gossip, complaints, and rumors.

I was the first person there, so I sat in an overstuffed chair at the back of the room. To my immediate right was a pair of computer desks with Dell computers for general use. The WiFi password was printed on a label on the front of each unit. To my left was a small kitchenette: a sink, refrigerator, coffee maker, electric kettle, Formica counter, dishwasher, and cabinets. My chair was the only cushy chair in the room, and I hoped I wasn't taking another teacher's spot. The placement would give me a good vantage point for watching the other teachers and observing their interactions.

When we'd looked over my schedule, Detweiler and I had learned that teachers rotated in and out of the lounge every two weeks, using this room for breaks and class prep. They took turns being on duty in the computer lab and in the lunch room. I was disappointed at what we learned. "It's possible that I'll be on duty with four teachers who can shed no light on what's happening."

My husband had sighed and said, "That's true, but this was the closest we could get to copying Luke's schedule."

I had nodded. "We can only do what we can do."

The door to the teachers' lounge flew open and in came two people, talking animatedly. I'd studied photos of the staff so I knew I'd been joined by Jessie Lionel, an English teacher and an aspiring author. She was forty-two, divorced, and had moved here from Tucson. Jessie was nicely dressed in a pink and green floral dress, white blouse, and a green cardigan sweater. Her nails and her lipstick were a matched shade of pink. Alan Bowman, age thirty-three, was a teddy bear of a man who must have been an athlete once because he moved with grace. He taught geography, sociology, and civics. He wore a nice suit, an Oxford cloth shirt, and a bright blue tie.

Alan was saying to Jessie, "He's alive, isn't he? That's what his brother told a group of kids."

"If Luke's alive, maybe we'll find out whether someone is behind all this? It's just creepy. Totally creepy," Jessie said.

"There's alive and *alive*," Alan said. "If he didn't get enough oxygen to his brain, his body might be alive but he might not be all there, you know? Besides, this is nothing but a bunch of stupid kids copying each other. What's there for Luke to tell? Nothing."

"I for one am sick of this. I have three job applications out to teach creative writing at prestigious colleges and all this bad publicity is making me look—" she spotted me. "Oh, hello. You must be the new substitute teacher. Welcome." She froze as she stared at my face and my mark of shame. "Oh, my."

After introducing myself, I repeated my explanation about the horse and the tree.

The door opened again and in came two more teachers, Drew Simchuck and Oleander Varney. Drew was the head of the PE department and the football coach. At forty-six, with bulging muscles and a burr haircut, he looked the part. Drew wore a gray track suit and red athletic shoes. Oleander, age thirty-two, taught French. She could have stepped off the pages of the Sundance catalog. Her hair was a loose tangle of red curls. Multiple bangles rattled around her wrist. A long skirt swept the floor. Each step exposed her leather huaraches.

The introductions continued, and my explanation about my problem with a horse was repeated. Handshakes were offered all around. Drew squeezed my fingers so hard I couldn't help but wince. When he saw me my reaction, he apologized. "Say, are you related to Patricia Detweiler?" he asked.

"Yes, she's my sister-in-law."

"Then you married Chad? Her brother? I remember when he worked stocking groceries. He was going to night school, right?"

I was in a pickle. I didn't want to admit my husband was a cop because that might limit what I could learn. On the other hand, Drew was angling to prove his superiority, and I didn't want to challenge the man on my first day, so I simply nodded. "That's my husband. A lifelong student. Of course, there's plenty of work at the family farm to keep him busy."

"Yeah, I bet. Once a farm boy always a farm boy," said Drew. "You can't get that love of the land out of us, can you?"

"No, you can't," I said.

Alan went to the refrigerator and withdrew a can of Red Bull. "Anyone?"

I couldn't imagine the sort of jitters a shot of Red Bull would give me. None of the others took him up on it either. Oleander moved to the electric kettle and flipped the switch to boil water. "Tea, anyone?"

"Yes, please," I said. So did Jessie. Drew asked Oleander to make him a cup of instant coffee. The way he said it, and the fact she didn't ask specifics, gave me the impression that she'd made the drink for him numerous times.

"Jessie and I were talking about our latest near miss, Luke Kressig," said Alan as he hoisted his pants, the way men do, as if we don't notice how they are rearranging themselves.

"Poor kid," said Jessie. "Near miss sounds so cavalier, but it's accurate. Luke tried to kill himself over the weekend. You've probably heard we've had a rash of teen suicides here at Jarvis Township High School. It's been horrid. The way the parents look at us? Such accusation in their eyes. As if we're the ones who need to stop this from happening!"

Here was my chance to learn more. "I heard a little about the problem. Through the media, you know? Copycats, right? I don't know very much about teen suicides. Is there something I should look out for?"

"Probably not," Oleander said. Raising a delicate hand with a leather bracelet, she brushed a curl from her forehead and added, "All you can do is be sympathetic. The students are grieving."

Jessie said, "We have no idea where this is coming from. None. No one knows. Could be the kids bullying each other." With a disinterested shrug she added, "We do what we can but we cannot be everywhere all the time, watching and babysitting, you know? The parents, they expect too much from us. They should do their jobs. Then this would stop. I get sick of how they blame us for everything."

"Not fair, Jessie, and you know it," said Oleander as she

poured hot water into mugs. "The Internet is a big part of all our lives. It's there, it's insidious, and who could monitor a child 24-7? No one. Especially if you have two jobs like a lot of these parents do."

She passed a mug of steaming hot coffee to Drew. He took it and said, "Sports. That's the answer. We need a more robust athletic department. Team sports keep kids focused on good behavior. Exercise is proven to help with depression. Sports and exercise build character. You notice that none of my football players has tried any of that nonsense."

"Not everyone can play sports," Alan interjected. "Music and art are helpful, too. Ask Joseph Scalia, the music director. He told me that his kids haven't been affected by the rash of suicides."

"You're suggesting that the kids who've hurt themselves were uninvolved? Not part of any organized school activities?" I hoped I wouldn't sound too bold, but to ignore the topic at hand didn't make sense, either.

"Yes, no, wait," Drew said with a frown. "That girl, Lisa Sorenson? She was in choir, wasn't she? She took pills and killed herself. So Joseph is blowing smoke."

"Lisa was in choir but then she dropped out." Alan covered his mouth to burp. He tossed his empty Red Bull can into the recycling bin.

I shivered.

Drew put a hand on my shoulder. "Not to worry. You're an adult and a productive member of society. You're safe. This is a matter of kids talking each other into stupid stunts."

Oleander's eyes grew moist. "These kids have their whole lives ahead of them. Everything. They hate being teens. Hate living out here in the sticks. They haven't found themselves yet. They get depressed and think this is the way the rest of their lives will go."

"You sound like you remember being an outcast," I said.

"I do. I was the weird one. The hippy girl. I spent my entire high school career on the outside looking in."

Drew smirked. "All better now?"

Oleander nodded slowly. "Yes. Yes, it really is. Most of the time."

---

24

*W*hen the bell rang, Drew Simchuck walked me to the computer lab. Along the way, he asked, "Do you know anything about computers?"

"A little," I said.

As we entered the lab, he jerked his head toward a bank of computers. "Come over here." Drew pulled a chair across the floor and plopped down in it, leaving the chair at the desk for me. His fingers raced across the keyboard as he booted up the unit. Talking over his shoulder, he lectured me. "This is the Intranet, the school computer network. I made you an account, KLDetweiler@JarvisTHS.edu. We get bulletins, reports, updates from the school board, and so on this way. This is the best method for contacting another teacher or turning in your grades. See that icon? It's the yellow letter J on a royal blue background. Of course, you aren't restricted to our internal communication system. You can also use the World Wide Web. Go to the browser icon and right click it twice."

"Isn't it risky to let students roam around the Internet? It seems like a waste of time when they should be studying," I said. I hoped he would tell me something we—Schultz, my husband, John, and I didn't know. Or even talk about the suicides.

"You bet it is. It's like letting a team on the field without a referee. Here's the deal: a lot of these kids don't have good Internet—or any Internet—at home. This area being rural and all. In this day and age, you can't get to the starting block in life without the Internet. Half of our graduating seniors are taking AP, Advanced Placement classes, and they are taught over the Internet. All of us assign our students homework and post it on the school's website. Much of their research is done online. Some of the seniors are already getting their college reading assignments, and those exchanges happen via the Internet. We do everything we can to screen out porn and keep our students safe, but blocking them from using the Internet would seriously handicap their academic careers."

He searched my face for a sign that I understood. I said, "My daughter is 13 turning 14 this summer. I'm astonished by how much of her study time is spent on the Internet. Back in the old days, I used to practically live in the public library; Anya couldn't find a book on a library shelf if her life depended on it."

Drew rumbled a low, "Uh-huh. Not only that, you were limited to whatever your library system could buy, beg, or borrow. For these youngsters, the sky's the limit. You'd be amazed at the sorts of cool research they can do. My ten-year-old was assigned a paper on Native Americans. Using the Web, he tracked down a tribal elder and interviewed the man via email. Not only was it a home run of a project, but my kid connected with another human being. Someone from outside of his immediate social circle. That was a powerful experience, for sure." Realizing that we'd been talking a lot while students were coming in, Drew tried to wrap things up. He tapped another set of buttons.

The screen blinked and changed. The icon for Outlook

popped up. Everything there was familiar, and I said as much. We use Outlook at the store. I could pick up my email messages from my phone, but I'm not as good at texting as my daughter. With Outlook being available, I could type longer messages from the computer lab and send them to Anya or even Clancy at the store. With a mental dope slap, I realized that that Schultz was probably monitoring any outgoing emails. I would use Outlook to communicate with Clancy if I had to, but I would be extremely careful about what I wrote. Long ago, I realized that if you had anything sensitive to share, you should do it in person or over the phone. Certainly not via email.

"I doubt that I'll do much emailing from these computers," I said.

"Up to you." Drew linked his hands behind his head and leaned back in his chair. "That's the nickel tour. You're good to go. When the students are in computer lab, they're supposed to be doing their homework. Don't fool yourself, they'll cruise the Internet at the drop of a pencil. You need to walk around a lot and check on them."

"Won't you be here in the computer lab while I am?" I took the opportunity to do a slow scan of the room. John was seated at a computer station directly across from where I was sitting. He gave me a barely perceptible nod of acknowledgement and went back to staring at his computer monitor.

"Depends," Drew said. "Usually I am, but not today. This is the time of year when I do my planning for our fall football season. Most of my notes are in the PE office. I'm heading there as soon as I know you're settled."

"If there's a problem with the computers ..." I let the question float in the air.

"Call me. The school secretary will track me down."

"What sort of problems might happen? What should I expect?" I asked.

"Kids do the darnedest things. One girl hit a bizarre combination of keys and lost her entire college essay. I was able to retrieve it. Another boy was working on his science fair project. He put his charts in Google docs, and then he couldn't access them to show his teacher. He was totally freaked out. There's always the occasional wise guy who's convinced he can watch porn without anybody knowing. We have monitoring programs that alert me when that happens, and it does, with regularity. You'd think we were a training academy for gifted gynecologists the way some of these boys act."

That caused me to blush.

"Power surges and outages cause havoc. Bad storms can knock our Intranet out. Tornados? Don't get me started." Drew shrugged and rolled his eyes to the heavens. "Who knows what Mother Nature has planned for us? Okay, you ready to take the helm, captain?"

With that, he left.

As per Drew's instructions, after introducing myself, I spent the first fifteen minutes roaming around. A few of the students didn't even turn on their computers. Instead they brought books to read or quietly did sudoku puzzles for extra math credit. Two, a boy and a girl, asked permission to work together. They were writing a play to present at a summer theater camp. I said fine as long as they kept the noise level down. After looking over many shoulders and finding nothing to concern me, I booted up a computer and created journaling boxes for my art students to use.

Journaling boxes are preprinted boxes scrapbookers can use to tell a story. Most scrapbookers don't like to journal (write information) while they're creating a page. Journaling boxes make it easy to add information at a later date. I call them SOFJ or Sites of Future Journaling. I like to design journaling boxes on the computer, using clip art and fancy borders. I make enough to fill up a page and print them on archivally safe paper.

When I finished creating a full page of boxes, I sent a copy to my Intranet address, KLDetweiler@JarvisTHS.edu and forwarded a copy to the store so I'd have it for my archives. The minute I hit "send," I realized that I should have put the copyright symbol, my name, and a date on my work. I did a second version, adding all those details, and sent it to my Intranet address and the store. A faint "ding" told me that my first version had landed in my Intranet email inbox. I quickly hit delete, moving it to the trash.

Then I had a brainstorm: If I went into the trash and hit "permanently delete," no one could access that first version. It would never get in the wrong hands. I'm not paranoid, but I have noticed how easy it is for people to share what they find on the Internet and not give credit to the source. My small business needs all the credit we can get.

I opened the trash and found four items, one of which was the first file with my journaling boxes but no copyright details. With two taps of the keys, I erased the original file forever.

The rest of the hour went by quickly. I was fortunate that the students had been on their best behavior. So far, so good. My first class had given me confidence. The teacher prep time seemed tame enough. The computer lab session had gone without a hitch. Maybe I was being overly optimistic, but I thought the people at Jarvis Township High School were a pretty nice group.

Except for the Devil who lurked behind the shadows and encouraged students to kill themselves. Brawny had warned me about being lulled into thinking I was safe.

The bell rang for my lunch period. The cafeteria was easy enough to find, but as I stood in the huge doorway, I felt sick. The sight of students and teachers lining up for food, the long tables, the trays. . . all of that conspired to bring back some of the worst memories of my teenage years. I had hated eating in the school cafeteria. Absolutely hated it. The lunchroom was where the worst teasing and bullying took place. Rather than walking into the Jarvis Township High School cafeteria, I froze. I was stuck there in the doorway with my backpack over a shoulder and a brown lunch bag in my hand.

I fought the urge to run back to the teachers' lounge. Oh, how I wanted to! But I couldn't. That would be shirking my responsibilities .At Jarvis Township High School, teachers were assigned lunchroom duty on a rotating schedule. That was the only way the staff could keep watch over the 342 members of the student body.

Of course, I was assigned the cafeteria duty that Mrs. Eowin would have normally taken. To duck out would be irresponsible. There was nothing I could do but take her place. My best option was to find a seat in the back of the huge room and keep my head down.

Not surprisingly, students and teachers had already staked out their chosen spots. Standing on tiptoe, I didn't see any unoccupied seats. I couldn't keep blocking the doorway. With my heart in my mouth, I scurried to the back of the cafeteria. I'd made it to the last row of tables when I noticed Oleander was sitting alone in a far corner. "May I sit with you?" I asked.

"But of course." She smiled kindly at me while she dished up a small spoonful of low-fat yogurt. From the looks of it, that's all she was eating for lunch. I could never manage on so little food.

She cocked her head and asked, "How's your first day going?"

"Pretty good." No way was I going to admit to being intimidated by the cafeteria. Instead, I picked an easy conversational tidbit to share. "Mr. Rusk isn't happy with me. The box of supplies that I sent on ahead was too heavy for him to lift."

"*Mon dieu.*" She waved off his complaint. "That man! Such a ninny. Honest. If there's such a thing as a male diva, he's that."

I opened my brown paper bag, set aside napkins and a wet wipe, and pulled out the tuna fish salad sandwich that Brawny had wrapped in wax paper. There was also a plastic bag of sliced cucumbers, carrots, and celery. A bottle of water and a cupcake were the finishing touches. Oh, how I love our nanny!

"Oleander? Do you know a teacher named Tammy Calhoun?"

"Middle school English teacher. Why?"

"She's a friend of a friend, and I was told to say hello. Speaking of teachers, the students told me that Mrs. Eowin didn't like messes. They said that they rarely used the art supplies. Is that true?"

Covering her mouth, she giggled. "Yes. Crazy, *n'est-ce pas?* Imagine if I tried to teach *la Francaise* but didn't allow the students to speak it. *Trés ridiculous.* That's why so many of them are behind on their portfolios. They are supposed to have them done, but ..."

I dropped my half-eaten carrot stick. "Excuse me? I was told that majority of the portfolios *are* done. According to the lesson plan, my job is to keep the students busy until the school year ends."

"*Non, non, non.*" Oleander stared at me with big eyes. "Janice Eowin did not even start the portfolios. Some of the seniors worked ahead without her. They were worried about getting their portfolios done because they cannot graduate without them."

"Look," I said as I pulled out my phone and scrolled through the pictures. I had photographed the lesson plan so it would always be at my fingertips. I stopped racing through the photos when I came to Janice Eowin's lesson plan. "See?" and I showed the image to Oleander. "*Most of the Seniors have finished their portfolios, so all you need is to keep them busy.*"

"*Mon Dieu.* She is lying, and I know why. If the school had any idea that the portfolios weren't done, Mr. Rusk might have cancelled her maternity leave. She is only six months along." With a quick glance left and right, Oleander cupped a hand over her mouth and whispered in my ear, "Janice lied about her due date. She wanted time to get the baby's nursery ready."

"Oh, boy," I said. "Good thing we had this conversation. What if I hadn't found out that most of the students haven't started their portfolios? They couldn't have graduated. It would have been my fault! I would have let the kids down. That would have been awful for them and for me! Can you imagine how upset everyone would be with me? I'd be upset with me, too, if I was the reason that kids didn't graduate." I babbled because I was shook up. This had been a very near miss.

"*Alors!* Things could be worse." Oleander lifted her shoulders and let them drop in a classic Gallic shrug. "These days I compare everything to students killing themselves. Nothing else matters, you know? Not really. The suicides have been so terrible. *Je ne sais pas.* I feel angry and hurt and disappointed in turns."

"Were any of the victims your students?"

"Yes. Elise Abrams and Tony Mangiano. Wonderful kids. *Trés adorable.* Not the most popular, not stars by any stretch of the imagination, but I thought they were doing all right. The news about their deaths came out of the blue. *Oh, c'est terrible!*" Her voice trembled and she sipped from her metal water bottle. "I dream about them. I hate going to sleep at night. If I didn't have my cat, LeChat, I would be so sad."

That led us to talking about our pets. I was happy for the change of topic because talking about the suicides had pushed Oleander to the brink of tears.

The bell rang, and we threw away our trash. Despite the shocker about the portfolios, I had enjoyed spending time with Oleander. "Only two more classes to go," she said with a smile. "Your first day."

"Right," I said, but in my head I was thinking, "One class down and forty-one more to go."

Was I nuts or what?

25

*D*etweiler was waiting for me at the end of the day. He'd driven his father's blue Ford pickup truck. The minute I climbed in, I told him about the portfolios. "That stinks," he said. "Someone in administration had to approve Mrs. Eowin's lesson plan. We need to find the person who did that. Sounds to me like you were set-up. You would have been blamed when the kids didn't graduate."

"What if Oleander hadn't said anything?" I agreed. "Can you imagine? Are we going to grab something to eat? I'm starved."

My last two classes of the day had been easy. The students were sophomores and juniors. They were happy to spend an hour learning to make trash journals. I got the impression that my classes provided a welcome stress release for the kids.

"John's meeting us at the Flying Horse Truck Stop," Detweiler said. "I figured you'd be hungry after a long day at school. The kids always are."

Entering the truck stop building, we quickly found John. He was sitting in a booth against the back wall. A waitress wearing a name badge that said, "Iola," stopped by to take our drink orders. She looked like an Iola. She was a cheerful bleached blonde with dark roots, and a gap between her front teeth. Iola wore blue jean cut-offs. Her britches were so short that the lining of the pockets stuck out below the hem. Her tee shirt said, "SuperSTAR" in gold foil letters. If it hadn't been for the change pouch she wore tied around her waist, you would have thought she was a patron of this fine establishment rather than a server.

I liked her immediately. She had spunk.

Sitting in the back of the restaurant gave us the chance to spot anyone walking in. As long as we kept an eye on the front doors, there was very little chance of someone surprising us. I told John what I'd learned from Oleander about the senior portfolios.

"That's weird," said John. "Didn't Mr. Rusk have to approve the lesson plans before Mrs. Eowin left? That's how they usually do it."

Detweiler gave a loud huff of disapproval. "We wondered who was in charge of approving the lesson plan. You say it's Rusk?"

John nodded. "I'm 99% sure."

"Mr. Rusk must have wanted me to fail. And fail spectacularly," I said. I had ordered a cup of hot tea and a lemon poppy seed muffin, and the men asked for coffee. Iola cheerfully brought us the drinks and my food.

"In a weird way, it makes sense." John fiddled with his plastic stirrer. "I bet that Mr. Rusk hoped a scandal over the portfolios would turn attention away from the suicides. See? It's twisted logic, but logic after all."

Detweiler sighed. "I'm not sure if that makes him a viable suspect for the suicides. A sneak, yes. A sociopath? No."

"He has no moral fiber," John confirmed. "Mr. Rusk accused Luke of keying his car. There was no proof, but Mr. Rusk insisted that my brother was responsible so he expelled Luke for a week."

"You can do that? Make an unfounded accusation and kick a kid out of school?" I couldn't believe what I was hearing.

"I guess so. My folks were furious. Ma wanted to talk to the school board but Luke talked her out of it. He said that Mr. Rusk would find another way to punish him. Luke told us about another incident. One of the students lost his scholarship because Mr. Rusk took his time getting the boy's transcript to the college. Of course, Mr. Rusk claimed he sent it, but this kid had been bugging Mr. Rusk to get it done, and it would have been easy enough to double-check since it was sent electronically. But Mr. Rusk refused to do that. Luke was convinced that Rusk held the grades back on purpose. My brother said Mr. Rusk always hated that particular boy. He made no secret of how he felt, either."

"Could Mr. Rusk be behind all this?" I asked my husband as I brushed the muffin crumbs off my hand. "He's a bully. He has almost unlimited power. He's vindictive."

"Maybe." Detweiler stirred his coffee. "Moving on, Schultz told me his department doesn't have the manpower to do extensive background checks into everyone who works at the school. What you're telling me is that we shouldn't exclude the school staff from our inquiries."

"I bet Brawny can help with that," I said. "She already volunteered to check people's social media accounts."

"Brawny? Your nanny?" John repeated incredulously. "Was that the older woman wearing black pants who was sitting at the picnic table with the kids?"

"Yes, she has skills and resources," Detweiler said. "And the less anyone else knows about her involvement, the better. John? We're trusting you to not say anything."

John hooted a laugh. "How could I? Who would believe it? Your nanny has resources? Like what? An extra copy of Dr. Spock's manual for raising kids?"

"She served in the SRS," I explained.

"You're kidding me? That's our equivalent of the Navy Seals, right?" John couldn't believe what he was hearing.

Detweiler continued, "Brawny's also a graduate of an elite school for nannies who serve families of the rich and powerful. In both jobs, she received training in a variety of covert activities. Her previous employer paid for her to take continuing education. She's taken extensive computer classes. She even has a private detective's license in California."

"And she's your nanny? The one who looked like a caterer? Black pants and white blouse?"

"We inherited her when we adopted Erik," I explained. "We're not rich or famous but Erik's late parents were."

"I see." John didn't seem convinced.

"You think an adult might be behind all these suicides? A staff member at the school?" I asked my husband.

"I have no idea. Not yet. But it makes sense to eliminate low-hanging fruit. Juvenile records are sealed until the offender is of age, but adult records aren't. Brawny can dig into the backgrounds of all the adults associated with the school. If her search comes up empty, we can turn all of our attention to the students."

That made perfect sense to me. "What does Schultz think about whodunnit? Does he have any pet theories?"

"He is convinced that there's a student behind this," Detweiler said. "Could even be a former student."

"A graduate?" John asked. "A person who has left the school but wants to hurt his alma mater?"

"Possibly," Detweiler said with a nod. "Could even be a student who didn't get into the college he or she wanted and blames Jarvis Township High School."

"Maybe we're looking for someone like the kid you mentioned earlier, John," I said. "Maybe there's a person out there who was denied a scholarship and wants to strike back at the school."

John chewed on the end of his stirrer. "How on earth would we catch him? Or her? We're on the inside, and the person you're describing would be on the outside."

"Right." Detweiler leaned in and lowered his voice. "Elimination of suspects is always useful in an investigation. The way I see it, we have three groups: admin and staff, graduates, and current students. Brawny can cover groups one and two. Eliminating current students as suspects is up to the two of you."

I opened my mouth to register a protest. John and I couldn't possibly vet all 342 Jarvis Township High School students. We didn't have the training, the resources, or the time. Detweiler anticipated what I was going to say.

"Honey, it's an impossible task," he said, setting his hand on top of mine. "But we're coming up on the end of the school year. If there is a student behind these suicides, the instigator is running out of time. Let's hope that he or she gets sloppy."

26

$\mathcal{T}$helma met us at the door. She blocked the entrance while wringing her apron between her hands. "Where have you been? I've been so worried about you. School's been out for more than an hour. Where did you go?"

Detweiler reached out and gave his mother a hug. "Mom, you know where I went. I had to pick up Kiki, and then we met John at the truck stop. It's halfway between Jarvis Township High and here. I figured going there would make life easier for all concerned."

"But you were gone so long." She turned the drama down a notch.

"I didn't think it would matter. You were working with Brawny on that new crochet stitch, remember?" he spoke gently to her.

"We got finished a long time ago," Thelma continued her whine. "I made cinnamon rolls for you, Chad. They're cold now, and not worth eating."

I piped up with, "I'll eat them!" She didn't have to ask me twice. My cheerful answer clearly annoyed Thelma because she ignored me and kept talking to her son.

"You went to a truck stop rather than coming home. For goodness sake. Why would you do a thing like that? I've been waiting for you." She suddenly seemed to notice me. "What if Ty had needed his mother? We would have had no idea how to get in touch with Kiki. The baby could have gone hungry."

"Brawny's fully capable of taking care of him, there's breast milk in your refrigerator, and I had my cell phone with me." I held mine up as proof. "You did, too, didn't you, honey?"

Detweiler raised his in solidarity.

Thelma pouted. "That's not what I mean. Cell phones go dead all the time."

Louis must have heard his wife complaining because he joined us in the kitchen. "Thelma, honey? Does it really matter? They're here now. See? They look jim-dandy fine to me. They're adults, honey. Got their own lives to live. I looked in on the baby. Brawny's got him. He's happy as a beaver in a mud dam. That little dickens is cute as can be. Such a charmer! He sure loves his nanny."

"He should be loving his mother," Thelma hissed under her breath.

"I would love a cinnamon roll," I added.

"Ty absolutely loves his mama," Detweiler added because he'd heard his mother's criticism. "He adores Kiki, and he's lucky to have other people in his world who shower him with affection. Our son will have a full life."

"Speaking of full," I said. "I'm starving. Could I have one of those cinnamon rolls?"

I was really tired from my first day at school. Immediately after dinner, I breastfed Ty, set out my clothes for the next day, and took a shower. The gauze bandaging was easy to peel off my arms when it was soaked. Brawny had suggested that I let the wounds dry overnight so I didn't replace the gauze. I'd probably get blood on Thelma's sheets but I knew how to get it out.

It was only eight p.m. when I crawled into bed. Before I closed my eyes, I checked to see if I had any messages. Anya had sent me a smiley face emoji in response to the photo of me with Bert, the wonder horse. Sheila sent a mangled "all is well" message because she's all thumbs when it comes to texting. Clancy and Laurel both emailed to tell me the store was fine. Satisfied that at least a portion of my life was under control, I fell asleep.

Detweiler slipped into bed after I was conked out. His arrival didn't even wake me. Tuesday morning over a breakfast of scrambled eggs, toast, and bacon, he smiled at me and said, "It's not too late to back out."

"Yeah, it kinda is." I tried to smile at him. "What did you do while I was sleeping?"

Detweiler said, "Brawny and I worked late. She's still checking social media. I gave her whatever data I had. Her sources are doing background checks. Today she hopes to find out what she can about Mr. Rusk. She's been running spreadsheets, trying to pin down similarities. Cross-referencing timeframes."

"And?"

"I'll let her tell you," he said, as our nanny came into the kitchen.

As usual, she was wearing her casual uniform of black slacks and a white blouse. Her gray ponytail sported a black and white ribbon. For her, that was a festive touch. Of course, she'd already dressed Ty in one of the onesies I'd purchased at Goodwill. Our little boy gurgled with excitement when he saw me and his dad.

Brawny mixed a watery rice cereal for Ty. While I fed him, she got us up to speed on her activities. "I did a second extensive computer analysis of all the data on the phones of the kids who died. Like the first analysis, none of it revealed any sort of messaging that might explain the victims' motives. No emails back and forth to anyone. Just goodbye emails right before they..." Her voice trailed off.

Using his fork as a hatchet, my husband divided the mound of scrambled eggs on his plate. I'd already cleaned my plate. When he's stressed, Detweiler doesn't eat much. I do the opposite. Last night I'd eaten three cinnamon rolls plus a hearty dinner of pulled pork, freshly roasted vegetables, and fruit. Because I am nursing, I burn up a lot of extra calories.

"What are you thinking?" I asked him.

"I'm thinking there has to be a communications trail," Detweiler said. "We just don't know where to look. Brawny? Could there be a message board or forum that they're viewing? Could the students be communicating with each other while they play a video game? One like *Grand, Theft, Auto*? I know the kids chat with each other while playing. There has to be a way that the victims receive a trigger, the command to kill themselves."

"Not a lot of girls play video games," our nanny said. "Of course, it still could be something to explore. Perhaps Schulz can tell you if they've checked into video game usage."

Detweiler continued, "Given the number of deaths, you'd think there would be something that waves a red flag, but nothing like that has shown up."

"Not that I've seen," Brawny said.

"Could it be a post on Pinterest, Snapchat, Instagram, or Reddit?" I knew about these sites because I'd discussed them with Anya. "Even a Subreddit posting?"

"Not that I could find." Brawny handed me a damp washcloth to wipe Ty's face. "Not yet at least. I am still working my way through the roster. I have called in favors. I even contacted a sociology professor who works with electronic communications, and he's stumped. His specialty is social media and how it can be weaponized. Doesn't that sound cheery?"

"Not especially," I said.

"By the way, don't worry about clearing the dishes. I'll take care of that for you. You two have a full day ahead," the nanny said.

My husband and I both thanked her.

"I do have this for you both to look over." Detweiler slid a piece of paper my way and handed one to Brawny. "This came via email this morning. I printed it while Kiki was getting dressed. It's a psychological profile generated from information I gave to a criminologist who teaches at Washington University. He's done work like this before."

Before I could pick up my copy, Detweiler set his hand on it. "Honey? This is bleak. No one would blame you for taking a pass on substitute teaching after you see it. I know you're your own woman, but this is upsetting stuff"

"At least let me see what he says," I said in an attempt to stall for time.

~

FORENSIC PSYCHOLOGICAL PROFILE
PERPETRATOR OF JARVIS TOWNSHIP HIGH SCHOOL SUICIDES

THE TYPE of person who is behind behavior like this is highly organized, methodical, able to control his impulses, educated, skilled, and has an above-average intelligence. This type of killer is smart enough to think three-dimensionally and control three different crime scenes: the approach to the victim, the scene of the crime where the killing occurs, and the scene where there is the disposal of the body. Because of his understanding of forensic techniques, he is very difficult to catch. He knows how to cover his tracks, and he has the self-control to plan and follow through in a way that leaves behind minimal forensic evidence.

Often a killer like this is charming and able to seduce other people with his personality. Frequently the killer is physically attractive and uses this to further his aims. This sort of criminal revels in his ability to manipulate other people, and he believes he is smarter than others. He is like a puppet master, pulling strings behind the scenes.

Because all of the victims are Caucasian, Christian, and local, there is a high probability that the killer is, too. Additionally, given the age of the victims, it is reasonable to assume the killer is very familiar with the lifestyle, thought patterns, and activities of teenagers. This does not mean the perpetrator is the same age, although he could be. The level of manipulation indicates a high level of understanding by our perpetrator, regarding the ways teens communicate.

This particular killer has a huge need for control, a need that's almost overwhelming. It's not an overstatement to say it gnaws at him.

Serial killers are so named because they tend to escalate their activities over time. A killer such as this must up the ante in part because the longer he gets away with his crimes, the more convinced he is that he's invincible. He also craves more and more extreme behavior to satisfy his emotional hunger. Therefore, with each day that passes, this person becomes more dangerous and more lethal. LEOs are advised to proceed with the utmost caution.

Respectfully Submitted,
P. Mellon, PhD

I set the paper down on the kitchen table. With shaking hands, I picked up my glass of water and gulped most of it. As I put the glass back down, it rattled against my plate, making a noise suspiciously like the chattering of teeth. When I thought I could speak calmly, I asked, "Why does this profiler use the male pronoun? Isn't it possible a woman is behind this?"

Detweiler brought over the coffee pot and freshened my cup. "Only one in every five or six serial killers is female. Most of them are very careful about disposing the body. We have bodies in this case, and they were left out in the open so the stats argue against this being a woman. Doesn't mean it couldn't be, but I think it's highly unlikely. The criminologist said the planning behind this is pretty in-depth, so he believes we need to look at one of the seniors or even a school worker or a teacher."

"Oh, my!" Thelma's exclamation caused us to turn around. She had been hiding in the living room and listening to our conversation. My husband's face tightened with anger. A muscle twitched in his jaw. His mother had really, really ticked him off.

But Thelma didn't seem to notice as she strolled into the kitchen. As if she'd been included in the conversation all along, she said, "An adult is behind all this?"

Her son shrugged, doing his best to act like nothing was amiss. "Not necessarily. Remember, most of the seniors are adults in the eyes of the law. Right this moment, we have no way of knowing who it is or how old the perpetrator might be. We're not even sure there's anybody egging students on. That's why what Kiki is doing is vital. We hope she'll see something that'll help us. It's also remotely possible that with the school year coming to a close, the suicide attempts will stop. It's also possible the killer might feel a loss of control with a new teacher in the mix. Or he might sense that there is a new pair of eyes watching him. Or her. At least, that's what we're hoping. Rather than sit on the sidelines and wait, we're heating up the situation. Stirring the pot. It's not a tactic I like, but it's a tactic, nonetheless."

"How on earth could Kiki possibly be of any help?" Thelma

took the chair next to her son. Although I could have taken umbrage, I decided it was better to shrug off her comment. Thelma *did* have a point. What possible good could come from my involvement?

"At the very least, the school needed a substitute art teacher, and Kiki's more than qualified for the job. Surely you can see that." My husband sounded pleasant enough, but he'd interlaced his fingers so tightly that the knuckles were turning white.

We have a saying in our marriage: Somebody has to be the hero. I think it is advice from Dr. Phil. The sentiment is absolutely true. When things go poorly, as they inevitably do, one of us has to step up and calmly take charge. This morning, right now, Detweiler was the hero. He was meeting Thelma's complaints head-on. I loved how he wasn't backing down.

My husband continued, "And Kiki was asked to do this job. Don't forget that, Mom. She didn't go looking for extra work."

"You ready?" Detweiler turned to me. His amazing green eyes had darkened to the color of holly, an indication he was not happy. However, he'd said his piece, he'd placated his mother, and it was time for us to mosey on down the highway.

"Be careful," said Brawny.

"Uh-huh." I kissed the top of Ty's head. "Goodbye, Thelma," I said.

"Slipping out like a thief in the night," groused Thelma under her breath. "Doesn't even bother to clean up after herself."

I heard that. Detweiler did too, and he stiffened but kept on walking. Rather than take the bait, we simultaneously reached for each other's hand. Linked that way, flesh to flesh, the energy flowed between us, forceful and reassuring. Thelma's critical remarks were not going to put a wedge between my husband and me. Not today. Not ever.

27

*N*ow that I knew the senior portfolio project was my A-1 priority, I was eager to get back to the school. I wanted to help the seniors finish their work. Mr. Rusk might have planned for me to fail, but I was having none of it. As a matter of fact, the challenge excited me, especially since we were talking about a gauntlet thrown down in my home territory.

As soon as the bell rang for first period, I said, "Kiddos, gather around. We need to have a talk."

They looked at each other curiously, but slowly they came over and made a tight circle around me. "Here's the deal. Nobody told me that your portfolios might not be done. In fact, I was told exactly the opposite. I hate it when people set me up to fail. Worse yet, it really stinks that you might suffer the consequences because I didn't get the proper information. I would never have suggested that we do the trash journals if I had known your portfolios weren't all done. So here's what's going to happen: We're going to get cracking on your portfolios, and we are going to crank those puppies out."

Becca, a serious-looking student with thick glasses, said, "Kiki? I have my portfolio done already. Some of the others have theirs done too. We worked ahead when we heard Mrs. Eowin would go on maternity leave before the school year ended."

"Great. Thanks for sharing that, Becca. Okay, show of hands. How many people are done?"

About half the class put up their hands.

"Oh, wow. That's good news. If you want, you can go ahead and make the trash journal. I'll show you how. Now, just so I understand, how many of you are mostly done with your portfolio?"

A couple more hands went up.

"Who hasn't even started?"

Four hands went up. Those students looked absolutely miserable.

"Not to worry. I'm the absolute LeBron James of getting last-minute papercrafts projects done." Then it hit me. Here I was making an assumption that I understood exactly what a Jarvis Township High School portfolio should look like. I'd already been tricked once. I didn't want to get tripped up again. "Does anyone have a finished portfolio that I can look at? I want to make sure I know what's expected. Becca, you wouldn't happen to have yours on you, would you?"

Shyly, she nodded. After a quick visit to her backpack, Becca handed me her portfolio. I wasn't sure whether the work was private or not so I opened the three-ring binder only part of the way and quickly scanned the pages.

I needn't have worried. I now knew that the students had been instructed to create the most boring portfolios in the history of mankind. Basically Becca had pasted a dozen home-work assignments on sheets of construction paper, three-hole punched the pages, and stuffed them into a common office ring-binder. This was the all-important portfolio?

"Could I see another example?" Surely Becca's was an

outlier, I thought. But when Tadd handed me his, it was the same story.

Rather than criticize the students, I held my tongue. Showing is better than telling, especially when you are trying to share a visual concept.

"Hang on a second," I said. I dug around in my FedEx box of supplies until I found what I was looking for, Anya's seventh-grade portfolio.

"If you are going to do a project, it ought to be fun. I love making memory albums. If you have to work on a portfolio, why not create something that will have meaning to you in the future? Let me show you an example. This is a portfolio my daughter did last year." I put Anya's project on the desk and opened it. My students gathered around. Tadd took the lead and flipped the pages.

The students were mesmerized. The book opened with a glorious title page. Anya had showcased her own personal motto, a phrase coined by Emily Dickinson: "Dwell in possibilities." Under the motto, Anya explained what the saying meant to her. The next page was a table of contents. After that came a variety of assignments. She had photocopied them at 70% so she could back them with colorful scrapbook paper. The first example of her homework was an English assignment. On the first day of seventh-grade, Anya had been instructed to write an essay about her feelings at the start of the year. My very emotional daughter chronicled her fears and hopes. The port-folio went on to share other assignments. At the end, Anya added extra pages to cover her interests.

"Since this is my daughter's," I said as I took the book away from Tadd, "I won't let you read her personal thoughts, but I assure you that they are here. You can't see them because Anya tucked them into pockets behind the photos. She's also added envelopes to hold journal entries she didn't want to share with a casual viewer."

Holding up Anya's portfolio and flipping to the middle of the book, I pointed to an envelope. "Inside that envelope are journaling pages she wrote about feeling lonely. At the time, she didn't have a best friend. Not yet. It was hard for her. Writing about her situation made her feel better."

"Why put the papers in an envelope?" asked Rhett, a boy with swarthy skin and jet black hair.

"Envelopes are useful when you have feelings you want to preserve, but not share publicly." I tugged on a corner of the papers from Anya's journal and exposed them so my students could see a square inch or so. Although my young friends couldn't read what Anya had written, the demonstration proved my point.

"I would also urge you to take photos and write about people, places, or things that really matter to you," I said. "Like pets. How many of you have pets?"

Almost all the hands went up. I said, "Here's a photo of our dog." A beautiful candid shot of Gracie's majestic head filled the entire surface of one page.

"That dog is wicked cool," one of the boys said. "Is he really that big?"

"Uh-huh. But he's a she. That's Gracie. She's our Great Dane."

"How much does it cost to feed a dog like that?" asked Carl, a kid who was a little on the hefty side.

"A lot," I said, and everyone laughed.

Next Anya included a photo of Martin and Seymour. The two cats were curled up around each other and snoozing. To the left of that picture was a short timeline detailing how we came to adopt our feline friends.

"Hey, Kiki," said a boy who was wearing a Miami Dolphins tee shirt. "You must have a real menagerie at your house."

"I do indeed. Wait until you see what's next," and I flipped to a picture of Monroe, the donkey who lives on our property in Webster Groves.

"Get out of town," hooted a short boy with a sprinkling of freckles over his nose. "Is that a donkey?"

"Sure is." I smiled at the students. "See? You don't know Anya. Not personally, but thanks to the pictures she chose and how she's displayed them, you have a sense of who she is, don't you? She chose those particular photos and journaling to make a point. What do you suppose that point is?"

"Dwell in possibilities," Becca repeated. "But I'm not sure I know what that means."

"It's a way of looking at the world and seeing that we have choices. We are creators. We can reshape ourselves. Anything can happen." I smiled at the rapt faces turned toward me. "You might not feel this way all the time. You won't win all the time, but you have to keep trying. There's a world full of abundance out there, and everything you need to succeed is yours! You just need to claim it."

The muscular student who had suggested that a beer cap might be ephemera snorted with laughter. "You sound like our assistant coach, Mr. Herbert. Or like that Tony Robbins guy I've seen on TV. "

"Good." I paused for a second, debating what to say next. "I grew up in a messed-up family. No one ever told me that life could get better or that I deserved more. You don't know me, and I bet you think I'm just another boring grown-up who's married with kids. I probably seem out of touch. That's mostly true, except I'm also someone who hated her life as a teen. Let me assure you that life does get better. Honest, it does."

The quiet that followed felt like a communion of sorts. I

looked into the eyes of the young people, and I willed them to be strong. I prayed that they wouldn't fall victim to life's dark moments. I hoped with all my heart that they would live to adulthood. I really, truly wanted them to succeed and I hoped they could sense that. I'd said my piece, and I'd been honest: Life can get better.

"Um," said a girl with beautiful red hair. "I'd like to make a few changes in my portfolio."

"Some of you need a portfolio for college, don't you? And some don't? But every graduating senior has to have one, right?" I asked.

Becca pulled up a screen on her phone. "Says here that in order to graduate, every senior must turn in a portfolio of no less than twelve pages. This portfolio should describe his or her senior year accomplishments. Each subject taken should be represented and mentioned. Samples of homework should be included. The finished portfolio must be 8½-by-11 inches. Candid photos are encouraged."

Finally, I had the information I needed. I appealed to the class. "If this is a requirement for you for graduation, why not make it fun? I realize I'm repeating myself, but I'm trying to make a point. Obviously, you need to put the required samples of homework in your portfolios to satisfy the requirements so you graduate. But it looks to me like you could also make a portfolio that's all about your life. Make a record of what you enjoy, what you worry about, what has meaning to you. Trust me, that'll change over the years."

They looked overwhelmed. The possibilities were too much for them.

"Let me show you another example," I flipped to a page in Anya's portfolio. "Here my daughter's talking about her grandmother who's having a problem with alcohol. After Anya wrote this, her grandmother went into rehab. Today my mother-in-law is trying very hard to stay away from booze. Maybe in 20 years, my daughter will look back on this. Maybe she'll see it when she arrives at a turning point in her own life, and she'll find the courage to hang in there."

"Man," said a boy with pale green eyes and a head full of unruly cowlicks. "That's deep."

"Enough talk," I said. "How many of you have a three-ring binder that's empty? Everyone? Good. Please bring it tomorrow. If you haven't even started on your portfolio, come over here next to me. If you have started and need more pages, help yourself to the pile of paper and supplies in this box. If you are done with your portfolio, you can make a new page or wait while I get the other folks started. Once everyone is working, I'll pass around samples of junk journals that use ephemera, okay?"

The hour had passed so quickly I forgot to set aside time for picking up. That oversight meant I needed to stay behind to tidy the room. Thus, I was the last teacher to walk into the lounge. When I arrived, Drew Simchuck smirked at me. "If it isn't our little rock star in the flesh. How does it feel, Kiki, to have all the kids in awe of you?"

I didn't know what to say so I shrugged. "I'm new, and art is fun. No big deal."

$\mathcal{F}$eeling his mean little eyes on me, I walked away from Drew and joined Oleander at the Formica counter. "I made tea for you," she said sweetly. Under her breath, she added, "Too bad we're all out of arsenic!"

That made me laugh. I took my cup of tea and sat down on one of the hard chairs around the table. Drew had taken the cushy chair. Drat. And just yesterday, he had seemed so nice!

Mr. Rusk burst through the doorway. "Luke Kressig is going to make it. I heard from his parents an hour ago. He's still not talking, but the news is good."

The reactions of my fellow teachers were mixed. Oleander seemed relieved, Jessie broke into a smile, Drew nodded, and Alan said, "That's great." I couldn't tell how sincere any of them were because I didn't know them well enough.

Mr. Rusk slapped the doorframe and said, "Okay. Just spreading the good word." And he was off.

"Thank goodness," Oleander said with a sigh.

Jessie, who was holding a CliffsNotes version of Shakespeare's *Romeo and Juliet*, added, "Let's hope no one else tries to kill himself or herself over the next few school days. If they're going to do it, I hope they wait until summer vacation so we don't take the blame."

Her callous remark landed awkwardly like a cow patty hitting the pasture. Drew blinked in shock. "I understand where you're coming from, Jessie. Really, I do, but does the timing matter?"

"I am sick and tired of this community blaming us for what's happening with their children. We're one small part of their lives." Jessie sounded defensive with a double-shot of snarky. "Their parents and families need to step it up and do their jobs. Pointing fingers at us is the easy way out."

I struggled to keep my mouth shut. This wasn't the time or the place to share what I knew. That information was classified. But Jessie's comments got me thinking. There's a question often cited in mystery novels: *cui bono* or who benefits? Who stood to gain from encouraging students kill themselves? Or on the flip side, who stood to lose? Who suffered most when the school's reputation was blemished? I made a mental note to discuss this idea with my husband and John Kressig.

Mr. Rusk popped back in. This time he handed out photocopied sheets of paper. He gave one to everyone but me. "Move the chairs into a circle. Let's go over what needs to happen on graduation day."

"Kiki? Want to share?" Oleander noticed I'd been excluded. Jessie and Alan dragged over their chairs. Drew picked up a straight-back chair and carried it to the circle.

"Kiki doesn't need a copy. She won't be here." Mr. Rusk glared at me over the top of the paper he was holding.

"But she'd be invited, wouldn't she? That's only polite." Oleander's voice wobbled as she pulled her chair into the circle. "Surely, you can do that much."

Mr. Rusk's cell phone rang, and he made a big deal of taking the call and talking loudly.

Drew looked over at me. "Forget it, Oleander. Kiki's lucky that she doesn't have to come. It's not like attending our graduation ceremony is a perk. No way."

"Mandatory sentencing," sniffed Jessie.

"If I were you, Kiki, I wouldn't spend any more time than necessary at this sad excuse for a high school," said Alan. "Trust us. I bet you can find a million better ways to waste a Saturday than sitting in our stuffy auditorium with a crowd of farmers and their wives."

"The lack of air conditioning does make it miserable," Oleander admitted.

Mr. Rusk ended his call and snickered. "Too right about all the farmers. Too bad we can't check everyone's soles for manure, right, Drew?"

I found their behavior appalling. All of them but Oleander were making fun of the families they served. If they didn't like the community, they should just move on instead of snickering up their sleeves.

"If you'll excuse me, I think I'll look over my notes for the next class," I said. The cushy armchair was empty. I walked over and got comfortable. Anya had taught me a neat trick. I shoved earbuds into my ears, even though the buds weren't connected to anything. The ruse worked pretty well for shutting people out. While the others talked, I studied them and wondered. Was it the same at my kids' school? Did the teachers at CALA hate the students and parents as much as these teachers hated their community? I sure hoped not.

29

*T*he rest of the day passed quickly. By the end of school, my voice was tired from talking. I cheered myself up with the thought that I was adding a total of seventy-one new scrapbookers to the wonderful world of papercrafting. I double-checked my math on a scrap of paper: twenty-two in the first period, twenty-five in the fifth period, and twenty-four in the sixth period.

When the final bell rang, my phone vibrated. I opened it to a photo of Anya and Erik grinning as they posed next to a costumed pirate. I couldn't help but smile back. It looked to me like the kids were having a good time.

Brawny had texted me to say she was on her way to pick me up. Detweiler was working late in Missouri, so she'd been dispatched to fetch me. My heart did a somersault of joy when she pulled up because Ty was in his car seat. I desperately needed a dose of baby love. He was happily waving a teething ring. "How are both of you?" I asked the nanny after I tossed my backpack in the trunk and closed it.

"Right as rain. We're meeting John at the Dairy Queen near the highway," Brawny announced from the driver's seat of the

Highlander. "I introduced myself to him over the phone. I am tasked with debriefing both of you."

I slammed the passenger door shut and buckled my seatbelt. "They officially announced that Luke is on the mend. I thought we'd agreed to keep Luke's condition under wraps."

Brawny frowned. "Aye, I thought so, too."

"Mr. Rusk, the dean of the upper school, announced John's status during the teachers' break period," I added.

"Aye," Brawny gave a brisk nod of her head. "Doesn't make sense to me. That's not what we planned on doing. Could put Luke at risk even though he still refuses to talk. His mother came over to the farm, bawling her eyes out."

"Mary Martha came over? That poor woman."

"Aye, Thelma insisted. Your mother-in-law introduced me to her guest. Mary Martha said she's scared her son will hurt himself again. She is thinking that if Luke won't talk, he's holding back, and she's taken that to mean he's got plans he's hiding from her."

"What do you think?" I reached behind my seat to touch my baby boy's hair. Ruffling the peach fuzz on the top of Ty's head made me deliriously happy.

"I believe the lad's not talking because he's afraid to spill the beans. He's worried that once he gets to talking, he won't stop. Seems to me like he's still loyal to someone or something. I can't tell what yet. But that's my guess."

The low green rows of soybeans stretched out on each side of us like parallel lines drawn in crayon on paper. Red-winged blackbirds perched on the fence posts that were rotten and barely standing. When our car drove by, the birds flew away. The bright red patches on their shoulders stood out like stop signs against the soft blue sky. The noise of trucks rumbling along the overpass grew louder the closer we got to the exit where we'd be meeting John. Those big beasts of burden could tow as much as

80,000 tons of weight, but you'd never know that by how nimble they could be. A steady stream of trucks hauling silver containers zipped past us before we turned onto the black asphalt parking lot of the Dairy Queen. A fiberglass tower of vanilla self-serve ice cream stood proudly on top of a yellow-beige building intended to look like a waffle cone. This particular fiberglass icon was a favorite Midwestern landmark, written up in many of the local guidebooks. I'd heard that the fiberglass ice cream was developing cracks along its base. Someday soon, the entire building would be knocked down to make room for a modern Dairy Queen with a lot more seating. That struck me as sad. I snapped a photo of the cone and a second picture of Brawny holding Ty in front of the building. I sent both photos off to the older kids.

We claimed one of the concrete picnic tables. The tops of all the tables were inlaid with bits of red and white glass tiles. I took Ty from Brawny, because I missed holding my little guy. She took my ice cream order and walked to the window while I bounced Ty on my knee. The server was counting change into Brawny's palm when John's pickup pulled in next to our High-lander. He introduced himself to Brawny and ordered a choco-late-covered vanilla ice cream cone. Then he and the nanny joined me at the table. I introduced John to Ty.

The afternoon sun packed enough heat to melt our frozen treats. Rather than discuss the investigation, we concentrated first on eating. After John wiped the last drop of ice cream off his chin, Brawny asked, "Are you ready? Detweiler asked me to do your daily debrief. What have ye got for us, John?"

He said, "I overheard two students talking about a challenge. They clammed up the minute I came near. I pretended I knew what they were talking about. I asked them if Luke had finished the challenge they were talking about. One of the kids said, 'Maybe. Maybe not. Luke knows better than to blab about it.'"

John shook his head. "That made me mad. I got ticked off with the kid."

"Did that work for ye?" Brawny grinned.

"Not really. The boy's name is Brian O'Sullivan. I told him that my brother tried to kill himself and when I asked him a question, I expected an answer. I told Brian I wanted more information about this challenge, and he totally shut down."

A tingle of excitement raced through me. "Totally? You weren't able to convince him to talk?" I didn't like the way John had threatened the boy, but I understood John's frustration so I focused on the nugget of information he'd gleaned. Was Luke's suicide attempt some sort of challenge gone wrong? If so, who issued the challenge? I touched my index finger to my ice cream and rubbed it on Ty's lips. The cold shocked him, but the sweet flavor caused him to wave his arms around happily. He wanted more.

"O'Sullivan told me that if I bothered him again, he'd tell Mr. Rusk and get me kicked off the property." John huffed. "Can you believe that? I guess Mr. Rusk has made it known we're persona non grata. You and me both, Kiki. He's made no secret of the fact he doesn't want either of us there at Jarvis Township High School. Makes me wonder whose side he's on."

"You're telling me nothing I don't know." I explained about Mr. Rusk and the invitation to the graduation. "Brawny have you been able to look into Mr. Rusk?"

"I have, and there's nothing suspicious. He has a mediocre set of credentials. That's about it. I'll keep checking."

"He was nasty to me today," I explained. "Malicious. That got me thinking, *cui bono*? Who benefits? Who gets blamed for these suicide attempts? Mr. Rusk is the dean of the upper school. But isn't Mr. Lambert the principal? I think his name is on that plaque as you walk in, but I don't recall meeting him."

"We didn't meet him because he has been out of town for an

educators' summit. He should be back tomorrow." John hesitated. "Are you thinking that Mr. Rusk wants kids to kill themselves? And the suicides would reflect badly on the principal, Mr. Lambert, right?"

Brawny jumped in and said, "If Mr. Lambert gets blamed for the suicides, he would probably be fired. If he gets fired, they'd look for a new principal. Would Mr. Rusk be in line for the position?"

"I have no idea, but that makes sense to me," I said. "What do we do next, Brawny?"

"You keep looking and listening. I'm still gathering information on the staff at Jarvis Township High School. I've gone about as far as I can with checking out social media. Tonight after dinner, I'll sift through what I have once more. Should be easy enough to figure out whether Mr. Rusk is in line for a promotion or not."

"Can you do that?" John asked. "Look into people like that?" He tossed a crumb from his cone onto the ground. Two sparrows immediately landed and began to fight over the food. Ty was enchanted. My little guy flapped his arms excitedly, and the birds flew off. For a second, I thought Ty would burst into tears. Fortunately, Brawny had brought along a plastic container of Cheerios and gave one to Ty to chew on.

"I have resources," Brawny explained. "It's best for all concerned that no one knows how I do my research. And it's a good idea that you don't share my activities with Schultz." Her smile was multiplied by the gleam in her eyes. Brawny loves tracking down bad guys. Good thing she loves my kids more or we would lose our nanny to the world of law enforcement.

"Gotcha," John said with a brisk nod of his head.

"I assume Schultz hasn't had any luck talking to any of the other students who attempted to take their own lives," I said. "Brawny? Have you heard anything?"

"From what your husband has said, no one will talk to Schultz or his investigators."

On that depressing note, we decided to end our discussions for the day. John said, "I'm meeting my parents at the hospital. Fingers crossed that we can get Luke to talk."

I wasn't feeling optimistic but I put on a cheery face. I'd concluded that either Luke was scared or he was embarrassed. Whatever the case, his commitment to staying silent was strong. Something was at work in the shadows. Something that made Luke clam up even though his life had been at risk.

"Nice meeting you, Brawny. See you tomorrow, Kiki. Goodbye, Ty!" John waved to us as he climbed into his truck.

30

*W*hen we got back to the farm, Thelma and Louis weren't home because they'd gone on their weekly Costco run. Gracie was thrilled to see me. Ty was ready for his nap, so I put him down. My husband wasn't home yet, so Brawny and I decided that we needed a snack of cheese and crackers to tide us over until dinner. Ice cream, I've discovered, does not stick with me.

Who am I kidding? Hunger isn't why I eat. I eat for a variety of reasons: nervousness, boredom, frustration, and obviously for enjoyment. I'll never understand people who eat to live and find no joy in food. Therefore, it goes without saying, I'll probably never be skinny.

"What are you thinking?" Brawny asked. "Better yet, what are you feeling? What's your gut tell you about all this? Have ye gotten a sense of what's happening? Who might be involved?"

"Not really. There's a weird undercurrent among the students. It's like they've closed ranks. I'm not surprised that John feels frustrated. I do, too."

I nibbled at a piece of Gouda cheese with bits of bacon in it. Savory and delightful all at once. "If only there was a way to get the kids to open up to me. I have such a short time to win them over."

"What has worked for you in the store? What do you do when you've got new customers? How have you won people over in the past?" Brawny looked at me with genuine curiosity.

That was easy: Food. I said as much and caught myself because another answer popped up in my head: "Photos. Pictures. People relate to what they see. Even if the picture wasn't taken by them. It's like this mental game of Old Maid starts and people comb their memories to match the image."

"Tell me more about the students' portfolios," she said.

"Primarily they are a visual representation of their senior year. All of the seniors have to make one to graduate. They're supposed to show off their school activities. Homework. Projects. Clubs. I talked with them about how to include more of their personal lives. Hidden journaling and so on. They totally lit up when they saw Anya's seventh-grade portfolio." I paused because that gave me an idea. "Photos are really cheap to develop these days. I ought to use the camera in my phone and take a lot of candid pics in the classroom. I can upload the photos to the nearest drugstore and bring in the developed pictures the next day."

"Sounds pretty pricy," Brawny said. "On the other hand, who can put a price on a student's life?"

"You're right on both counts. The cost isn't such a big deal. Detweiler and I aren't spending money on a real vacation. His parents are feeding us. The school is paying me as a substitute teacher. Spending money on photos for my first period class is sort of a wash."

"Hello, my scrapbooking queen." My husband came up behind me and planted a kiss on my neck.

"That reminds me," I said. "Your parents aren't here or I'd

ask them. May I take three of the scrapbooks I made for your family into school with me tomorrow? To show the kids?"

"Go right ahead. How did your meeting with John go?"

While I retrieved scrapbooks from the drawer of Thelma's breakfront and shoved them into my backpack, Brawny talked to my husband. "Unfortunately, it doesn't look like we've gotten very far, except that there are challenges involved. That's about it."

I explained about my *cui bono* notion. "We think that Mr. Rusk might be in line for the principal's position if it becomes available. He's been a thorn in my side since the day I arrived. Today he made a big deal about how I wasn't invited to the graduation ceremony. Not that I care. It's the way he did it in front of other teachers with this Mr. Grinch smile on his face. Positively nasty."

Brawny added, "John told us that he planned to stop by the hospital. His parents are there already. John's thinking maybe he can coax his brother into talking."

"We can only hope." Detweiler sounded like he didn't think it would happen.

"If he doesn't talk today, maybe he will in a day or so." There I was, being optimistic again.

Brawny glanced at her watch. She wore a red Mickey Mouse watch on her left arm. When I asked about it, she told me, "I like it because it reminds me that 99% of all the problems I'll face in a day are nothing but Mickey Mouse." Getting to her feet she said, "If you two will excuse me, I've been entering the information you've given me in spreadsheets. I'm hoping we'll see patterns that way. If Thelma asks for me, please tell her I'm busy. It would be best if I could work without her interference. She seems determined to look at what I'm doing even though I've asked her not to."

Ty's half-hearted whimpers floated downstairs. That was his

way of telling us he was done with his nap. I told Brawny, "Go. I'll take care of him. I bet he needs a diaper change."

Brawny hurried up the stairs. I stared after her. I couldn't get over the fact that Thelma kept prying into our business. I got to my feet and started toward the stairs, too.

"Wait." Detweiler put a gentle hand on my arm. "I'm going to talk to my dad about this. I can't figure out why Mom's so intent on interfering. I've tried to be reasonable. It's time for the big guns. I'm going to bring it up to my dad."

"All right." I did my best to smile. "Now for that diaper change."

As I climbed the stairs, I had an epiphany. I was Detweiler's third wife. Sure, his first wife had been his high school sweetheart, and too young and immature to make any of the sacrifices a young couple starting out has to make. His second wife had gotten hooked on drugs. But wasn't it also possible—even probable—that Thelma Detweiler had been a meddling mother-in-law? That she'd found ways to insert herself into her son's marriages? Ways that caused problems?

I thought so.

In my head, I held a conversation with Clancy. So often, she and I would have a confab in the privacy of my office at the store. Clancy was both a good listener and a straight shooter. Mentally I imagined Clancy asking me, "What are you going to do about Thelma? How do you intend to handle this? Is it smarter for you to wait her out than to confront her about the way she's acting?"

Detweiler said he would handle it. That should take care of the problem. That's what I would have told Clancy, even though I didn't really believe it. Thelma had proven herself to be ruthless in getting what she wanted.

The next question my fantasy version of Clancy asked was, "Is Thelma so determined to get attention that she might jeopardize your efforts at Jarvis Township High School?"

The answer scared me.

As I lifted Ty from his bed, I reviewed my choices. Once upon a time, I would have been certain there was a right answer and a wrong one. Fear of making an incorrect choice would have paralyzed me. After I made a choice, I'd second-guess myself for months. I've grown up a lot since then. There wasn't a right or wrong, black or white, answer to any mess. People are much more fluid than that. You make a move and other people counter. I now knew that I could try one solution, and then if that didn't work, I could try something else.

The smartest option was for me to ignore Thelma. This was not the place to confront her. We were living under her roof. I wasn't on my home turf. I didn't have anywhere to hide if I needed an escape from her. And I was already in a stressful position with my work at the school

I should let other people carry the load for me. Brawny was wise to her tricks. Detweiler planned to talk to his dad about his mother. Ginny knew what her mother was up to. Thelma was isolating herself, although she might not realize it yet.

I decided to wait and see what happened next. My responsibilities as Ty's mom and my work at Jarvis Township High School had to be my priorities. That was more than enough to keep me busy. I was two days into my first week in my new role as an art teacher. That left me with three work days, a weekend, and another five days to go. Surely I could stand up to anything Thelma dished out.

I'd lived through much worse.

31

*B*rawny rustled up sandwiches for the three of us for dinner. We ate quickly, hoping to be out of Thelma's way when she got home. Detweiler had to go back to work. As tired as I was, nursing Ty and climbing into bed made it a full day for me. I fell asleep, but it was a restless slumber. I woke up several times during the night.

The next morning, I got up extra early. I must have been dreaming about Anya and Erik because I felt a terrible pang. I physically ached for my two oldest children. I hurt. Getting dressed was a real chore.

My husband met me at the foot of the stairs. His eyes were drooping from the late shift he'd worked the evening before.

"We need to see John. We can eat breakfast with him at the truck stop. Can you feed Ty while Brawny is busy on the computer?" Detweiler asked as he handed me our son.

"Of course." I fed Ty his rice cereal and burped him. He was so sweet. I loved the tiny bubbles he blew. All I wanted was to go upstairs, sit in the rocker, and spend time with Ty. But I had other responsibilities. I ran upstairs and changed Ty's diaper.

When I came back downstairs, I handed my sweet baby to

Brawny. She took him while I shrugged my backpack onto one shoulder. I was wearing a nice pair of black pants and a black blouse with white polka dots, an ensemble I'd found at Goodwill. I waited at the back door for my husband.

"Mom? Dad. We have an early morning meeting. See you later," he said.

"Why couldn't you have met here?" Thelma asked petulantly. "There's plenty of food to go around."

"John asked if we could meet him at the Flying Horse Truck Stop," Detweiler explained. "He texted me first thing. He spent a lot of time last night at the hospital, I was more than happy to let him choose our location."

Thelma harrumphed a little, while Louis asked, "How's his brother?"

"Better. At least, we think he's better. We won't know for sure until we talk." After quick goodbyes, my husband drove us to the truck stop restaurant where John was holding a table for us. He'd already alerted the waitress that we'd need caffeine and lots of it, so she came to our table and immediately set down a steaming hot pot of coffee before taking our orders. I blessed that woman repeatedly for her timely intervention.

Detweiler and I asked John how his brother was doing.

"Nothing has changed. I mean Luke is awake but he refuses to talk. He's out of the woods—or so they say—but it's as if he's had a nervous breakdown. No matter what time of day it is, he's curled into a ball facing the wall, acting like the world has come to an end. Ma sits by his bed, hour after hour, hoping he'll say something. Anything! She talks to him but he won't answer her. She doesn't even acknowledge she's there. This is killing her. Dad's a bit more stoic, but it's eating at him, too. A psychologist keeps telling my parents that it'll take time and not to push it."

We ordered. Detweiler had scrambled eggs, whole wheat toast, and a bowl of fruit. I asked for biscuits and gravy with bacon on the side. John had an omelet and whole wheat toast. After the server walked away, John asked me, "Do you feel like you are making any progress? The students seem to like you a lot. Especially after you shared your daughter's portfolio. They think you are cool."

"I appreciate the vote of confidence," I said, "but that might or might not translate into the students telling me anything of value. I worry that I'll get so involved in our projects that I won't notice an important clue." I gently stirred creamer into my coffee and watched the clouds in a brown sky mingle and disappear. The waitress brought our orders and asked if we needed anything more. We said no, thanks, and she walked away

"What do you think, John?" Detweiler asked our young friend, after spearing a piece of pineapple with his fork. "I'd even entertain your guesses at this point. We have so little to go on."

"I'm doing my best to fit in. The kids don't want to include me, much less share with me," John said. He told Detweiler all about Brian O'Sullivan and the challenges. "I wanted to throttle the kid because I was so frustrated. What is going on in that school? Why won't anyone tell us? I'm not sure I'm doing any good. Feels like a colossal waste of time!"

"It's early days," I said, quoting Brawny with that pithy Briticism. "Maybe we're expecting too much too fast. I woke up last night around one and noticed Brawny's light was on in her room. She must have been working hard, inputting information. Maybe she'll have something for us soon."

I explained how I planned to take loads of photos during the first period class. "Brawny reminded me that sharing photos seems to loosen the tongue. I'm cautiously optimistic."

"Could you use your phone to take pictures of their portfolio pages? Then you could share those with John, Brawny, and me," Detweiler suggested.

"The students who are done with their portfolios don't always bring them to class," I said. "But I'll photograph whatever I can."

We walked out into a light rain. The dark clouds and drizzle matched our moods. We had decided that I'd go on to school with John so that Detweiler could get back to the farm and make follow-up phone calls. He was working a case in St. Louis. The paperwork for his investigation would consume hours of his time.

"At least working at home will make my mother happy," Detweiler said. "Unless she tries to force-feed me, that is." When John and I laughed, he added, "No joke. I think it's another strategy for needling information out of me, but at this rate I'm going to gain ten pounds and she'll have nothing to show for her efforts."

"Could be worse," said John, as we walked toward the cars. "Thelma could be serving you cafeteria food. Kiki? You've been smart to pack a lunch."

"Drat!" I yelped. "I forgot all about my lunch. I remembered my backpack, but forgot my purse and my lunch! Golly, and there isn't enough time to run back to the farm."

"Here." My husband reached into his wallet and handed me a crisp ten-dollar bill. "I'll turn it in on your expenses. Don't go hog wild with all that money."

That made John and me both laugh. I kissed Detweiler goodbye. "Now you know exactly how much one of my kisses is worth," I said.

"Honey, they're worth a whole lot more than ten bucks. I promise you that." He waved and got into his car.

John unlocked and held open the passenger door of his pickup truck for me. The raindrops splashed dusty water on the truck's finish, making a runny polka dot pattern. I looked down at my blouse and decided it was a polka dot sort of day.

"How much are carrot sticks?" I asked John as he pulled away from the truck stop.

"I'm not sure," John admitted, "but they can't be expensive. I bet you can buy a round of carrot sticks for the kids, if you are so inclined. Make that a round of French fries and you might make new pals for life."

"I am not going to bribe people to like me," I said. "Okay, I take that back. I bribe people to like me all the time at the store. But those are grown-ups. These are kids. I draw the line at high-jacking young minds."

"Do you really? If it'll save someone's life, I will not only bribe the kids, I'll do whatever it takes to get them to spill the beans. Problem being, I obviously don't know what it takes. Kiki, are we on a fool's errand?"

"Hmmm." Rows of green flickered past us. There was a meditative quality to driving through farmland. "Let me channel my spiritual advisor, okay?"

"You have a spiritual advisor?" John asked. He was only halfway joking.

I answered him honestly, "Yes, her name is Rabbi Sarah."

Now John looked surprised. Obviously he didn't know that I attended temple.

I went on talking, "If Rabbi Sarah were here, she would say that we've been given a rare chance to do good. To save lives. Not everybody gets the chance to do something that might make an important difference. At the end of our days, whether we are successful or not, we won't have to apologize for turning a blind eye. All things considered, Rabbi Sarah would say, the outcome doesn't really matter. Yes, it would be nice for us to catch the creep who's behind all this. Or creeps, plural. But Rabbi Sarah would tell us that we might never know if our presence at the school made a difference or not. She would stress that good deeds, mitzvahs, are like rocks tossed into the center of a pond. They create ripples, concentric circles reaching out."

John didn't say anything.

I added, "I think Rabbi Sarah would also point out that we are certainly not doing anyone any harm by attending Jarvis Township High School, are we?"

"No," he said as he shook his head. "We're not. I'm trying to make friends with the students. Mainly the other guys. I'll try to be like a big brother to them. If they need me, maybe I can help. Except for Brian O'Sullivan. That kid better hide when he sees me coming."

I laughed. "That's how I see my job as a teacher. I'll try to be an adult friend. Even if one student sees me as shoulder to cry on, that might be enough to save a life."

John turned off the paved road to take a gravel road that would come out behind the school. "If I get too caught up and don't get the chance to say it, I want you to know that my family really appreciates what you are doing. Of course, Chad Detweiler is family. He's my brother's brother-in-law. But you don't owe us anything, and here you are, trying to help. I can see that Thelma is being a pain in the butt. That means you're having to put up with her and teach a class and be an undercover cop all at the same time. It's a lot to ask of anybody. Much less someone who isn't blood kin. So thank you."

"Not blood kin." I smiled at him. "My husband and I aren't blood kin to each other either."

I'd surprised John for the second time in less than ten minutes. I was on a roll, so I said, "And you are entirely welcome."

32

*M*y first period students were totally thrilled with my idea of taking their photos and getting them developed. During Tuesday's class session, they'd only had time for a quick look inside the box of scrapbooking goodies. Today, I would give them the whole hour to see what I'd brought.

First, I wanted to inspire them. I took the three albums I'd made for the Detweilers out of my backpack and opened them flat on an empty table. I said, "I brought more examples for you. You are welcome to come and look at them."

The students took turns filing past the completed memory albums. "You did all this?" Eldon, a narrow-shouldered boy with a broad forehead, pointed to all three scrapbooks.

"Yes, I did."

"Was it a kit? I bet it was." Delphine was a slight girl with frizzy brown hair.

"Nope. I bought the paper, I drew or made the embellishments, and I designed and executed the pages."

"Was it hard?" Bluette, a young woman with bad skin, asked in a timid voice.

"Not really. I've been scrapbooking for years and years. If there's anything you want to know how to do, ask and I'll show you. We have a whole hour. You can start your portfolios, finish them, or add to them. You can make a trash journal. All I ask that you only take two sheets of scrapbook paper at a time so that other people can have cool choices, too. After you use those two sheets, you are welcome to take two more. Either Saturday or Sunday, I'll make a trip to my store in Ladue and pick up more paper. If you see a paper you love, take a photo of it. If we run out, I'll grab more from the store. Send me the photo so I'll know what to get. Here's my email address," and I rattled off: TimeinaBottle2001@gmail.com.

"You're trusting us with your email address?" The girl with freckles, Sandra, stared at me as if I had told her a joke she didn't understand.

I laughed. "Sure. Why not? How else can you get in touch with me? I'd give you my phone number, but I turn off the ringer at night."

Along that line, I continued, "In fact, if you need to ask me a question or talk for any reason, just email me. I can always call you back. I'm only going to be here through the end of next week, but I'll always be available to you. Always. I care. I remember what it was like to be your age and not have an adult who would listen. I will. You have my word."

Twenty-two pairs of eyes stared at me. A couple of the girls actually rubbed their eyes in disbelief. One boy cocked his head as if studying me the way a bird does a bug. The beanpole boy, Ralphie, snickered softly in disbelief.

That was okay. I had this day and eight more to show them that I was who I said I was. Actions speak louder than words, so I began by encouraging them to pick out paper. "After you have chosen your two sheets, you can come over and pose for me or grab a friend and pose together for me. I'll also wander the room and take a few candid shots. Feel free to stop me if you need assistance."

As with any creative venture, folks dithered a bit before settling in. When Bluette couldn't choose two pieces of paper, I advocated the "eeny-miney-mo" method which got her giggling but moved the process forward. Ralphie wasn't sure whether the colors he'd chosen matched each other. "I'm color-blind," he explained. I worked with him to help him differentiate the various options.

John sidled up to me and whispered, "Me, too? I don't want to waste your stuff."

"Play along, please," I said quickly. "Besides, you might learn to like this."

Of course the tape-runner gave the students fits. It always does at first. I explained it's like a hand-held tape dispenser but it only puts down adhesive instead of a strip of clear cellophane with an adhesive backing. I demonstrated using the tape-runner four or five times, and then I showed the kids how to correctly use the personal paper trimmer. A couple of punches stuck when the kids tried to use them. That's typical. I knocked them against the floor until the spring re-engaged. Once in a while, I would interrupt the class to show off a special technique like using an emery board to smooth the rough edges of cut paper. I also encouraged them to pass around a laminated sheet with a list of different glues and what each product did best.

"Could I have a copy of this?" asked Sandra. "My mother likes to do crafts. She's always having trouble getting glue to work."

Eldon ambled over to me. "My portfolio is done, but I want to add more pages. What themes do you suggest?"

"Good question." Clapping my hands, I raised my voice.

"Listen up, people. I will brainstorm a list of possible themes and write them on the board—but I don't want to do all the work for you. I'll start the list and I expect each of you to contribute at least one idea. Put your initials by your idea so I can see that you participated."

My list included: sports, hobbies, friends, pets, chores, family, religion, clubs, choir, travel, driving, trips, farm life, music, and siblings. One by one the students added: movies, sports teams, politics, cooking, home, sewing, fashion, makeup, prom, college, decorating, crafts, challenges, drawing, shop, carpentry, dreams, military service, fortune-telling, restaurants, jobs, fast food, grandparents, my crushes, and video games.

"Do a lot of you play video games?" I asked. My heart sped up. Maybe I'm stumbled onto the way that students were communicating with each other.

"Nah," said Ralphie. "I like *Grand, Theft, Auto,* but the ping is too slow here for most multi-player games."

He went on to explain that "ping" was a signal sent to a host that requested a response. If the ping was slow, as it was out here in rural areas, you would be slow while making moves in a game. The other players would have a decided advantage.

"Our access out here is a lot slower than what you get in town," Ralphie said.

Our conversation seemed to encourage everyone to talk. Students asked me all sorts of questions about scrapbooking, but the one asked most frequently was, "What if I want a special image, and I can't find it in the stickers or embellishments or even in the scrapbook papers?"

"Easy-peasy," I said. "Tomorrow I will teach you the magic of paper-piecing. Right now, please clean up your supplies so you make it to your next class on time."

The teachers' lounge was quiet when I arrived. I was late

again and the other teachers were involved in working on their grade books.

I didn't care that I was the last teacher to arrive. My students had been reluctant to quit working on their various projects. The kids were now talking a lot both to me and to each other. That was super! I would have happily talked about my class-room success, but everyone seemed hard at work. The computer wasn't being used, and it occurred to me this was a good time to type up the list of topics from the first period class. I would compile the results into a handout.

I was excited when I took a seat at one of the Dell computers. Because this computer was the same brand as the one I use at work, I had no trouble at all logging in and getting my list created. When I finished, I hit the save button. After emailing a copy to myself, I created a folder and put the document in it. Tomorrow I would add any new ideas the students shared. That would give me a master list of topics I could use later at the store as a handout.

No one else seemed eager to use the computer, so I took my time. I decided that I might as well create a lesson plan, explaining what I'd done in the classroom. Maybe one day, another substitute teacher might want to emulate my scrap-booking and journaling projects.

A couple of false starts later, I had an outline committed to paper. I also had made three worthless attempts. I dumped those, hitting the delete button. When I checked, all three files were sitting in the deleted files folder by themselves. My defini-tion of a trash journal and a step-by-step breakdown of how to make one went pretty well until I realized that I didn't have any photos of trash journals in my phone.

With that in mind, I decided I'd come back to the trash journal and the scrapbooking lesson plans later. Tomorrow I would add in photos of trash journals as the kids made them. I would also create a supplies list. By the end of the week, I would have a nice presentation that I could share with other scrapbookers. Laurel and Clancy could use it to teach classes. A lot of my customers are also teachers. They would appreciate my work. In fact, I might even put the handout on the store website. Even if I wasn't spending time at my store, I was creating new materials we could use at a later date. That made me feel great!

33

To my surprise, Brawny didn't come to pick me up. Instead, Thelma was there in the carpool lane at the end of the school day. I was astonished to see her. Even more surprising, Ty was with her, sitting in his infant safety chair, facing backwards, and busily exploring his rattle.

I opened the passenger door and said, "Hi, Thelma. Thanks for coming and getting me."

It always takes me a minute or two to shrug off the backpack. Then I have to decide where to put it. I was half in and half out of Thelma's blue Prius hybrid when Becca and Sandra from my first-period class hailed me.

"Kiki! Giving us your email address, that's so out there. Nobody does that." Sandra fairly quivered with excitement.

"We won't misuse it," Becca said. "Honest we won't. But there've been times when, you know, a student says he'll do a stupid stunt like covering all the stripes on the parking lot with black paint, and if I could have told an adult, I would have. When Trixie tried to kill herself, if I could have called a teacher, I would have warned someone. As it was, her mother walked in when she was tying a knot in the—"

"Who is Trixie?" I thought that I had memorized all the names of students who had committed suicide. "Are there more students who tried to kill themselves? Students other than Luke Kressig?"

Of course, Schultz and John had said as much, but maybe there were even *more* failed attempts than the two of them knew of.

The young women looked at each other and finally returned their gaze to me. "Ladies? Have there been more attempts?" I tossed my backpack into the back seat of Thelma's car to get rid of it. I wanted to concentrate on what the girls were telling me. I had one foot inside Thelma's car and the other on the curb.

"Sure. Way more. There's Ainsley Hubbard, Lester Carne, and yeah, I know of two more at least." Becca spoke as though reciting a laundry list instead of talking about fellow students who almost killed themselves. She was that numb to the carnage.

"Did they say why? What happened?"

Sandra elbowed Becca and gave her a look so withering it could only mean, "Shut up!" She followed the scathing glance with, "Becca, are you nuts? You can't blab—"

Beep! Beep! Beep! Thelma laid on the horn. She literally pressed both palms against the rim of her steering wheel and didn't let up. The blast knocked me off balance. I would have stumbled and fallen to the sidewalk if Sandra hadn't grabbed my arm. The horn kept going with its unearthly howl as I regained my footing.

"Thelma?" I shouted to her over the noise. Ty had dropped his rattle. He was gulping air as a prelude to screaming. "Thelma? Could you please?"

"We've got to go. I have lasagna in the oven. I didn't expect you to take all day, Kiki!" My mother-in-law's face was red with fury.

When I turned around, Becca and Sandra were running to catch their bus.

"Becca? Sandra? Wait!" I yelled but Thelma hit the horn again. This time, Ty shrieked in unison with the ungodly noise. Everyone was staring at me. All out of options, I threw myself into the passenger seat beside Thelma.

"About time. You have no respect for other people. None."

With that, Thelma peeled away from the curb. Tires squealing. Baby crying. People staring. Me fumbling to click my seatbelt. I'm sure the expression on my face as we drove off made me look like I'd been car-napped. In a way, I had been. Thelma Detweiler was taking me to places I didn't want to go, against my will.

Thelma continued to yell at me all the way to the Detweiler farm. She called me ungrateful. She questioned why her son ever married me. She criticized my parenting. She was incoherent. Fortunately, I'm a graduate with a post-doctoral degree in verbal abuse. I hummed under my breath and told myself repeatedly, "Sane people do not act this way. Her behavior has nothing to do with me, and everything to do with whatever mess she's got in her head."

My mantra kept me from bursting into tears, but Ty was sobbing in the back. My mother-in-law was still spouting torrents of abuse, as she watched me struggle to grab my backpack from behind the seat after she parked. She didn't even take a breath before launching into how disrespectful I was. Meanwhile, Ty had worked himself up into a full-blown meltdown. It took me a while to unbuckle him because I wasn't familiar with this particular infant seat, and because the noise was distracting. Between Ty crying and Thelma screaming, I couldn't think straight.

Thelma followed me into the farmhouse, calling me everything but a human being. Ty was bellowing at the top of his lungs. Thelma was yelling, too. Brawny came flying down the stairs, taking them two at a time. "Who's hurt?" she yelled over the din.

"No one," I said, trying to be heard over Thelma. I let Brawny lift Ty from my arms because I figured that if she could get him away from Thelma, he might settle down. Brawny took the baby and turned her back on Thelma, even as my mother-in-law threw her keys on the floor like a petulant five-year-old. I followed Brawny upstairs to my bedroom and kept my fingers crossed that Thelma would not come after us.

She didn't.

It took Brawny and me fifteen minutes to get Ty calmed down. I explained to Brawny what had happened at the school.

My nanny was appalled. "That will never happen again, I promise. I was finishing my research, and when she tapped on the door and offered to take Ty for a ride and pick you up. I thought she was being conciliatory. Please believe me, I had no idea. And she cut off that girl? While she was opening up to you?"

"Yes. Becca was on the verge of telling me more about the near-misses when Thelma hit the horn. Sandra, the other student, intervened, but I almost had an answer out of Becca. Brawny, that might have been our best chance for finding out what's happening!" I buried my face in my hands and burst into tears. Thelma's abuse brought back years of buried memories. They surfaced like an explosion of Mount Vesuvius, and since I was tired, hungry, and far away from my own home, I had none of the usual weapons I could use to stop old memories from swamping me.

"Ye poor wee mite." After setting Ty in his crib, Brawny sat next to me on the bed. She wrapped me in her arms and rocked me. "Aye, and ye probably had a miserable day to boot. That woman's one-half harpy, I swear she is. So what if Thelma had to wait a while? She had no reason for fussing at ye. None at all. That's abuse, pure and simple."

Under stress, Brawny's Scottish accent becomes more pronounced. Fortunately, I've learned to tune my hearing to Scots 101, and I understood what she was saying.

"Detweiler himself will be home in ten minutes or so. How do ye want to handle this?"

"Let's play it by ear. I'm not sure what I want to do. Not yet." I mopped my eyes on my sleeve. Walking into the bathroom, I found a washcloth and ran cold water over it. After I wrung it out, I wiped my face repeatedly. The swelling would take a while to go down, but my mood had calmed considerably.

Thelma served dinner as though nothing had ever happened. In fact, she seemed to be in a terrific mood. Her lasagna was fantastic. Detweiler said, "Mom, you make the best lasagna in the world."

"She sure does," Louis agreed.

Brawny sent me questioning looks that gently asked if I was okay. I gave her a half-smile to indicate I was.

After dinner, the three of us went outside to the picnic table. "Any luck today?" Detweiler asked the nanny. If he noticed my swollen eyes, he didn't remark on them.

"Aye, a couple of bits and bobs," she responded. "I think the idea that Mr. Sidney Rusk is involved is a non-starter. He's up for retirement next year. He doesn't have a good reason to want the job as principal."

"And you?" Detweiler turned to me. How could he not notice I'd been crying? Was he in denial? Okay, two could play at that game.

I explained about creating the list of topics for the students' additions to their portfolios. "The students brainstormed after I got them started. I will work more on the list tomorrow during the period where I'm in the teachers' lounge. The other teachers are finalizing their grades. I don't have to calculate grades. Mrs. Eowin turned hers in before she left for maternity leave. The students don't realize that. At least, I don't think they do."

I hesitated, "I thought I had a lead on another girl who might have tried and failed to commit suicide, but I didn't get enough information."

Brawny sighed.

"I did learn we can forget about the students using video games," I said. "At least if the game is a multi-player format. The ping is too slow here."

"Unfortunately, I have to turn right around and go back to St. Louis," my husband said. "One of my cases is going to trial next week. I have to be ready for that. There's no way we can let this creep back out on the streets. I'm planning to work until the wee hours, so I'll sleep at the house in Webster Groves. I'll give Rebekkah a ring before I get there so I don't scare her. We don't want to lose a good cat sitter. I might even need to go back in to work tomorrow morning."

And so, my husband left before I had the chance to tell him how his mother had stopped Becca from giving me a list of students who had tried and failed to kill themselves. Those kids, like Luke Kressig, had information we badly needed to track down a murderer. Or to put to rest our theory that only one person was behind this mess.

Either way, we'd been stymied.

Although I considered grabbing my husband by the arm on his way to his car and giving him an earful, I couldn't see how that would help. The best way to validate what had happened would be to have Brawny chime in and explain what she'd witnessed. Otherwise, Thelma's behavior was nothing short of unbelievable. I didn't even know whether Detweiler had spoken to his father about Thelma yet. It was going to take an all-hands-on-deck approach to make that woman stop all this nonsense.

And that could not be accomplished in a quick five minutes. The sad truth was that Detweiler couldn't do anything about his mother's unacceptable behavior. Not tonight.

It would have to wait. While I nursed Ty, I tried not to obsess about how sneaky Thelma had been. Her moods seemed to change on a dime. Cradling Ty in my arms, I took the time to count my blessings.

But I crawled into bed later feeling teary-eyed. Thelma's behavior would take me a long, long time to forget. If ever.

I had bad dreams all Wednesday night and woke up soaked with perspiration. Thank goodness Gracie had climbed into the bed and taken my husband's place. Waking up to her was almost as good as waking up to him. Well, maybe not. But she certainly was a great comfort. Researchers have found it takes only ten minutes of stroking a dog's fur to lower your blood pressure. I needed a good fifteen minutes on Wednesday morning.

Brawny always knew how to make me feel better. On this particular morning, the smell of frying bacon drifted upstairs. The vanilla-scented fragrance of pancake batter soon followed. That was my favorite breakfast, bar none!

Ty was in his high chair when I got downstairs. I gave him a kiss. Our nanny greeted me with a sad smile. "I heard ye call out in the night. Looked in on ye. Must have been a whopper of a bad dream. Are you okay?"

"I guess. Eating your terrific breakfast should help." I was wearing a simple khaki denim skirt and white blouse with sleeves long enough to cover my injuries. Fortunately they were scabbed over. On my feet were cute brown sandals. They had a braided strap joined to a beige leather sole. I'd actually put on a little mascara to help disguise the puffy skin around my eyes. I was looking my best, and that helped to bolster my mood.

I added, "Sorry if I disturbed your sleep, Brawny."

"No bother. After all you went through yesterday, I wasn't surprised at the turmoil. Took every bit of restraint not to knock your mother-in-law silly. 'Twas only respect for her husband and son that kept me from doing serious damage to her. What utter nonsense! And then to learn that Detweiler had to turn around and leave. Of all days!"

She was right. I'd gone from a waking nightmare to a sleeping one. I rubbed my temples. "I think I need a couple of Advils. Let me run back upstairs and get them and my backpack. Can you drive me to school this morning?"

"I'd like to see somebody try and stop me," she huffed. "Today's a good day to pamper you in every way I can. I've already packed a lunch for ye. Go on and get what you need. I'll fill a plate for you."

After downing two Advils and grabbing my backpack, I took my place at the kitchen table where the promised plate with two blueberry pancakes and three strips of crispy bacon were waiting next to a tall mug of hazelnut coffee with almond milk and Stevia. Brawny had also provided a mug of freshly squeezed lemon juice in warm water with Stevia. She claimed it was good for the digestion, full of vitamin C, and an all-around healthy tonic to start the day.

Halfway through my pancakes, Thelma wandered in. Taking a quick look around, she said, "I hope you aren't expecting to leave me with this mess, Brawny. I won't stand for it." As she spoke, she moved so close to Brawny that she'd entered our nanny's personal space. The gesture was unnervingly provocative. Did Thelma have any idea who she was tangling with? Apparently not!

Brawny did not back down. Instead, she pulled herself up to her full height and squared her shoulders before answering, "Mrs. Detweiler, have I ever not cleaned up after myself? You know the answer to that. I would never do such a rude thing. As soon as I drop Kiki off at school, I'll come right back and see to it that the kitchen is put to rights. I promise you'll have no reason to complain when I'm done."

At that very moment, Louis came in from the barn. Wisps of hay were stuck to his jeans. As the pieces fell off, they left a trail behind him on the floor. His eyes darted from his wife to Brawny and back to Thelma. His wife's back was to him, but he had to have seen the look of alarm on my face. He immediately took his wife by the elbow and said, "Thelma, sweetheart, did you forget I promised to take you out for breakfast this morning? I thought we'd go to that Bob Evans over by the highway."

Crisis averted.

On the way to the school, Brawny shook her head. "There's something wrong with that woman. Truly there is. I'm wondering if she needs to be on medication."

"Beats me. All I know is that I'm tired of her. This week is almost over. I plan to drive back to St. Louis for the weekend. I can't stand living at the farmhouse any longer. Do you mind making the trip with me tomorrow?"

"Mind?" Brawny whooped. "I would have offered to drag you and young master in a pony cart if you hadn't brought it up yourself."

After she let me off, I shook off the Thelma cooties and hurried into the school. I used the ten minutes before class to get my thoughts organized. When the students were seated and the bell rang, I said, "Okay, I promised to teach you how to turn line drawings into scrapbook embellishments. Are you ready to learn?"

They gathered around and watched as I explained that you

could temporarily affix a photocopy to a piece of scrapbook paper and use the photocopy as a pattern. "Which image should I do first?" I spread out on the desk three cartoon images I'd chosen at random: a spooky Halloween house, a sports car, and a whale.

Unanimously they chose the whale. "Make it blue," suggested Eldon. A few of the others gave him a scathing look. I wondered what that was all about.

"Guys, this isn't hard. Trust me. Watch. I use the temporary tape-runner to put sticky stuff on the back of the photocopy. I adhere the photocopy to the blue patterned paper. Using the photocopy as a pattern, I cut out the image of the whale. See? A blue whale."

Ralphie glanced around at his classmates and giggled nervously.

"Any questions? Okay, then let's get to work. I printed out a variety of line drawings for you. I'd like for each of you to make an embellishment so I know you understand what you just saw."

"D-D-Does it have to be a b-b-blue whale?" asked Delphine. She looked really uncomfortable.

"No. It can be whatever you want. Remember? We're working on your personal pages or finishing your portfolio or doing a trash album. Choose any image you like. If you have trouble finding one, let me know so I can help."

By the time the class bell rang, I had twelve blue whales. The kids showed so little imagination that I was disappointed. Or maybe because I'd demonstrated the whales, the kids gravitated to what they'd seen me do. I wondered if the blue whale was a school mascot. Whatever. I decided that in the next art class, I'd choose a panda bear as an example.

With that decision cheering me up, I hurried to the teachers' lounge. Although I was the last person there, I was still able to use the computer. No one else wanted it.

"We're all working on grades," explained Oleander when she noticed me lingering at the computer desk.

Fine by me. I booted up the computer and went to work. I had decided to alphabetize the list of topics. There are alphabetizing programs online that you can use for free. I've seen Anya use them. The first program I pulled up scrambled a few of the letters in the words when I emailed it to myself at the school. I chose to delete that effort. There were three deleted emails in the school computer system when I finally turned off the computer at the end of my session. The bell rang for lunch, and I turned my thoughts to other matters.

At the threshold of the lunchroom, I stopped and scanned the tables, looking for a place to sit. Oleander waved to me. She had kindly saved me a seat at her side. She ate yogurt again while I ate the ham salad sandwich that Brawny had packed for me. Today we talked about paper-piecing, which is the name of the papercrafting technique I'd taught the students.

"How brilliant! They must have loved it because they came into my class and talked about it on and on. They were so happy. I have not seen them excited like that in weeks. What a wonderful way to take their minds off the suicides. You brought paper from your stores? *Vous êtes très gentil.* I am happy you are here. When school is over, I would like to visit this store of yours."

"I would be delighted to have you come and look around. Maybe you could even teach a class on France and the French culture. I bet my scrapbookers would enjoy that. They love learning new things."

She and I exchanged cell phone numbers. We talked about teaching methods and about dealing with uninvolved students. "There is so much fear. I feel it, don't you?"

I had to admit that there was something in the air. Whatever it was, the students were edgy. All I could do was redouble my efforts to be watchful.

And grateful. Whenever I get blue, I make a special effort to count my blessings. Today, as I walked out of the lunchroom, my list included Oleander. I enjoyed spending time with her and felt like I was making a new friend.

After school, I waited at the curb, not knowing who would pick me up. Oleander drove by in a blue MINI Cooper, every bit as cute as she. "Need a ride?"

"Thanks, but not today!" I waved at her right as the car behind her tapped his horn. It was Drew and not surprisingly, he drove an older model Porsche Carrera. The color was a dark navy. His license plate read: MO6Y.

Decoding license plates is a game Anya and I play and seeing that cryptic plate made me miss my daughter. An ache began in my heart. Instead of crying, I clamped my eyes shut tightly. When I opened them, Detweiler was driving up slowly in his unmarked cruiser. He leaned over and popped the passenger side door open for me. "Brawny will meet us at the Flying Horse Truck Stop. She was on the computer and needed a minute to close it down. I wanted a little alone time with you because I've been assigned to the Major Case Squad. That's a pain in the backside. I'll have to spend more time at the office, coordinating the investigation. I plan to eat dinner at the farm tonight, but I'll have to get up early and drive back into St. Louis first thing tomorrow morning. I don't know when I'll get to see you after that."

"I understand." The Major Case Squad was a way to get all 91 of the metro St. Louis municipalities to work together and share information. For the most part, only the best of the best law enforcement officials were invited. That meant that Detweiler's time with the Major Case Squad was particularly well-spent because he picked up new skills along the way.

He continued, "By the way, I ran by the store this morning when I was in the neighborhood. Clancy told me she's doing just fine but she misses you. You should have seen the store ... neat as a pin. I don't doubt that after every purchase, Clancy walks around and restocks the sold merchandise."

"Sounds like Clancy to me. She's great at keeping the store looking terrific. It's in good hands. How were the cats?"

"Happy to see me. They miss all the activity in the house, I think," he said.

Our conversation ended when we arrived at the truck stop, and Detweiler pulled into one of the designated spaces set aside for cars and small trucks.

35

*J*ohn was standing by his truck and wearing an anxious expression on his face. His hand were jammed deep into the pockets of his jeans. After a quick acknowledgement we'd arrived, he led the way to the same booth we'd chosen before. Once we were there in the back of the restaurant, John fairly threw himself down onto the vinyl seat.

"What's wrong?" I asked.

"I can't believe what a jerk Mr. Rusk is being. He's decided that if my brother can't get all his schoolwork finished in the next month, he'll have to repeat his senior year or get his GED."

Detweiler cursed under his breath. "That's great. That'll really help your brother to open up and talk. Additional pressure is not what he needs right now."

"You know it." John fairly seethed. "Is Brawny coming?"

"Yes." Detweiler said. "She should be here any time."

Iola, the waitress, came by. Today she was wearing shorts with cut-outs above the pockets so her skin showed through the holes. Seriously weird. One look at John's glum expression was all she needed. "Somebody's having a bad day. This definitely calls for three pieces of pie. We've got peach, apple, cherry, and lemon meringue. What's your pleasure?"

Brawny walked up behind the woman and said, "I want apple, please." To Detweiler, the nanny explained, "Your father has the baby. He insisted on a little man to man bonding time."

The rest of us ordered—lemon meringue for me, peach for Detweiler, and cherry for John. After Iola walked away, Brawny listened to the news about Mr. Rusk's demands. "I wonder if you can take this up with the superintendent?"

"Better yet," suggested Detweiler, "have Luke's psychiatrist write the superintendent a letter."

"Luke has a psychiatrist?" I wondered if he'd had problems before. If so, that might put a new slant on what happened.

"Hospitals always assign a psychiatrist to patients who've shown signs of self-harm," Detweiler explained to me. To John, he said, "Have the psychiatrist explain to the superintendent how detrimental additional stress will be to Luke's health."

That made sense. Iola brought the slices of pie. She'd topped them with generous scoops of vanilla ice cream. I savored the combination of tart lemon and the silky ice cream. Detweiler attacked his peach pie, and John dug into his slice of cherry pie. Brawny was tucking into her food, too. For a while, none of us spoke. After we slowed down, I said, "I realize this is a foregone conclusion, but there's something definitely going on at that school. I've seen the seniors at CALA. They're almost giddy when it gets this close to graduation. Not these kids. They're scared."

"You can say that again," John agreed. "In the locker room after PE, I walked past one of the senior boys and realized he was sobbing into his towel. He wouldn't talk to me. You know him, Kiki. It was Billy. All the other kids avoided him."

"Billy ... oh, yeah. The boy with the funny cowlicks."

"Right. He was red-eyed and hiccupping. Since I was wearing a towel and he was naked, the whole situation was awkward with a capital A. I wrote down my cell phone number. I told him to call me if he needed to talk."

Detweiler let his fork clatter against the tabletop. "What is it with these kids? They obviously need help. Why won't they talk to you?"

"I have no idea," John said. "None."

I reported my brief conversation with Becca and Sandra. "Unfortunately, it was cut short," I said.

"Why?" My husband asked.

Brawny gave me a sideways look.

"Um, your mother was in a hurry to get back to the house." I tried to sound nonchalant.

John flagged down Iola and ordered a cup of black coffee. Detweiler wanted one, too.

"My brother Luke and I have always been like that," and John raised two fingers wrapped around each other. "Now I can't get him to talk to me. He won't say a word. Won't answer my questions. Nothing. But I did see something when I dropped by this morning that might be helpful. As Luke was rolling over, moving away from me to face the wall, the covers pulled back from his arm, and I saw an image on his skin."

"A tattoo?" Detweiler raised an eyebrow.

The young man shrugged. "That's what I thought it was at first. I figured maybe my brother got one and hid it from our parents. I leaned over the bed and got a good look at it. It's *not* a tattoo. Not a professional one at least. Looks to me like he used an ink pen. He'd drawn a blob—"

"A blob?" That made even less sense. I sat there with my mouth open. Why would a teenager draw a blob on his arm in ink? That sort of behavior was what I expected from somebody Erik's age.

"Here, I took a photo." John dug his phone out of his jeans' pocket. Thumbing through the pictures, he came to one and pulled it up on his cell phone screen.

"That's not a blob," I said. "I'm used to interpreting people's artwork. That's a *whale*. My students made blue whales for their scrapbook pages. It's the school mascot, right?"

"No. The Jarvis Township High School mascot is a cougar," John said.

"What?" I was totally baffled.

Brawny got a wild look in her eyes. She reached into her messenger bag and brought out her notebook computer. When Iola came back with the coffees, Brawny requested the truck stop's WiFi password.

Iola said, "PieInTheSky6440."

After tapping a few keys, Brawny turned the computer around so we could see the screen. "Look at this."

Under a photo of a blue whale, the copy read: *Blue Whale Suicide Club Claims Lives of Local Teens.*

"Oh, my word ..." I felt like someone had knocked the air out of me.

Detweiler's eyes flashed with anger. "Clubs like that have sprung up in other parts of the world. But locally? I would have never guessed it could happen here."

"What on earth is a suicide club?" My mouth suddenly went dry, and my lips were sticking to my teeth.

"The Major Case Squad got a briefing on this two years ago. That headline is wrong. The name is actually The Blue Whale Challenge, and it's a secret society," Detweiler rubbed his forehead. "If this is what I think it is, it's horrible news."

His reaction didn't make sense. We'd had a breakthrough. At least now we knew what we were dealing with. So why was my husband so upset? I ventured to ask, "This is helpful, isn't it?"

"Dealing with secret societies is a tough assignment," Brawny spoke softly. "There's an induction, a hazing, and if you pass, you undergo an initiation. Challenges are issued to members as a way of testing their loyalty. They often use a secret code, secret handshakes, and the like. All the elements are designed to keep the members under the spell of groupthink. After a while, peer pressure takes over. Most importantly, there are severe penalties for talking to outsiders. That makes secret societies very difficult to crack."

"They're that strong?" I asked.

"Think of Jim Jones and Guyana, David Koresh and Waco, and you'll answer your own question. Those are two of the most well-known secret societies. These groups exert the sort of pressure that can drive people to commit to acts that are totally irrational," Detweiler said. "You never know what to expect from the members because you can't penetrate the wall of silence."

"Who in her right mind would dream up a club that encourages people to kill themselves? That's crazy." John smacked the Formica tabletop with his open palm. "Who would join a club like that? How did these kids come up with an idea like this?"

"I bet our creep stumbled on it through social media and appropriated the idea." Detweiler sighed. "These clubs have sprung up in other places. India, China, Egypt, and the UK. A disgruntled 21-year-old grad student thought up the Blue Whale Challenge after he was tossed out of his university. He was a psychology student. The game was his way of cleansing the student body, or so he said. According to him, the weak members of society would get involved and self-select themselves as candidates for extinction."

My heart was racing. Were we onto something? If so, could we do anything to stop the club from claiming more lives? I asked, "Okay, so this grad student invented the Blue Whale Challenge. That doesn't answer the question: why join? Who would go along with something so lethal?"

"Kids who feel under pressure, isolated, and unsure of their futures," Detweiler said. "In other words, anyone who has ever gone through high school."

"You've got to be kidding me!" I could barely contain myself. I didn't want to believe what he was saying, but in my heart of hearts, I knew he was right. CALA puts a high premium on good grades and getting accepted into good colleges. Of course, that's one reason we wanted Erik and Anya to be enrolled there. But there's a high price to pay besides the $30,000 a year tuition. Those high expectations translate into a lot of pressure to succeed. Each year at exam time, students walk around looking haggard. Dark circles ring their eyes. They either gain or lose a lot of weight. Their skin breaks out. Their poor physical condition reflects their mental duress, and each year students catch mononucleosis or the flu or break out in hives. I ticked off the variables: under pressure, feeling isolated, and unsure of their futures.

No wonder an online club would be so appealing! It would be accessible anytime, anywhere. It would function as a distraction, giving students a way to blow off steam. As an adventure, it would be new and exciting. As a club, it would offer a sense of belonging especially during a time when kids felt isolated and adrift.

John said, "Before all this happened, Luke told me he'd joined a club. One where he'd met a lot of people."

"Emily told us Luke had challenges," I reminded my husband. "She likened them to the ones Hercules faced."

"The part about the challenges should have tipped me off," Detweiler said. "The tasks start simple but are aimed at moving members out of their comfort zones. Participants are assigned tasks like listening to a specific piece of music. Watching a horror movie—"

"That explains it!" John practically jumped out of his seat. "Ma told me that Luke had rented two horror movies. She couldn't believe it, and I couldn't, either. Luke always hated anything spooky. He was a gullible kid, easily scared, and he never went to scary movies with us. Ma was surprised. Shocked even. If he's a part of this mysterious club, that would explain the sudden change of heart. It also explains why he opened a Pandora account. I bet if I look at his musical selections, I'll see artists he never listened to before."

I couldn't believe what I was hearing, but it certainly made sense.

"Of all the possible explanations for what's happening with these kids, the Blue Whale Challenge fits this situation the best," Brawny said. "It explains the secrecy, the different methods for committing suicides, the motives, and the timing. In the original Blue Whale Challenge, participants went through a grooming period that indoctrinated them by giving them a series of fifty tasks. Along the way, they were told that their computers had been infected with malware and that the malware was recording all their deep, dark secrets. The malware scam convinced the victims that self-harm was a better choice than having their secrets exposed."

I shivered. "That's so manipulative and cruel."

"And effective." John scuffed the floor with the toe of his shoe. "Small steps, group think, peer pressure. Every organization uses it to whip members into line. Unfortunately, this organization serves no benevolent purpose. None."

"Does that mean there's a student out there who's encouraging his or her classmates to kill themselves?" I wondered. "Is that what we're thinking?"

Detweiler nodded. "Apparently so. Now all we need to do is find the person who runs the Blue Whale Challenge."

"Or find out what they use as a messaging system," said Brawny.

Detweiler signaled Iola that he wanted to pay the bill. "All we can do is see this through. Sooner or later, somebody will crack and tell us how to get inside this mess. Let's hope one of us is there when it happens."

36

When we got home, Louis was watching baseball with Ty on his lap. Thelma had spent all day in the kitchen. At dinner, she set out an amazing spread of sauerbraten, green beans and spaetzle, red cabbage with apples, and fresh homemade rolls. I ate until I thought I'd burst. Brawny and I offered to clear the table, but Thelma haughtily insisted that she didn't trust her good china to anyone.

I covered my mouth, burped and thought, "Fine by me. Be that way." After so much tension during the day, and such a big meal, I was ready for bed. Detweiler carried Ty upstairs. I nursed him in the rocker and read him one book after another. He liked *Goodnight, Moon* best and chewed off a corner to prove he found it delectable. After putting him in his crib, I went downstairs and joined the others, except for Brawny, as they watched a sports channel on TV. The men were excited about spring training for baseball. That reminded me of what Tadd had said about "Beau the Bumbler." I waited until the commercials to ask, "What does it mean when a football player fumbles the ball at the one-yard line? Is that bad? Especially if his team is behind by five?"

"You're darn tooting!" Louis laughed. "You'd have to be an idiot to drop the ball at the one-yard line."

Detweiler gave me a very gentle one-armed hug so as not to hurt my healing skin. "If Team A is down by five points and they fumble the ball on the one-yard line, Team B would automatically win. Why?"

"Just wondering."

~

THE NEXT MORNING, I automatically rolled over in bed and reached for my husband. Of course, he wasn't there. He'd taken off earlier to beat the morning traffic into St. Louis. That made me sad, but I cheered up immediately when I realized that this was Friday. Just eight more hours of working as a substitute art teacher, and I could enjoy a weekend at home in Webster Groves.

By the time I dressed and packed my few belongings, Brawny had my breakfast sitting on the kitchen table. "I'll text Rebekkah and let her know we're coming home for two days," said the nanny. "Don't want to freak out our favorite cat sitter."

I agreed. Rebekkah is a sweetheart, and I appreciate the way she helps us out. Ty grinned up at me as he chewed on a piece of scrambled egg. I picked him up and cuddled him. My sweet little guy sat on my lap while I ate my cereal and drank my iced coffee.

"Another day, another attempt to save these kids," I told Brawny. "Not that we're making much progress. By the way, where's Thelma?"

"She was here earlier. She said she was tired out from last night."

"That was quite a feast."

"Aye, it was." Brawny went on to tell me that she'd reminded my mother-in-law that we were heading back to Webster Groves this evening. "I wanted to make sure Thelma didn't forget and expect us for dinner."

"Any new background information?"

"Nothing we can use, but I might have found an interesting pattern. I'll share it with you and John when we meet at the truck stop after school. I need to double-check my work to make sure I'm right."

That put a skip in my step. I was wearing a pair of khaki slacks, a black tee shirt and Keds with pictures of dogs all over them. My spirits were soaring. It was a Feel Good Friday for sure! A day to celebrate the end of five days of working hard.

I eagerly awaited my first period students. When they filed into the classroom, I was surprised at the downtrodden mood. "Is something wrong?"

I was answered by murmurs of, "No," but the kids refused to look me in the eye. "Are all your classmates okay?"

"Fine," someone said in the back.

"Everyone is okay," Becca assured me. I watched the students carefully and tried to decipher what they were thinking. One thing for sure, they were twitchy. Most of them played with their pens or chewed on their fingernails or twisted paperclips into odd shapes.

Maybe this was their way of gearing up for the weekend. Perhaps this was a delayed reaction to Luke's suicide attempt. I couldn't tell. Maybe being busy would help.

Delphine seemed the most jittery and weepy. I figured she must have had a fight with a friend, because throughout the class she sniffled into a tissue. In fact, she sniffled so much that I finally moved the classroom box of tissues over to where she was sitting. At one point, I actually saw a tear roll down her face.

"Are you okay?" I asked.

"Yes," she said, but she quickly looked away.

Becca flagged me down. The tape-runner had jammed. She needed my help untangling the mess. "Remember to lift it straight up after you put down a strip of adhesive," I said.

All the kids seemed fretful. Tadd couldn't find a color of paper he liked. Ralphie cracked his knuckles, one by one. Sandra chewed on a hangnail until it bled. Rhett kept shuffling his feet. Sam stared out the window for most of the hour. Every stinking one of my students had adopted some sort of self-soothing behavior.

"Would you mind telling me what's going on? You are all clearly upset."

I was met by blank gazes that couldn't maintain eye contact. *Oh, well.* I reminded them, "You have my email address if you need me."

After the students rushed out of the room, John circled back to talk to me. "What is going on? Any ideas? These students are nervous as a bunch of long-tailed cats in a room full of rocking chairs, as my grandfather used to say."

I had to agree. "Something is up. Something has changed since yesterday, but what? They seem to be depressed. Extra quiet."

John heaved a long, deep sigh. "I'll keep my ear to the ground, but seriously, I doubt that anyone will let something slip. It's like they've all gone into lockdown mode."

I had to agree. I quickly picked up the trash before leaving the classroom. Among the offcuts of scrapbook paper, I found a scrap of white copier paper. Fish Fry Friday was scrawled on it. Wadding it up, I tossed the piece into the trash and made a mental note of it because I love fried fish. Did that mean we were having fish and chips for lunch? I wouldn't doubt it. Yum, yum.

If the students were subdued, the teachers were just the opposite. Jessie and Drew had finished calculating their grades and turned them in. Drew popped the top on a can of Red Bull and toasted the end of the school year. Jessie hunched over her cell phone and read through emails. I assumed she was hoping to find out whether she'd gotten a job offer from another school. Alan was watching videos on his phone and laughing. Oleander was reading a novel in French.

I was surprised when my phone showed that I had incoming emails. First was a photo of Erik and Anya on a beach. Erik looked sunburned. Anya looked cross. Obviously, they were fine. The second was a message from Clancy. She suggested that I add location information to the handouts I'd created. "We want people to come and shop here," she explained.

Of course, she was right. I went over to the computer and pulled up my files. In short order, I added the store address and phone number. After emailing the new files to Clancy at my store, I trashed the old files. As usual, I checked to see that the files had actually gone into the deleted file folder.

As the "working" icon spun around, I did a double take. The number of deleted files had grown tenfold overnight. That didn't make sense. Or did it? I looked at the label on one of the files: Fish Fry Friday 321. Another said: Fish Fry Friday 621. Someone had been working on the cafeteria menu. The numbers were clearly dates.

The first bell rang for the computer lab, and I quickly shut down the Dell in the teacher's lounge. At least I had lunch to look forward to. If they were serving fried fish as I suspected, I planned to ditch the peanut butter and jelly sandwich that Brawny had made and eat the cafeteria food instead.

The menu definitely did not include fried fish. Total bummer. The rest of my day dragged on and on.

I threw myself into the car when Brawny picked me up. Ty was in his infant car seat, gurgling happily when I got in. Our rendezvous with John would be at the truck stop again. This struck me as funny, because this was the most time I'd ever spent at a truck stop in my life. My giggles were contagious and when I shared my thoughts with Brawny, she snickered, too. "From the truck stop, we'll run back to the farm, pick up Gracie, and then drive straight to Webster Groves. I've packed everything Ty needs and I need. I know you packed last night."

"Home," I said. "Sounds like heaven."

"Aye, Thelma and I had a bit of a row this morning. She fussed at me for taking you to school and leaving the mess in her kitchen. I told her that she knew I'd be right back, and she accused me of spoiling you rotten. That's when I let her have it with both barrels of the shotgun. I told her that if anyone deserved spoiling, that person would be you."

"You didn't have to do that," I said, "but it was kind of you to stick up for me. If that's giving it to her with both barrels, you must have loaded your gun with cotton wadding."

That made her laugh some more. "Cotton wadding? That's a right funny idea. Seriously, I don't know what's eating at her, but she's been a right git, as the Brits say."

"I don't know either, but ..." and I told Brawny what I had been thinking about Thelma's relationships with Detweiler's first two wives.

"Aye, sad to say, that makes perfect sense. I can well believe that Thelma drove those girls away. Some women are like that: no one is good enough for their little boys. Except, that's only the tip of the iceberg. Deep down, they feel a possessiveness about their sons. The experts call it an 'enmeshed relationship.' The son becomes a sort of surrogate spouse. While I believe Thelma loves her husband, she admires her son in a way that's almost unhealthy. You're her competition, and you'll never be good enough for him."

We would have discussed the matter more, but we'd arrived at the truck stop. As Brawny killed the engine on the Highlander, she told me, "I'm eager to share with you and John a pattern I've found. I think it will be helpful."

Shortly after we took the booth in the back and got Ty settled in a high chair, John joined us. His face looked thunderous. So much so, that my tummy did a flip as I worried whether Luke had taken a turn for the worse.

"Your mother-in-law phoned me as I was driving away from the school. She wanted to know if I was meeting you on the sly. Seems she thinks we're doing dirty something behind her son's back. Can you believe that?" John slammed himself into his side of the booth. The crease between his eyebrows was deep, and his mouth was set in a tight frown. "I was polite to her, but only barely. I remember overhearing Patty say that her mother was particularly nasty to Chad's wives, but I never thought she'd go so far as to accuse her own daughter-in-law of adultery."

"Wow," I said. I was all out of words.

Brawny stiffened and spat out, "Aye, well, she's got the entire weekend to herself, she does. I told her you needed to check on your store and that we'd be back Monday. She wanted specifics, so I explained I would pick you up, we would have a quick meeting with John, and then we'd run back to the farm to pick up Gracie. I couldn't leave her in the car in this heat. That would be cruel, so I had to leave the dog at the farm. Once we have Gracie, we'll drive straight back to Webster Groves."

"And she said?"

"You know how Thelma mutters under her breath. Sounded like she said good riddance. She's stirred the pot, she has. I plan to tell her son that his mother needs to rein herself in. Calling you while you were driving away from the school, John? What if you'd had someone in your truck? She could wreck this entire investigation!"

"There's more," John said. "Thelma told me there is no *real* investigation. According to her, this is all Kiki's way of getting attention. I set her straight on that. I explained that we're gathering important information, and you're trying to look after students at the same time. I also told her she better not say a word to anyone about what we're trying to do."

"How did she respond?"

John dropped his gaze to the tabletop where Ty had ripped open a packet of sugar. "Mrs. Detweiler was very annoyed that I took your part, Kiki. She told me she was shocked that I'd dare to speak to her that way, and she intended to speak to my mother."

I groaned.

"She went on to say she could do what she wanted, and she wasn't taking orders from anybody, including me, and especially from her daughter-in-law."

I buried my face in my hands. Ty reached over and awkwardly tried to pat my hair. That left me with a glob of wet sugar on my scalp.

I considered phoning Thelma right then and there and having it out with her, but when I tapped buttons on my cell phone, Brawny grabbed it from my hand. "Not a good idea. Get a hold of yourself. Take the long view. Don't jeopardize what you're doing, lass. Let your husband handle his mother."

37

_S_he was right. My call to Thelma could, and should, wait. Iola arrived in time to distract me with the news that they had freshly made lemon meringue pies. I ordered two pieces—I said that one was for Ty and one was for me, but of course Ty's too young to eat pie. John and Brawny had also decided that lemon meringue pie was just the ticket. John and Brawny ordered cups of coffee, and I asked for a tall unsweetened iced tea.

Brawny took control of the conversation. "Forget Thelma. She's a wee fishy and we're hunting for the Loch Ness monster. One of my friends in Scotland had a suggestion. He's dealt with Blue Whale copycats before. He believes we need to find the place where the administrator is posting the challenges. They maybe even in code. He says that for the perpetrator to accomplish its goals, he must activate each challenge, and of course, we know the challenges end with killing yourself."

"That's not anything new. We sort of figured that," said John.

"Right, but he and I were able to narrow down where and when you should look for the challenges. I did a spreadsheet." Brawny pulled papers out of her black leather messenger bag.

She handed one to me and one to John. "Notice the timing. See how each death and each attempt at suicide occurs over the weekend. Stands to reason that the victims get their challenges on a Friday. They're instructed to carry them out on a Saturday or Sunday. All of the suicide attempts have been on those two days. Even the ones that failed. At least, the ones we know of."

"You followed up on the failures?" I'd been bothered by the fact I'd gotten so close to learning about them, until Thelma had interrupted my chance to find out more.

"Aye. I went through the local hospital intake forms. I won't tell ye how, as it's not legal, strictly speaking, but I did it. Four other students besides Luke have been taken to the local emergency room with what appears to be botched attempts on their lives. All four tried to hurt themselves over a weekend. Another part of the puzzle is this: no *long* weekends were involved. These attempts were always restricted to a Saturday and Sunday. None happened when Monday was a holiday. Again, that points to the challenges being issued on a Friday. And what happens on a Friday? The students are in school. Stands to reason, the challenges are issued at the school."

"So the puppet master wants to know almost immediately if his or her instructions have been honored," John surmised. "With a long weekend or a school break, the creep might not hear all the gory details for days or even weeks."

"Right." Brawny smiled and thanked Iola as she passed out four plates with generous slices of lemon meringue pie. My unsweetened tea was the perfect counterpoint to the sweet dessert. Ty happily mashed bits of meringue between his swollen gums. When I gave him a taste of the filling, he puckered up at the tart flavor and grinned like a toothless jack-o-lantern.

"We're back to where we were yesterday. We need to figure out how the messages are shared, right?"

"That's right." Brawny speared a piece of pale crust with her fork. "Notice that none of the kids have died together, or in pairs. Only one by one. 'Tis almost like this monster is dragging out the drama. If these were copycat murders, you'd think that kids might die in tandem. But that isn't the case, is it?"

I said, "I can't imagine how awful this is for the Jarvis Township parents. This has to be driving them nuts. They must spend every waking hour worrying that one of their kids could be next. The pressure must be enormous."

John nodded his head. "I can vouch for that. My mom and my dad never used to fight. Now all they do is quarrel. Ma didn't like it when Luke stayed out late. Dad thought she was being overly protective. When Luke tried to kill himself in his own room, they blamed each other. They're barely talking to each other."

I pinched my nose rather than tear up. I knew the wedge that Thelma was driving between Detweiler and me. I wiped my nose with my paper napkin and tried to focus. "We need to hunt for a messaging system."

"Aye, and let's narrow it down, shall we? I can't imagine Anya or her friends passing paper notes to each other, can you?" Brawny gave me a patient smile.

I disagreed. "On the other hand, paper might be just the ticket. Who writes anything down these days? No one under the age of forty. Passing a note might be so low tech that nobody has noticed it."

"Detweiler told me that the police are monitoring all outgoing emails from the school," Brawny said. "He said they've also been monitoring the school's Intranet and found nothing."

"They can't tap every student's phone," I said. "John, they reviewed your brother's phone use, didn't they?"

"Yes. They found nothing. A few messages looked like they might be code, but when I looked at them, I could easily explain that they were bona fide communications. 'Don't forget to put the bales of hay in the truck,' meant exactly that. So did every note from Luke's friends. Yes, one of them had purchased a little weed, and they all smoked it at one friend's house. Big deal. Nothing so personal or weird that I couldn't read it and figure out exactly what my brother was saying."

Brawny had been listening carefully. She said, "Let's go back to the fact that all of the kids have died or made suicide attempts within the 48-hour period immediately following a Friday when school was in session. Doesn't it follow that the message was passed during school hours?"

"Let's brainstorm ways a message could be sent." I flipped over the paper place mat that had been under my cutlery. "We've got students passing notes, right? Talking to each other during school hours?"

"Or using designated drops, like spies do, leaving messages in designated places for later pick-ups," Brawny said. "The administrator of the game might even put a note inside a student's locker."

"I've read that spies create a physical code," John said. "That could be an action like moving a plant to a certain window or using a certain color of chalk on the message board outside the lunchroom."

"But those would be triggers and not the challenge itself," I said. "Remember, the administrator has to be able to communicate with the players. I took that to mean 'message' and not just leave a sign. It also suggests two way communication. Detweiler said that one way the administrator controls the players is by telling them that malware has been installed ..."

"So the player would have to have access to his or her own personal computer," John said. "Otherwise, the malware threat wouldn't matter. I read up on this last night. It's like Detweiler said. The administrator tells the club members that he's been spying on them all along. He has incriminating information that'll be shared publicly if the club members don't commit suicide."

"Kids really believe that?" I asked.

"You have to remember there are challenges along the way," John said. "Fifty to be exact. Those challenges are designed to encourage the victim to share embarrassing secrets and to participate in activities that might be illegal or immoral."

"Or embarrassing," Brawny tossed in.

"But how are these messages going back and forth?" I felt like we were banging our heads against a brick wall.

"It has to be via computer. I'll go back to my sources and ask them to look over all the electronic data one more time." Brawny picked up the bill and waved it at Iola. "There must be an electronic delivery method that we're overlooking."

I thought the subject was finished when Brawny handed Iola money and told her to keep the change. But the nanny had one more thing to say, and it was important. "John? You have to get your brother to talk. You cannot let him stay silent. Not when so many lives are at risk."

"We need to know who the administrator is," I said.

"Or how the members communicate," Brawny added. "That might even be more important. If we can stop the messages, we can stop the game."

John stood up next to the booth. Jamming his hands deep in his pockets, he rocked back on his heels and stared out the huge plate glass windows. Trucks of all sizes, in all colors, shifted positions like gumballs in a candy machine. The young man said, "I'll do my best."

38

$\mathcal{T}$he plan was for Brawny to run into the farmhouse and grab Gracie. She did, and therefore, I was able to avoid another encounter with Thelma. To give myself even more time to cool down, I turned the ringer off on my cell phone. I'd had enough of my meddlesome mother-in-law for one day. The drive from the farm to Webster Groves was pleasant, and our stop at the Muffin Man, a local bakery, was a treat. The young owners, two sisters, loaded me up with pastries, cupcakes, and iced cookies.

All of our errands took time, and our driving around proved beneficial because we missed rush hour. As usual, I let Brawny drive, and to my surprise, I actually snoozed a little while resting my head against the car door window. Dusk was falling gently, darkening the sky and softening the edges of the landscape. Vivid colors turned gray as night was falling.

We were a mile from home when my cell phone rang. The voice on the other end was tremulous and shrill. My caller was so upset that I couldn't figure out who was talking or what the person was saying. I asked, "Excuse me? Who is this, please?"

"S-s-she tried to commit," the woman seemed to be saying, she was crying too hard for me to understand.

"I'm sorry," I said, "but I can't make out what you are saying. Please. Take a deep breath and slow down. I'm listening."

Brawny had stopped at a light at a major intersection in downtown Webster Groves.

"*C'est horrible! Je suis* Oleander."

"Oleander? You'll have to speak English," I told her.

"Have you heard about Delphine Abernathy?" she asked. "She tried to kill herself today after school. You have her in class, don't you? Delphine swallowed Tylenol and vodka. Her mother found her but Delphine might not make it. It damaged her liver." A sob interrupted Oleander's recitation. "She sent me a text saying this was her only option. She had no choice," Oleander said.

"Oh, no." I repeated that over and over. And then the call dropped. I stared at the phone and used my sleeve to wipe the tears from my eyes.

"What is it?" Brawny asked tentatively.

"Another suicide attempt! This time it was one of my students. Her name is Delphine. She took Tylenol and vodka. Ruined her liver."

Brawny kept driving. After a bit, she asked, "Who called you?"

"Oleander Varney. The French teacher. We've gotten friendly. I shared my cell number with her. She planned to come to the store this weekend. I can't believe Delphine tried to kill herself. That's crazy. She was such a slip of a girl. One of my art students! And now she's dead—dying. Her mother found her. She's in the hospital but ..."

In the half-light from the overhead security lamps, I could see a deep frown creasing Brawny's forehead. "Aye, no doubt the poor lass has damaged her liver something frightful, she has.

And here I was praying that the deaths might stop until the next school year. It never occurred to me we'd lose one of your students."

She hesitated. "I don't mean to sound callous but this points to that girl getting her instructions today. On a Friday."

"I told the kids they could email me. Any time, any place. Why didn't she? Why didn't she try to reach out?" I beat my fists against the dashboard.

"Have ye checked your emails lately?" Brawny asked as she turned onto the main street that leads to downtown Webster Groves.

I hadn't checked my emails because I'd been avoiding Thelma Detweiler. I dug my phone out of my backpack and opened up my email inbox. There it was: *Sorry. This is the only way. Delphine.*

Hot tears ran down my face and dripped off my chin. "Brawny? I didn't make any difference. Not to her. What good am I doing? Maybe Thelma is right. Maybe there isn't really an investigation. I'm wasting my time *and* everyone else's by playing at being a detective. Shoot, I'm not even an effective teacher. Delphine didn't try to talk with me."

"Aye, and you've only been on the job, what? One week? Five whole days? You're a wee bit unrealistic if you're thinking that's enough time to truly make a difference. Nice as you are, gaining a teenager's confidence probably takes more than five hours, don't you think?"

When I didn't answer, she added, "I best send John a message so he knows."

While we waited at the last red light before our house, her thumbs flew over the buttons on her cell phone.

I knew Brawny was right. I had only been on the job for five days. Detweiler had worked cases that lasted much, much longer. However, I couldn't help but feel defeated. After the light turned green and we pulled forward, I told the nanny, "Delphine has frizzy hair. She reminds me of myself at that age. What possible reason could she possibly have for ending her life?"

I squeezed my eyes shut to try to stop the tears, and I saw Anya. My own daughter was less than confident, although she was growing emotionally more resilient as the years went on. She was coltish with knobby knees, and she'd always been thin. Delphine could have been my child. The pain of losing Anya, even in my imagination, knocked the air right out of my lungs. I gasped and choked out a sob. Concerned about the strange noises I was making, Gracie stuck her big head between the driver and passenger seats and licked my cheek. I rubbed her velvety ears and cried harder.

"Aye and you've had a rough, rotten week," Brawny said as she guided the car into the garage. She glanced down at her cell phone. "John got my text. He'd already heard about that poor wee girl and was trying to get more details before he contacted you. Let's get you and Ty inside. I'll pour ye a nice glass of wine and you can curl up on your sofa while I heat food from the freezer, eh? You take care of yourself. I'll bring the baby in."

Gracie stayed right beside me as I stumbled into the great room. She watched as I put a Firestarter log on the chunks of wood in the fireplace. I struck a long match and got the blaze started. While I worked on the fire, Gracie climbed up on the sofa and waited patiently for me to join her. Brawny changed Ty and handed him to me to nurse. The comfortable domestic scene soothed me. I cried, but I was only sniffling when my phone rang.

I answered it, while praying that Delphine might defy her poor prognosis and be all right.

"Sweetheart? Are you all right?" My husband's voice was thick with emotion. "John told me about Delphine."

"Uh-huh." I sniffled. "It's awful, isn't it?"

"Where are you?"

"We're home. Webster Groves."

"Glad to hear it. My mother was so worried. She had no idea you, Brawny, and Ty were leaving. She called me almost in tears because the dinner she made was getting cold. I was worried that something had happened to you at school so I phoned John. He told me about that student trying to kill herself. Mom is worried. She doesn't think people will blame you. She hopes you don't worry too much."

"Pardon me?" I couldn't believe what I was hearing. In a round-about way, Thelma was suggesting people *might* blame me for Delphine's suicide attempt. Could that even be possible?

Well, yes, it could. That was the sort of passive-aggressive behavior that Thelma Detweiler did best.

Brawny had heard the phone ring. She hurried into the great room and stared at me. I put my husband on speakerphone. Detweiler's voice came through loud and clear: "Mom is really concerned about you, honey. She knows people will talk because that girl is in your art class. She says her friends are already phoning her."

Brawny's mouth dropped open.

I was so angry that my blood pressure spiked, and I thought I was going to pass out. Brawny took one look at me and took Ty out of my arms right before I exploded. "Seriously, Detweiler? Your mother is afraid people will blame me? Because this poor girl was in my art class for, what? Five hours over the past eighteen years of her life? Boy, oh, boy. Do I ever work fast! Can you hear yourself? Have you lost your mind?"

I was shaking with rage. Did he have any idea how toxic his mother was being?

Brawny hurried up the stairs with my son in her arms. I could tell she was thinking she needed to get Ty away from me because I was going to blow my stack. And she was right.

I held onto the phone while Detweiler kept talking. He spouted gibberish about his mother and her worries and her friends who had kids at Jarvis Township. Brawny must have put Ty in his crib and taken the stairs two at a time to get back downstairs and make sure I didn't have a stroke.

"Brawny?" I said, handing over my phone to her. "Please tell Thelma Detweiler's precious son that I'm not speaking to him. Not tonight. Not tomorrow. Maybe never again! He doesn't even need to come home. He's welcome to hang onto his mommy's apron strings. That should make them both deliriously happy."

39

*L*eaving Brawny to talk to my husband, I marched upstairs and straight into the master bedroom shower. I stood in the stream of hot water for at least twenty minutes. When I got out, I changed into yoga pants and a hoodie. It felt good to get out of my nice teaching clothes and into garments that were soft and cuddly. My khaki slacks and my nice black tee shirt sat in a pile on the floor. Would that every problem in life could be thrown off so easily.

I wanted to talk to Clancy. She knows a lot about marital problems because she's had them. I wanted to tell Clancy about how Thelma was acting and how my husband had sided with his mother. Clancy would understand. She'd been married to a jerk, too.

My mind plummeted into a worst case scenario. What if Detweiler and I split up? I knew how much his family meant to him. Particularly his mother. What if she had managed to ruin our relationship? What was that phrase Brawny taught me? "Throw a spanner in the works." Yes, that pretty much described it. I could picture Thelma tossing a wrench into a fine-tuned motor. That's what my mother-in-law was doing to my marriage.

I stood there staring out the bedroom window. Seymour, our striped gray cat, jumped on the sill and rubbed against me. I should have felt comforted, but my emotions were as dark as the night sky. I didn't want to end my marriage. I didn't want to get divorced. Until this week and our time at the farm, we'd done so well. Erik was adjusting to being our middle child. Anya had matured and found a new role for herself as the oldest child. And then there was Ty. Adorable, perfect, and so very much like his father.

This was definitely a house filled with love, but a house couldn't stand if it was divided against itself. Thelma Detweiler was skilled at doing exactly that.

My tummy growled. I walked downstairs to the kitchen. Brawny was bustling about, reheating a homemade stew and toasting whole grain bread.

"I spoke to your husband. He won't be coming home tonight. He has to go back to the police department," Brawny said, greeting me when I took a seat at the kitchen table. "I told him that you and I both had specifically told Thelma we weren't staying for the weekend. I also told him about his mother's phone call to John, suggesting you two were having an affair."

"Do I want to hear his response?" I walked over to the kitchen cabinet and grabbed a bottle of California red wine. After stabbing the cork and breaking it with the corkscrew, I grabbed a knife and proceeded to chop the cork into tiny pieces. They floated on the top of the wine. Without a word, Brawny handed me a tea strainer. I held the strainer to the bottle and poured two big glasses of wine. I gave one to Brawny who was watching me with amusement.

"Your husband was gobsmacked."

"Translation, please." I lifted my glass. "Cheers."

"Cheers. Gobsmacked means shocked speechless."

"Good."

"Ye realize, I am certain, that he has a bit of reckoning to do. He's not a stupid man. It has to have dawned on him that his sainted mother is doing everything she can to wreck his marriage. Again. It has to pain him to realize she's done this before and gotten away with it."

"Good for her, eh? That's her game and she plays it to win. Before the marriage Thelma is nice as pie. After the marriage, Thelma drives a wedge between her son and his wife. The upshot? She gets her son back, at least temporarily. Then Thelma busies herself, buzzing from one member of the community to another and spreading tales about how awful her daughter-in-law is. Or was. And who's going to stop her? Not Louis. He turns a blind eye. Not Detweiler. She's his mother. He trusts her. Not her daughters. They have their suspicions, but they're loyal to their mother, as you might expect."

After pulling a rack of toasted bread slices from the oven, Brawny set the metal grid on a hot pad. While I grabbed the butter from the refrigerator, she ladled out two bowls of hot stew. "I froze this a couple of weeks ago when I made it. Tastes even better the second time around, I think.

"I agree," I said as I put two toasted slices of bread on plates and spread butter on them. Brawny and I carried our food to the kitchen table. The wine worked its magic, softening the world around me and relaxing up my muscles. The stew tasted terrific. And warm bread with Kerry Gold butter? It can't be beat.

"A weekend away from my husband might be exactly what the doctor ordered. Teaching tired me out. Golly, Thelma tired me out. I felt like I had to be constantly on my guard. And the news about Delphine? My heart is breaking. That poor child."

As if my thoughts had been broadcast to the Universe, my phone rang again. This time, John was calling. "Good news. Sort of, at least. Turns out there's an antidote for liver poisoning, N-acetyl cysteine. They had to dispatch an ambulance to St. Louis to get a dose. The countdown has started, but if they can administer it within 16 hours after the Tylenol was taken, Delphine might make it. And without liver damage!"

My knees went weak with relief. "Hallelujah," I said.

(A mean little voice inside me said, "Boo-ya, Thelma. Take that. She's going to make it.")

"I know. I'd never heard of the antidote. I thought for sure she was a goner. Man, I hope the ambulance hurries there and back. I'm sure he or she will, but even so ..." John let out his breath with a loud whoosh. "I've been dreading any calls, thinking that I'd hear Delphine had passed. What a relief! At least she has a chance now. She sure didn't before."

"Any luck with your brother? I'm guessing you can talk to him and point out that we almost lost Delphine. Maybe that'll encourage him to tell you what's happening behind the scenes." I didn't want to push John, but the timing seemed optimal. I was worried that if I didn't plant the seed, we might miss the opportunity.

"I'm planning on it," John said and we ended the call.

The wine, the full tummy, and the good news served to mellow me. I shared John's news with Brawny. She was thrilled to hear it.

"Brawny? Can you take over? I'm going to go to bed early."

She gave me the kindest smile. "Aye. Sweet dreams."

40

*I*nstead of sweet dreams, I had one nightmare after another and woke up feeling tired the next day. I managed to drag myself into the shower and turn on a blast of cold water. That jump-started my senses. After the Arctic downpour, I moved the dial to a more comfortable temp and cleaned myself up.

Donning underwear, another clean pair of yoga pants, and a Wash U sweatshirt, I was ready to rock and roll. The prospect of spending time in my store put a bounce in my step. Playing with paper was much more fun when you didn't have to worry about a killer on the prowl! Hurrah! I would catch up with all my friends at work. I couldn't wait.

Ty squealed with joy when I walked into the kitchen. I lifted my adorable son out of his high chair and blew raspberries on his neck. This brought on more laughter. Blowing air on his chubby belly made him shriek with delirious joy.

Dressed in her black slacks, white blouse, and black brogues, Brawny served me a plate of pancakes and bacon. She was making this a red-letter day. "After I clean the kitchen and the litter boxes, I'll come over to the store. If you'll email me the photos you took of your art class, I'll get them developed. Shall I bring Ty with me or do you want to take him now?"

"How about if you bring him and Gracie when you come?"

"With pleasure."

"Any news overnight?" I half-expected to hear that my husband had emailed her or me. Since I'd turned off my phone, I wouldn't know if he'd tried to make contact.

"Only a message from John. They picked up that medication for Delphine. Slight complication. Seems that she had mixed a few other drugs with the Tylenol, so they're not as certain of a positive outcome as they thought. I think she might have gotten her hands on some Valium."

I sank down into my kitchen chair and groaned, "Oh, no."

Brawny clamped a strong hand on my shoulder. "Keep saying those prayers. The lass has a good chance of survival. I refuse to believe otherwise."

"Okay, maybe she survives, but if she has severe damage, is that for the best?"

"I don't know, lass. 'Tis up to the Lord."

I poured warm maple syrup over the stack of pancakes. "Any word from my husband or the other Detweilers?"

"Nary a peep."

To swallow down the lump in my throat, I cut off a big bite of the hot pancakes, dripping with syrup. Talking with my mouth full, I said, "Oh, well. I guess when I said I didn't want to talk to my husband, he listened. I can't expect much from that end."

Taking the chair opposite of mine, Brawny nodded at me. "You have to know he's licking his wounds. Maybe even getting an earful from his mama. Or sorting out her story. I wonder if Louis recognizes his wife has a problem. He's very observant. Even if he does, I can't imagine Louis calling her out. Especially in front of other people. It might be that this is something their family has to work out in private."

I thought about the problems my late husband, George, and I had been faced with. In most cases, he had sided with his mother. Not entirely, but frequently. Shortly before he had died, he had stood up to her more often. Using that as my guide, I said, "Families tend to circle the wagons when trouble comes."

"Aye, the question is can Detweiler see what his mother is doing?" Brawny's face settled into a frown. "Obviously, this is a pattern and it's well-established. Here's another thought: What if you break the cycle?"

I laughed out loud. "How could I? Duct-tape Thelma's mouth shut?"

"No, lass," said the nanny. "In the past, Thelma has succeeded in running off all of her son's wives. You can make a hash of her plans by sticking around. Have ye ever read *The Art of War*? It's by Sun Tzu. He says, 'The supreme art of war is to subdue the enemy without fighting.' I'm suggesting that you don't fight Thelma. You win by ignoring her. She can only split you and Detweiler apart if you allow her to cause friction between you."

Brawny had a point.

"Let me think on it, okay? I don't need to decide how to handle Thelma right away. After all, I won't see her again until Monday evening."

"Right you are. I'm sure a little time away from the problem will help you clear your mind." Brawny poured me more coffee. "It always does. And going to your store will remind you who you are. When you're under someone's thumb, it can be easy to forget your own strengths, especially if another person is harping on your weaknesses."

41

I was happy, happy, happy when I turned onto Brentwood Boulevard and saw my store up ahead. The Time in a Bottle building is the proud survivor of several incarnations. One day a developer will buy the block we're on, and there will be a forced sale of our humble concrete block building. That developer will bulldoze our entire street, my store, and all the sagging houses in our neighborhood. Out of the rubble will rise commercial real estate worth a hundred times the current value. That will be a sad day, but it's inevitable. Until then, I'll earn a modest living doing what I love best.

Our parking lot was nearly full, which surprised me. In fact, I'd been holding my breath and didn't realize it until I turned off the engine on my old BMW. When I'm not working on the retail floor, I always worry that no one will come shop and my store will go bust. That's pretty silly, but I suppose it's natural. I have a lot of financial responsibility and I take it seriously.

Margit must have heard my car because she met me at the back door. The German widow reminds me of a sparrow, tiny, curious, and always on the go. She has the same coloring as the small bird, too.

"*Guten Morgen,*" she said. "I have missed you. Let me help."

I was loaded down with boxes of treats from the Muffin Man. Margit grabbed several cardboard containers, making it easier for me to get through the door.

"There are more in the car," I said.

"Laurel?" Margit stuck her head around the doorframe and called to Laurel, who's the youngest of my co-workers. "We need help."

"Hello, stranger. Glad to see you." Laurel threw her arms around me and gave me a heartfelt hug. Her baby bump came between us, and we both laughed about it. Her tummy was growing, a very good sign indeed, considering how sick she'd been at the start of her pregnancy.

"Kiki brought treats from the Muffin Man," Margit explained. "Could you bring in the boxes from her car? I'll put them in the refrigerator." Turning to me, Margit added, "Clancy is waiting on customers on the sales floor."

After the treats from the Muffin Man had been put away, I walked onto the sales floor and over to my work table. I could overhear Clancy talking to a trio of customers who were interested in using alcohol inks.

I had my own agenda. I had asked the students in my art classes to send me photos of papers they liked and any particular requests. Opening my phone, I discovered they'd taken my offer seriously. I took this as a very good sign, indeed. Their responses meant that they cared, they were interested. My heart felt a little lighter.

I went about the job of collecting the paper that matched the students' requests. In essence, I went shopping in my own store. A few patterns were out of stock, but most weren't. Digging around under my worktable, I found a plastic case that would protect 12-by-12-inch paper. The case was perfect for my needs. I was gathering pieces of striped paper when Clancy walked over.

As always, my friend was impeccably dressed. Today she wore black slacks, black loafers, and a black-and-ivory striped sweater that she wore tucked in with a black leather belt. Her sleek auburn hair swung around her face as she moved, rocking back and forth like a pendulum. She doesn't like to be hugged, but I gave her one anyway. "I've missed you," I said. In reply, she just smiled.

"Let's go to lunch together," I said. "How about it? I want to thank you for picking up the slack for me. You choose the place."

"Brio? Near Frontenac? You're on."

At eleven thirty, Brawny showed up with Ty and Gracie. As always, the arrival of the baby and the Great Dane lifted everyone's spirits. Laurel was drawn to Ty and asked to hold him. I could tell that she was wondering what her own child would look like. Margit fussed over Gracie, while ignoring Brawny because the two of them don't always see eye-to-eye. Fortunately, they both love my dog and my kids. They've come to some sort of truce, and I'm glad. Everyone played nicely with each other, taking turns loving up Ty and Gracie.

After we played several rounds of "pass the baby," everyone went back to work. I held Ty while Brawny made another trip to the car to retrieve her messenger bag and Ty's diaper bag. Ty is a very social baby so Brawny set up his playpen in the needle arts area. I carried him out onto the sales floor and put him in his playpen. That way he could people-watch while his nanny took yarn inventory. After Ty was settled, I went into the back room. Margit had put cupcakes on a plate. I peeled the wrapper away and ate one while standing at the kitchenette counter.

My next priority was checking our sales figures. I grabbed a second cupcake and walked into my office where Laurel was seated at the computer. She asked me, "When was the last time you ran a diagnostic and backed this thing up?"

"Not in a while. Why?" I tore the wrapper off and ate the cupcake in two bites.

"It's running really slowly. I'll take care of that right now." After tapping a few keys, Laurel sat back to watch the computer do its work. Gracie lumbered over to her. Laurel rubbed my dog's ears while the program ran. Laurel leaned closer to the monitor. "Kiki? No wonder this machine was running like refrigerated molasses. The deleted files folder hasn't been emptied in forever."

"My bad," I said. I didn't dare admit that I was paranoid about dumping the trash files at Jarvis High School, but blithely irresponsible own turf. Instead, I ducked out of the office and snatched another cupcake.

I carried the treat into my office. I took the seat across from Laurel and put the cupcake on the desk in front of me. I was trying not to give in and gobble it down.

Laurel handed me a memory stick. "I backed the computer up to the cloud and to this memory stick. It's important to duplicate your data and store it in more than one location. That's called geographic redundancy. I copied the hard drive and I'll give Clancy a copy on a memory stick, too."

I tucked the stick into my back pocket and stared at the cupcake on the edge of my desk. "Wouldn't it be nice if we could keep people safe as easily as putting data on a memory stick?"

"Working at Jarvis Township High School is stressing you out, isn't it?"

"Who said that I'm working at Jarvis Township High School? I never mentioned the name of the school where I'm teaching," I said as I put my hands on my hips.

Laurel laughed. "You didn't have to. It's the only high school within driving distance of the Detweiler farm. Not to mention, they're having a rash of suicides and you're drawn to trouble like bees to clover. Of course, the real giveaway was when you sent

Clancy emails. The ISP, or Internet Service Provider, was Jarvis-THS-dot-edu. So, if you thought you were being secretive, sweetie, you blew it."

My face went red. I should have realized all of that. I'd left a trail of clues any smart cookie could follow, and Laurel is as smart as they come.

Laurel's eyes were moist with empathy as she continued, "Living in another woman's home, being away from your own home, and taking on a new job would be enough to stress anyone out. Add to that the fact you're trusting your other in-laws to take Erik and Anya on a vacation without you? Good grief, Kiki. That has to be incredibly hard on you."

I nodded because I couldn't talk without crying. Laurel came over to where I was sitting and opened her arms for a hug.

"Another Jarvis Township student tried to kill herself yesterday," I said as she put her arms around me. "She was in the art class I teach."

"Oh, no!" Laurel stroked my hair as I buried my face in her shoulder. She was in an awkward position, half squatting and half bent over.

"Oh, *yes*," I said. Laurel straightened. She stared down at me with sad eyes as I continued, "They treated her with a drug that's supposed to save her from liver failure, but she took a cocktail of pills. We're not sure if she's out of the woods yet." Then I grabbed the third cupcake and began peeling away the liner.

"We figured that the whole point of you taking this little vacation on the farm was to *prevent* suicides." Clancy had walked up behind me. Her tone was so sharp that I dropped my cupcake. Cupcake #3 landed icing side down on the desk. Using the handy-dandy 5-second rule, I determined the cupcake was still edible so I stuffed it into my mouth. Unfortunately, it didn't make me feel better. Clancy's comment had cut me to the quick. I swallowed the tears that threatened. "Y-y-you two are too smart for me. I can't put anything past you. Yes, you're right. That is why I'm teaching at Jarvis Township High School. I went there to prevent more suicides, and so far I've failed."

I burst into tears.

"Clancy, that was uncalled for." Laurel got up to grab the box of tissues I keep in a desk drawer. "Just because the Jerk has been hurtful to you lately doesn't mean you have the right to be unkind to Kiki."

The Jerk was our name for Clancy's ex-husband. He ran off with a woman younger than his daughter, divorced Clancy, left his young lover, moved back in with Clancy, and more recently he'd moved back out again. Clancy refused to share the details of his last departure, but we all knew his decision had made her miserable.

Clancy stood over me, wringing her hands. "Kiki, I'm sorry. Laurel's right. That was uncalled for."

Laurel being Laurel, and an imminently practical person, she went over to the refrigerator, brought out a Diet Coke for Clancy and a Diet Dr Pepper for me. Shoving the cans into our hands, she said, "Drink up. If I had anything stiffer, I'd give you a glass of that, too. Sheesh."

Margit had been counting paper on the sales floor. She wandered in, looked into my office, and realized that Clancy and I were both distressed. Margit froze, unsure of what to do. She hates displays of emotion. Laurel walked over, put her hands on the older woman's shoulders, and pointed Margit toward the sales floor. Laurel said, "I suggest you go out there where it's calm and leave these two to slug it out."

Margit did just that.

The cold drinks were exactly what Clancy and I had needed to get ourselves under control. I wiped my eyes. "I am okay. I will be okay. My feelings are on the tender side. I overreacted. That's all. It's been a rough week."

"Really?" Clancy said sarcastically. "I thought these two weeks would be like a vacation for you. You love teaching. You got a change of scenery. No kids to worry about, and Ty's no trouble. Thelma would be cooking. That's the way you presented it to us, remember?"

"I didn't have a choice, Clancy. I wasn't supposed to talk about the real reason I was teaching at Jarvis Township High School. For the record, yeah, Thelma's part of the problem."

"Really?"

"Really," I dried my eyes. "Are you ready for lunch?"

"Lunch? You've eaten three cupcakes. Are you hungry?" Clancy asked.

"Of course I'm not hungry. Who could be hungry after three cupcakes? That's not the point. I still want to go to lunch. You coming or not?"

"Let me get my purse," Clancy said. "We'll go in my car because I don't want dog hairs on my clothes."

"So you two are leaving?" Laurel asked.

"We're going to go eat lunch and drink wine," I said as I got to my feet. "Clancy? You've got that Uber app on your phone, right? How about if you drive us to Brio and then we use Uber to get back to the store?"

"Kiki, are you sure you want to drink wine? It's the middle of the day." Clancy was reapplying her lipstick.

"Good. At least we won't be stumbling around in the dark."

42

I told Clancy everything. I mean, I spilled my guts. I whined and wined and whined and wound up feeling a whole lot better. Clancy couldn't believe what a harpy my mother-in-law was being. "There's a classical word for that. It's termagant. Pretty cool, eh?"

"Good to know your degree in English lit has its practical uses."

She snickered. We were on our second bottle of wine. We'd decided to eat lightly which meant we'd ordered all the hors d'oeuvres on the menu. Then salads. Then we ordered dessert.

"You still aren't talking to Detweiler?" Clancy raised an eyebrow.

"Nope. I've turned off my phone. Everyone who matters to me knows they can call you or Brawny and get in touch with me that way. Robbie and Sheila know they can call Detweiler or the store. Besides, we were warned that cell phone coverage on the cruise ship is practically nonexistent. I think they dock this coming Wednesday. It was a ten-day cruise."

Clancy licked the fork that was decorated with a few crumbs from her portion of tiramisu. That's how I knew she was tipsy, too. Miss Manners has nothing on Clancy ... when she's sober. "Have you heard anything from Erik and Anya?"

"Sheila and Robbie have sent photos. Anya messaged me along the way and when they got into Orlando. Can you count a smiley face emoji as a message? They've sent me photos from Disney World. More photos with characters when they boarded the cruise ship. I think they're having a terrific time."

"They're fine and you look so sad." Clancy chided me. "Thelma's not worth that. Honest."

My phone vibrated. Detweiler was calling. I ignored it. Clancy realized what I was doing.

"You will have to speak to Detweiler eventually." She stared at me thoughtfully. I could feel the intensity of her gaze, and I knew she was gearing up to say something weighty. With a quiet determination, she said, "At the risk of overstepping my bounds, here's a bit of hard-won advice."

And then she leaned halfway across the table and said, "My ex-husband has been a thoughtless jerk from the day I met him to the day he walked out on me with a woman young enough to be our daughter. I am hard-pressed to believe that he ever truly loved me. I put up with him and his shenanigans almost two decades longer than I should have. I am telling you all this to underscore a simple, important fact: My situation is not the same as your situation."

"Hmmm?" I was only listening to be polite. I didn't need a lecture about my marriage. Not right then.

"Chad Detweiler is a good man. A confused man. A man being manipulated by his mother. But at his core, he's a good man. He worships the ground you walk on. He adores the kids. Don't stay mad too long or you'll ruin a good thing. Get over this and move on."

SHOWING up three sheets of scrapbook paper to the wind would not be good for my business. Clancy's Uber app came in handy. A dark-haired young man named Fayid was our driver. He basically poured Clancy and me into his car. He refused to pull out of the Frontenac parking lot where Brio is until we had buckled ourselves in. Once we got going, he cranked the A/C down to near freezing to keep Clancy and me from getting sick to our stomachs.

I called Laurel to say we wouldn't be coming back to work. She nearly wet herself laughing at how loosey-goosey I was.

"No need to worry about the store. With Brawny here, Margit and I have the store covered. I love cuddling with Baby Ty. Sounds to me like you and Clancy have kissed and made up. Good! You aren't driving are you? Tell me you aren't driving and talking after drinking."

I explained we'd left Clancy's car in the far corner of the Brio parking lot and were using Uber to get to my house in Webster Groves.

"Once you get home, take a couple of Advils, drink a Gatorade or two, and go to bed. Be sure to eat eggs when you wake up. Wash your hands before you fall asleep. In fact, do that as soon as you get home. Alcohol suppresses your immune system. Any germs on your hands will increase the likelihood that you come down later with a cold or the flu."

"You sound like you're an old pro at this," Clancy hollered into the phone. The way she bellowed out her comment, you would have thought we were two little kids talking with two empty soup cans and a string. I don't know why she thought yelling would help Laurel hear her.

Fayid must have agreed with me because the Uber driver's shoulders heaved with laughter.

Laurel took it in good humor. "I'm not an old pro, but I am definitely a seasoned one. Don't worry about the business. I'll close the store. Brawny can take Ty and Gracie back to your house, Kiki. Now I've got to go. Two customers just walked in."

"I suppose I should be ashamed of myself. The only other time in my life that I got this tipsy, I wound up pregnant," I said as I hit the "end call" button on my phone.

Clancy snorted. "You're safe with me."

Fayid was from Afghanistan, and he was a perfect gentleman who ran to open the car doors for us when we arrived at my home. He watched to see that we made it into the house. Laurel's suggestions made sense to me, so I washed my hands, found the Advil bottle, and grabbed two Gatorades from the refrigerator in the garage. I took the purple sports drink and Clancy took the red. After we took the pain pills and drank the Gatorade, Clancy tottered off to the guest bedroom. I wobbled my way to the master bedroom where I fell face-first onto the bed. I woke up around eight that evening. Detweiler had phoned me ten times. I didn't call him back. I still was steaming mad.

THANKS TO LAUREL'S good advice, I didn't have a terrible headache when I woke up at eight p.m. that Saturday night. I did have a bruise on my butt where I'd rolled over on the memory stick in my back pocket, but that was minor. All things considered, I was fine with the exception of being hungry as a bear who's crawled out of cave after hibernating all winter. I could hear Clancy rustling around in the guest bedroom. I would have knocked on her door but I was lured downstairs to the kitchen by the luscious fragrance of chopped onions, bell peppers, and American cheese.

"Good evening," said Brawny as soon as I grabbed a chair.

"Good evening to you, too. How's Ty?"

"I heated a bottle of refrigerated breast milk for him. He's fast asleep," Brawny said.

Gracie ambled over and put her head in my lap. Brawny poured the eggs and veggies into a sizzling skillet and cooked a delicious omelet for me. Clancy came creeping down the stairs and joined me at the kitchen table. Looking around, she noticed Ty was missing. "Where's the baby?"

"Sound asleep," Brawny said. "Past his bedtime. After his bottle, he conked out. He had a big day, greeting everyone at the store. Being passed around and fawned over takes a lot out of a little man."

"Did we miss anything?" I buried my toes in Gracie's fur.

"Nary a thing. The afternoon was quiet so I did follow-up work on our special project."

"Clancy knows," I said.

Brawny smiled. "Aye. So I heard. The email from the school was your downfall. So, I've been working on a new spreadsheet."

"Why?" Clancy frowned

"Charting is useful in many ways. We tend to look at information according to our own biases. Getting data down on paper gives us new ways to look for patterns. For example, there's a field of study called geographic profiling. The theory is that a criminal is likely to commit crimes in the same geographic areas where he or she spends the majority of his or her noncriminal time. By figuring out where the crimes have been committed, or even where the suspects have been spotted, you can more accurately predict where new crimes might occur."

Clancy nodded, then winced because the motion of her head pained her. "Could I have more Advil? Please?"

"You might be dehydrated." While Brawny got the Advil bottle, I hopped up and ran to the garage to grab more cold

Gatorade. This time I gave Clancy the red while I kept the purple.

My friend uncapped her bottle, tossed the Advils into her mouth, and swallowed. "Thanks, ladies. Brawny? What you're saying makes sense. You wouldn't go to a place you were unfamiliar with and commit a crime. You couldn't limit your risk factors."

"Exactly. You wouldn't know how to escape, where to hide, and what obstacles you might run into," Brawny agreed. She continued, "Another use of spreadsheets is temporal analysis, looking at the times when the crimes occurred. I also charted specific characteristics of the victims like age, class schedules, method of suicide, club or team memberships, outside interests, number of kids in the family, generational data, and so on. Once again, I'm looking for a correlation or an anomaly. For most law enforcement agents, this is instinctive. They call it having a hunch. I'm convinced it's actually a skill set involving the sorting of information. Comparing it. Seeing patterns."

Sounded like a lot of busywork to me. Could all this comparison of data help us figure out who the Blue Whale administrator was? I had my doubts, but I hoped I was wrong.

"Fingers crossed that your work bears fruit because I've been a total failure." I tipped my plastic Gatorade bottle left and right, watching the colorful liquid slosh around.

Brawny jammed her fists against her hips and stared at me. She had a spatula gripped in one clenched hand and a deep scowl on her face. "Aye, you're being awfully shortsighted, lass. Think about it and you'll know it's true."

She had a point.

After eating, we found a movie the three of us would like, or so we thought. *Michael Collins* is more truth than fiction and watching the struggles of the Irish leader was both inspiring and depressing.

Not surprisingly, when I finally went back to bed and fell asleep, I had bad dreams. Maybe the violence in the movie caused them. Maybe it was because I missed the warmth of Detweiler next to me. Or maybe the stress of the previous week had caught up to me. I grind my teeth when I'm under pressure, and not surprisingly, I woke up with an aching jaw.

43

*S*unday morning when I looked at my phone, Detweiler had called three times. I couldn't bring myself to call him back. The longer I waited, the harder it seemed to capitulate. What would I say? "Your mother is out of her mind? A master manipulator? A one-woman marriage-wrecking ball?" I couldn't construct a comment that would be both accurate and civil in tone.

I stepped into the master bathroom shower, sat down on the little plastic-and-metal stool, and let the water pour over me. When I closed my eyes, I could almost—but not quite—pretend I was on a cruise with Erik and Anya. Another image popped up: a whale. Did they even have whales in the Caribbean? How on earth were we going to track down the administrator of the Blue Whale Challenge? I squeezed my eyes shut and tried to let my creative juices work on the problem. Frustrated, I gave up and tried to relax, letting the water massage my muscles. I probably sat there for half an hour. My fingers were wrinkled like baby prunes when I finally turned off the water. The glass shower door was completely opaque with steam. I couldn't postpone the inevitable.

I stepped out of the shower ...
And straight into my husband's arms

WE MADE UP. There wasn't a lot of talking involved. Afterward, as I was getting dressed, he said, "I know my mother is being difficult."

"Yes, and she's your mother. I understand how challenging a difficult parent can be. I don't expect you to shut her out of our lives."

He nodded. His arms were folded under his head and he was staring at the ceiling. I loved the way his biceps bunched up. Such a gorgeous man and a good man, too. Clancy had been right: he was a keeper. I vowed to myself that we would get through this. I was not going to let Thelma Detweiler ruin my marriage.

"I love watching you dress," he said as I pulled a tee shirt over my head. "Of course, I love watching you undress even more. Matter of fact, I love you. Please never forget that."

"I won't," and I crawled onto the bed to cuddle with him.

THE FRONT DOOR SLAMMED. We had a visitor. John's voice drifted up from the foyer. Detweiler and I made ourselves presentable and hurried downstairs. Clancy was bright-eyed, dressed, and raring to go. She popped Ty into his stroller. "It's been forever since I had a little person to enjoy. Mister-mister and I are going to take a long walk. Don't expect us back for at least an hour."

That was her subtle way of saying, "Get caught up. I won't be around to eavesdrop." I appreciated her thoughtfulness. Instead of spelling all that out, I settled for, "Thanks. What about your car?"

"Brawny drove me back to Brio, and I picked it up while you were, uh, occupied." She blushed. "I grabbed toilet articles and fresh clothes from my car. I keep a small bag in my trunk for emergencies."

Of course she does.

After Detweiler carried the stroller to the sidewalk for Clancy, he joined Brawny, John, and me in his office. Everyone had a cup of coffee, except for me. My beverage of choice was more Gatorade. I chose yellow this time.

"Let's see where we are," my husband said, by way of getting us started. "I've dug a little deeper into the suicide club theory. Although that idea seems to fit, we might be following a red herring instead of a blue whale. There's a high probability we're talking about an urban myth. No one has found any conclusive proof that Philipp Budeikin, the supposed creator of the Blue Whale Challenge, ever convinced anyone to commit suicide. There was a worldwide panic that the Blue Whale Challenge was spreading and that it was being perpetuated by predatory adults, but that's been proven to be patently false. Research into the Blue Whale administrators showed them mainly to be 12-to-14-year-olds. That said, there have been a couple of cases worldwide where adults copied the challenge formula. One such administrator claimed the game was his hobby."

"You're saying there is no Blue Whale Challenge? We need to look for another reason these kids are dying?" I asked. "Or is it that we're looking in the wrong spot? Should we be searching the middle school for an administrator?"

Detweiler folded his hands and rested them on his desk pad. "I'm cautioning us to keep open minds. Someone might have been inspired by the Blue Whale Challenge, but we can't be sure how closely the original scheme has been duplicated. And yes, the administrator might well be a middle school student. I wouldn't have guessed that, but the research backs it up. John, have you been able to get Luke to talk yet?"

John shifted his weight in his chair. "When I told him about Delphine, he cried. He admits he's part of a club, and it's called the Blue Whale Club. Of course he didn't call it a suicide club. He swore to me that he doesn't know who the administrator is. When I asked him about the messaging system, all he would say is, 'Computers,' and then he started sobbing. The nurse came in and gave him a drug through his IV. It was supposed to calm him down. Instead, it knocked him out."

At that point, we all wilted with frustration. We'd been counting on Luke for help. Now I wondered if he would ever be forthcoming about the Blue Whale Club. With his depression, the injuries to his brain, and his psychological ties to the suicide club, Luke seemed incapable of telling us what we needed in a timely manner.

"At least we know now that the students think of this as the Blue Whale Club," said Brawny. "That gives us a name to put to the problem. The students may or may not have researched the original scheme."

"But what Luke said doesn't make sense," I said. "It can't be a computer-generated message. The experts have monitored all the incoming and outgoing messages."

"It *can't* be." Brawny's tired face said it all. "Those are famous last words, aren't they?"

～

DETWEILER HAD to leave and go back to work shortly after our meeting. Since he wasn't going to be around, and Clancy was enjoying her time with Ty, she decided to stay at my house Saturday night.

Consequently, Clancy was sitting next to me at the breakfast table on Sunday morning when Anya texted me a picture of her and Erik on an inflatable raft, floating down a shallow creek. Both my children beamed with happiness. I noted with relief that they were wearing life jackets. I smiled and silently thanked Sheila and Robbie for being diligent caregivers.

"Nice photo. Looks like they're having fun," Clancy said as she handed me back my phone. She had a bite of blueberry pancake in her mouth, and I nibbled on my fourth piece of bacon. We both were enjoying fresh cups of Kaldi's coffee with cream. Brawny joined us after taking Ty upstairs for a diaper change. Clancy asked if she could feed our little man his rice cereal.

"Of course. I'll mix it up for you," said Brawny.

"A baby is God's opinion that life should go on," Clancy said, cooing over my son. "Carl Sandburg said that, and he was right. Ty has his whole life ahead of him. I'm so lucky you named me his godmother."

Ty seemed to agree because he squealed at her with happiness. Gracie wandered over to make sure he was all right. I patted her head and said, "He's fine. Go lie down."

"By the way, if you don't want to stay at the farm, you're welcome to bunk up at my house. It's a longer drive than from the farm to the high school, but at least you wouldn't have to cross the river." Clancy brushed a lock of auburn hair out of her eyes. Even on a Sunday, she was the picture of good taste with her boatneck navy-and-white striped jersey top and crisply ironed jeans.

"That's kind of you." I'd been deep in thought most of my waking hours. If I wasn't thinking about the Blue Whale Club, I was thinking about Thelma. The fact I was lumping two such different problems together was cringeworthy.

"Have you decided how to deal with your mother-in-law?"

Clancy knew I had nothing to hide from my nanny. After all, Brawny had seen Thelma in action.

"If you don't need me right now, I'd like to go back to my spreadsheets," Brawny said. "Let me know when you're hungry for lunch." She was asking me for permission to work on her computer even though she didn't need to. That was one of the many reasons I thought the world of her. She always put our needs first.

After I said, "Of course," I continued discussing my marital problems with Clancy. "Nope. As a matter of fact, I haven't decided anything about dealing with Thelma Detweiler. I've been trying not to let her ruin my weekend, but it's hard. Detweiler knows she's interfering but he's not sure how to handle the situation. He hasn't really caught her in a lie. The idea that she played a role in ruining his first two marriages makes him physically ill. You can literally watch the color drain from his face, although he's quick to say both marriages were doomed from the start. I kinda feel sorry for him."

Clancy cocked her head to one side like a thoughtful spring robin. "I have an idea."

"You do? Spill."

She got up and refilled my coffee cup and then hers. "You know that coming between a mother and a son is not a winning strategy. And that's exactly what Thelma expects you to do: try to pry her son away from her. If you do, you'll be playing into her hands. Wouldn't it be interesting if you paid no attention to her bad behavior?"

I smiled. "That's exactly what Brawny suggested. She pointed out that Thelma's goal is to cause friction and drive a wedge between my husband and me."

"Great minds think alike," Clancy said. "Think how frustrated Thelma will get when you refuse to let her bug you."

"I'm not sure I can ignore her jabs." I shrugged.

"Sure you can," Clancy said as she tapped my hand with an index finger. "Make a game of it. Keep track of the number of times she mutters under her breath. Write down every time she snipes at you. Tally up all her temper tantrums. After all, this is a game—and one you really need to win. Trust me on this. You don't want the misery of a divorce. When you have children together, you can never be free of each other. Better to work together than to let her tear you apart. What's that line in the marriage ceremony? Let no man put asunder?"

I nodded. "I don't want to get a divorce. I love him. He's a good father."

"I know." Clancy checked her vintage Cartier tank watch and said, "As much as I'd like to spend more time with Ty, I should hit the road. I need to drive back to Illinois. My plants will need to be watered."

After she left, I pulled out a notebook I keep in the kitchen. I scribbled all my thoughts about Thelma on the right side of a piece of paper. On the flip side, I added all the advice I'd gotten. Getting everything down was helpful. I felt better. When I viewed my notes objectively, I realized that in the near term I needed to outlast Thelma for five more days. I counted up the hours I'd be awake and not at the school. I came up with a total of thirty-five hours, and that didn't subtract the time I'd be spending away from the Detweiler farm in meetings with John, Brawny, and my husband. After that, I would not have to put up with my mother-in-law for any extended period. Ever again.

I took my shower, washed my hair, and brushed my teeth. Standing in front of the bathroom mirror, I stared at my reflection and said, "I can do this. I know I can."

This time I fixed lunch for us, even though it was peanut butter and jelly sandwiches. When we were done, Brawny told me she planned to do laundry and work on her computer. She was happy to watch Ty. "By the way, I had the photos developed for you. I put them in your backpack so you'll have them when you go back to school on Monday."

I thanked her, got in the BMW, and drove to the store in time to open up. Laurel, Margit, and I worked together all day. We enjoyed each other's company. While I was helping customers, I had an idea. I went to the die cut machine and punched out two dozen whales from sheets of blue paper. I tucked the paper whales into my backpack. Around five, I came home. I brought with me the new supply of scrapbook paper for my art students.

Brawny had made spaghetti for us. I tossed a salad of Bibb lettuce, hearts of palm, chunks of avocado, and tomato slices for us. We ate and then I nursed Ty. After I put him to bed, I organized my clothes for the next week and packed my suitcase.

"Come on, Gracie," I said. "Time for bed." The big girl easily jumped up onto Detweiler's side of the bed and with a grunt of contentment, crossed her front paws and rested her head on them. The cats, Martin and Seymour, curled up next to the dog. I turned on my Kindle and read *The Marsh King's Daughter* by Karen Dionne until my eyes got heavy. I thought I'd drift off to sleep, but I didn't. My mind was spinning like the busy icon on a computer.

Folding back the covers on my side, I climbed out of the warm bed. Getting up was silly. I needed sleep because we would have an early start tomorrow. Brawny would drive me to school and then take Ty and Gracie to the farm. I really should have stayed in bed and rested, even if I couldn't drop off to sleep.

Instead, I tiptoed across the room. I eased open our bedroom door and took the stairs, one at a time. By hugging the wall, I managed to keep the treads from squeaking. Gracie padded along behind me. She was wondering what was up.

Together we stepped outside. Detweiler had hung a rope swing from a branch of the big maple tree in the center of our yard. Ignoring the slight chill of the night, I sat on the swing and pumped with my legs until I was flying up, up, and up into the jet-black darkness of the sky. The scent of green grass stuck to my toes. When I concentrated, I could smell the pale pink sweet peas that were just now blooming along our fence. With each arc upward, my body was weightless. No cares could tie me down. I loved the way the wind messed up my curls. Gracie stood watch over me, a silent sentry standing next to the tree.

I was strong.

I was invincible.

Neither Blue Whales nor Thelma Detweiler were going to drag me down.

44

On the ride to Illinois the next morning, Detweiler phoned to say good morning. "I called in a few favors. Our technical team has been all over Delphine Abernathy's cell phone. And her computer. We searched her locker with her parents' permission. Haven't found so much as a whisker that might help us out."

"Do whales have whiskers?" I asked as I studied the embroidery edging my white peasant blouse. The top had looked so cute when I found it hanging from the sale rack at Target that I bought it without trying it on. This morning I regretted it. I looked like I was wearing a pillowcase that had been decorated with Magic Marker. All I needed was a pair of white pants instead of my dark blue ones and I could double as a piñata.

"Actually, whales are one of the few mammals born with facial hair that resembles whiskers. Scientist theorize these hairs help them detect turbulence in the water. Or food."

"Maybe that's my problem. I have too many whiskers that keep trying to detect food," I said. "I think I'll take up shaving my face."

Once my husband and I got off the phone, Brawny and I

discussed the Blue Whale theory. I was determined to track down the administrator no matter what.

Brawny said, "My spreadsheets found another anomaly. Might be meaningless, but I'd be amiss not to mention it. All of the victims or failed-attempt victims have been children of alumni. And all the alumni graduated from the same class, twenty years ago."

"That's freaky."

"Isn't it just?" she agreed. "I plan to drive to the nearest public library and see if I can put my hands on a yearbook. I'm wondering if our answers will be in the pages of that publication."

"But Detweiler thinks middle schoolers might be involved."

"Aye, and that's why I'll cross-check those families for students in the middle grades, as well. Both the elementary school and the middle school in Jarvis Township do their own versions of a yearbook. Nothing fancy, but I should be able to work out who's related to whom."

"Sound like a plan. While you're busy in the library, I'll go to the teachers' lounge and download all the files from that computer onto a memory stick." I had grabbed a fresh memory stick from my desk on Sunday when I was at the store.

Brawny kept her eyes on the road. "It's not likely the experts missed anything, but who knows?"

Walking into my classroom that morning, I was a woman on a mission. After the first period bell rang, I said to my art class, "I brought more paper, and I had the photos developed from last week, but first let's make get well cards for Delphine." I passed around card blanks. "Tadd? Would you grab these matching envelopes and pass them around, too?"

"Is a get well message appropriate?" asked Billy. "She isn't sick. She tried to off herself."

I counted to ten before I lost my patience. In every class I teach, there's at least one person who gets tripped up in the details. "Okay, how about 'thinking of you' cards? Something to show that you care."

I hoped the students would talk to each other while they were making the cards. Maybe I could glean useful information that way. If the cards didn't work, I had another trick up my sleeve. Once all the kids got down to working on their cards, I passed out the paper that students had requested. I spread the photos across an empty desk so they could choose the ones they wanted.

"I made a bunch of blue whales for you to use as embellishments to decorate your portfolios or scrapbook pages. Several of you asked for them. They're up here with the new paper. Help yourselves."

Next to each student who took a blue whale, I put a check mark on my class list. Perhaps Brawny could add these names to her spreadsheets. Maybe I was closing the barn door after the blue whale had swum out, but more information was better, wasn't it? After all, whales eat by straining large volumes of ocean water through their baleen, a sort of screen in their mouths. The process leaves behind bits of food that are captured and swallowed.

Operating on that same principle, I said, "I'd like to see your portfolios, please. I want to snap a few pictures. My accountant will want proof that I took these supplies out of stock so I can claim the loss on my taxes."

Who can argue with the IRS? Not these students. Reluctantly, they dragged out their portfolios and set them on an empty table. While they worked on their cards, I took photos of every blue whale I could find. Four students had included the image: Ralphie, Bluette, Eldon, and Billy. At the very least, we might be able to warn their parents to keep a close eye on these kids. Even better, if we couldn't get Luke to talk, maybe one of these students could tell us who the Blue Whale administrator was.

John knew exactly what I was doing. This morning he came over to the table where the portfolios were spread open. Turning my back to the students as they worked on their "feel better" cards, I opened my notebook and showed him my roster sheet with the checkmarks. He nodded and whispered, "Did my brother finish his portfolio?"

I answered, "I don't know. Did you look in his locker? Or check his room?"

"No. I just now thought of it."

"Then I suggest you try those two places. If he hasn't, I'll set aside paper for him so he can do it over the summer."

"Thanks. I will."

OLEANDER MET ME OUTSIDE THE TEACHERS' lounge. Her puffy red eyes and blotchy skin suggested she'd been crying. "Delphine was a particular favorite of mine. I can't believe she hurt herself."

I gave my new friend a hug. "I had my students make cards for her. Do you know how I can get them to her?"

"Yes. We can pull up her postal address on the Intranet."

When we walked into the lounge, we discovered that Alan was using the computer. "Sorry, girls. Mine is broken, and I have end-of-the-year reports I have to get done."

I tried not to show my disappointment. I'd been counting on getting to the computer and downloading all the files onto my memory stick. Alan seemed to be taking his sweet time, and that made me even more antsy. To keep from going nuts, I dragged my sudoku book out of my backpack and spent the hour trying to solve the puzzles.

The ringing bell offered relief. Okay, I hadn't been able to access the computer in the teachers' lounge, but at least I could use a computer in the computer lab. Merging into the river of bodies moving from one room to the next, I made it to the computer lab in less than a minute.

However, Drew Simchuck had beaten me there. He was taping signs to all the computer screens. "Out of Order," they said.

"You're kidding me! All of them at once?" I felt the tingle in my fingers that precedes raw panic.

"No." He grinned at me. "They aren't really out of order. They're dead. There's a wiring problem. I bet we'll find a dead mouse back there in the fuse box. Notice we don't have any overhead lights in this room? Only light from the windows? We should be able to get these babies up and running by the end of the day. I can't fix the problem right now because I'm meeting with a college scout."

Fortunately, the students seemed to have plenty to keep them busy. Most of them dragged out paperbacks and opened them. When I asked what was happening, one girl reminded me they'd gotten their college reading lists.

Once again, I whipped out my sudoku book. I'd finished all but one of the puzzles and that last grid took me no time at all. I was left twiddling my thumbs. My phone vibrated. Brawny had sent me highlights from the yearbook that coincided with the years the victims' parents attended school at Jarvis Township High. The words ran together in a blur: homecoming queen crowned, homecoming bonfire, new dean of middle school, football team loses game against rival, regional spelling bee, all honors choir takes state, and on and on. I had no idea what I was looking for. None. Did any of this drivel matter? I quickly sent her a message to that effect. Her response was: *Will put in spreadsheet.*

"Great," I muttered. Another day, another spreadsheet. What difference did it make?

⁓

LUNCH PROMISED to be a miserable affair and it was. Thanks to my sleepless night I had no energy. I could barely shuffle to the cafeteria. Oleander had saved a place for me. She waited until I was seated before saying, "I keep thinking about Delphine. *Pauvre petite.*"

Soon Oleander was crying into her yogurt. She wasn't the only one feeling emotional. All around the lunchroom, girls were sobbing. I tried to choke down my tuna salad sandwich. Since food is my natural "go to" when I need to be cheered up, I went to the lunch counter and bought myself two packages of sea salt and vinegar potato chips. After pouring a liberal amount of ketchup onto the open bag, I dipped one chip after another into the sweet red sauce. Lucky for me, Oleander didn't want any. Or maybe she was afraid to compete for the food. I was going at it pretty hard.

I was halfway through the second bag when Oleander hopped to her feet and waved at a striking brunette who was walking our way. "Kiki? Meet Tammy Calhoun. You two have a mutual friend, don't you?"

I struggled to my feet, feeling miserable. I had spilled ketchup down the front of my white peasant blouse. Thanks to the humidity outside, I was sporting a blonde Afro. I had so many bags under my eyes that I would have been charged extra on an airplane. In short, I did not look like a woman that Chad Detweiler—or anyone else except Bozo the Clown—would find appealing.

Tammy was a knockout. I took in her fashionable pumps, her pencil skirt, the tucked-in poet's blouse, and her chic French braid. She was also perfectly groomed. Her amber eyes studied me intently as I offered my hand and said, "Hello."

After we sat down, Tammy said to Oleander, "I heard about Delphine. That's a crying shame. You'd think the authorities could have figured out what's going on by now. That poor child. I know she was one of your favorites."

Oleander deferred to me. "Kiki had her as a student, too."

People were standing up, picking up their messes, and getting ready to leave before the bell rang. I tried to hide the two empty bags of potato chips by shoving them into my backpack.

"I used to date Chad." Tammy's smile seemed genuine. Turning to Oleander, she explained, "That's Kiki's husband."

"Yes,"" I said. "Um, Thelma told me."

"Thelma," Tammy said with a chuckle. "She's one tough cookie, isn't she? Actually I ran around more with Chad's sister, Gina. There was whole group of us who hung out together. We had a lot of good times."

She paused because she had spotted Alan. Tammy gave him a quick wave hello. "Alan was part of the group, too. He was riding high back then. Hey, nice to meet you. Got to run."

The bell rang and I needed a bathroom break. As I washed my hands, I caught my reflection in the mirror. My eyes were bloodshot, my nose was red, and my lips were chapped. The woman looking back at me had been through a lot. But that woman had never experienced the loss of a child, thank goodness—and suddenly I got mad. Absolutely furious. "I am not going to take this lying down. I promise you, Delphine. Someone is going to pay!"

I had an idea. Anya's school had redone their wiring in a piecemeal fashion as they brought in computers. Maybe Jarvis Township High School had done the same. That would explain why the outage hadn't impacted the computer in the teachers' lounge—and I knew that computer was operational because I'd seen Alan working on it. I was determined to copy the hard drive from the Intranet. I decided get my fifth-period art students started working on get well cards for Delphine. Once they were, I would run down the hall and duck into the teachers' lounge. Surely, Alan would be done by now! If all went as planned, I could use that computer to transfer information onto my memory stick.

I needed to move quickly. I raced into the art room and greeted my fifth-period students. Even though this class was a mix of sophomores and juniors, the school was small enough that they all were aware of what had happened. Several of the girls were crying. The boys tried to look like they weren't bothered, but of course, they were. I got them started working on cards for Delphine. Once they were busy, I raced down the hall to the teachers' lounge. Instinct cautioned me not to yank open the door. Instead, I peeped inside.

Alan Bowman was sitting at the computer. Again! Didn't that man have classes to teach?

I had to get him to leave! I hesitated. I looked left. I looked right. I reviewed my options.

No one was roaming the halls but me. I didn't have time to find a student who could take Alan a message that might drag him away from the computer. I didn't have the man's phone number so I couldn't call him and invent a reason for him to leave the teachers' lounge. If I asked him to step aside and let me use the computer, he might ask questions.

I thought about Delphine—and that increased my determination. This couldn't wait. I had to get this done. Lives were at risk.

Brawny had told me to be creative. To look around. To use what I found in my environment. I did all of that. I pulled the fire alarm.

45

Woop-woop-wooop-woooop-woop!

The shriek was deafening. I raced down the hallway and into the art room. "Fire!" I yelled. "Everybody out!" I shooed my students away from their get well cards. They went running out and joined the stream of bodies moving in the halls. When the last student left the art room, I entered the throng, but instead of going with the flow, I turned the opposite way toward the teachers' lounge.

By the time I got there, that portion of the hallway was deserted. I yanked open the door to the teachers' lounge and closed it firmly behind me. The place was empty. Fortunately the computer was still booted up. Good. At last something was working in my favor. I shoved the memory stick into the USB port. I clicked on the hard drive and hit copy. The "it's working" icon spun around and around. My fingers ached with nervousness. Outside, the fire alarm kept shrieking. I sat down and my foot rolled on an ink pen that had fallen to the floor under the computer desk. I picked it up. I drummed the pen against the computer desk. "Come on, come on," I said.

The PA announced, "This is not a drill." Even with the door

closed, I could hear voices in the hallways. Kids were talking, adults were shouting orders, and locker doors were being slammed. The ruckus was a low roar. I willed myself to concentrate on the task at hand. I switched from tapping the pen against the desk to beating it against my thigh.

"Hurry up," I told the computer. "You're going too slowly."

Like magic, the icon quit spinning. The hard drive had been copied. I right-clicked the paste command in order to move the hard drive data to the memory stick. Once again the icon went spinning around and around and—

"What are you doing here?" Alan Bowman towered over me.

"Um, I had to ..." I stopped.

That's when I knew who the Blue Whale administrator was.

With his right hand, Alan grabbed the back of my blouse and hauled me out of the chair. He lifted me like a cat takes a kitten by the scruff of the neck. I was choking. His grip on my peasant blouse was cutting off my air. My feet were scrambling against the tile.

"You little ..." He called me a very bad name. I dropped the ink pen.

Alan cocked his left fist. "I'm going to pound you into the floor."

I struggled to get away. My shoes slipped on the linoleum floor. I flailed around, trying to grab at the desk, the chair, anything! I kicked at Alan. My foot didn't connect. My lungs were bursting. I was starving for air.

And then, I remembered practicing a similar scenario with Brawny. I let myself go limp. Alan hadn't expected that. The sudden shift of weight threw him off balance. We tumbled to the floor. I landed on top of him. His head bonked against the linoleum. I rolled off him and onto my knees. The ink pen was sticking out from under him.

In my head, I heard Brawny saying, "Anything can be used as a weapon."

I grabbed the pen. Alan picked me up, flipped me, and threw me flat on my back. I hit the floor so hard I saw stars. Both his hands were on my throat. He was a big man, and he was trying to crush my windpipe. I had one shot. One chance to save myself.

I rammed that ink pen into his arm as hard as I could. I jammed that sucker in at least an inch.

"Ow!" Alan screamed in pain. He let go of me to paw at his wound. His howl brought footsteps running to the teachers' lounge. While Alan bellowed with anger, I scrambled away from him, but I wasn't fast enough. With his good arm, he clubbed me up the side of the head.

Everything went dark.

46

I regained consciousness in an ambulance. Oleander and John were leaning over me. At the ER, I demanded to be released into Brawny's care rather than spending the night at the hospital. The doc insisted on writing me a script for painkillers. Brawny ran it down to the pharmacy and had it filled. After taking one, I stuffed the pill bottle in my purse. You never know when an OxyContin will come in handy. The ride to the Detweiler farm was blessedly quiet because the painkiller made me sleepy. Thelma met us at the back door and immediately yammered on and on about my irresponsibility. Brawny slipped an arm around my waist and hauled me upstairs to the bedroom. She helped me strip to my undies. Once she was confident I was settled, she went downstairs to tend to Ty— and to tell Thelma Detweiler to back off or else. Even though I was upstairs, I could hear Brawny bark at my mother-in-law. My nanny sounded amazingly ferocious.

My husband made it home the next morning after wrapping up his case. He sat at my bedside with Detective Randall Schultz as I wrote out my statement:

Brawny confirmed that all the victims were children of alumni from one specific high school class. I didn't know that Alan Bowman was an alumnus until Tammy Calhoun mentioned that he used to hang around with her back in the day. It made sense that Alan Bowman might be the administrator of the Blue Whale Club. There was something else Tammy said: "He was riding high back then." My first day at Jarvis Township High School, a student pointed out the display case with all the trophies. He mentioned a football player who'd fumbled the ball on the one-yard line. I thought he called the player, "Beau the Bumbler," but he was actually saying, "Bow the Bumbler." Alan Bowman had been teased unmercifully for his failure on the football field. The Blue Whale Club was his way of getting revenge. My suspicions were confirmed by his license plate, MO6Y. The six represents the letter "b" turned backwards to spell out MOBY, as in Moby Dick, the whale.

I quit writing as I took a sip of Slippery Elm tea.

"Why did you insist on copying that hard drive?" Schultz asked.

I croaked out the words. "The experts looked for communications going in and out of the school. I noticed that the deleted files on the Intranet were growing at an astonishing pace. That got me thinking: What if the messages never left the building? All the suicides occurred in the 48-hour period immediately following a Friday when classes were held. What if the administrator posted their next challenge each Friday in the deleted file folder?"

"That doesn't make sense." Schultz wagged a finger at me. "How would participants be able to tell which file was meant for them and which was real trash?"

"Drew labeled their files: 'Fish Fry Friday' and assigned each player a number like 'Fish Fry Friday 321.' It was his idea of a joke." I sipped more tea. "I found a scrap piece of paper with Fish Fry Friday on it. I thought it had to do with the cafeteria menu. It didn't. When I looked at the trash files in the Intranet, I saw Fish Fry Friday on many of the labels."

After another sip, I asked, "Any word on Delphine?"

My husband smiled. "Good news. She's going to pull through."

Grateful tears filled my eyes. I was so happy. Maybe my time as a substitute teacher hadn't been a total waste.

"That's enough for now," my husband said and ushered his friend out. I ached all over, so I took another OxyContin and went back to sleep.

While I was out of it, I missed the fight Detweiler had with his mother. According to Brawny, it was a real doozy. I spent the next two days in bed being pampered by Brawny and my husband.

On Thursday, Oleander called to ask if I'd go after school with her to see Delphine. Of course I said yes. To disguise the bruises on my neck, I carefully wrapped my throat with a blue silk scarf that Clancy had given me. I borrowed one of Detweiler's light blue Oxford cloth button-down collar shirts. It stopped four inches from my knees, so I added a pair of black yoga pants. The mirror told me I looked surprisingly chic.

Even Oleander remarked on my outfit when I climbed into her car. The day dawned blustery. The fat-bellied clouds crowded the skies, blocking the sun. She drove us to a double-wide at the end of a dirt lane. The white house had electric blue shutters. Purple petunias grew in plastic pots carefully positioned around a small wooden stoop.

Delphine's mother, Anita, answered the door and threw her arms around Oleander and then me. She thanked us profusely for coming. I'd brought the girl a small gift, a bag filled with scrapbooking supplies. Anita noticed it right away and said, "That's totally unnecessary. You've done more for us than you can ever imagine. Everyone's talking about that monster and how he tried to choke you to death."

Delphine was propped up in her bed. She was wearing a Wash U sweatshirt over a floral nightgown. She greeted us with delight. Oleander and I took turns hugging her.

"So you'll be going to Washington University?" I asked. "That's not far from my store. If you need a part-time job, come and see me."

"Really?" Delphine lit up with joy.

"Really."

Delphine and Oleander conversed in French. I caught a word here and there. Mainly, I was happy to be there. Happy to be alive. Happy, happy, happy.

EPILOGUE

*A*s soon as I heard the Mazda SUV pull up in the drive of our house in Webster Groves, I ran out of the front door. Anya tossed open her car door and jumped into my arms. Erik pushed her to one side and demanded to be included in the hug, too. Both my children were wearing Mickey Mouse-themed tee shirts. Both had gotten tons of sun. Anya was lobster red and Erik had darkened to a yummy shade of bronze.

While the children threw themselves at me, Detweiler contented himself with greeting Sheila and Robbie. When the kids let go of me, I gave Sheila a hug and a kiss. I did the same for Robbie. Both grandparents looked a little ragged around the edges. Later I'd learn that Erik hadn't slept at all on the ride back to St. Louis. He'd been missing us too much.

Gracie cavorted and pranced and generally made it known that she was beyond thrilled to have her family reunited.

"Robbie? Sheila? Would you like to come in? Brawny made muffins," I said. Anya and Erik were loving up Detweiler.

Robbie waved away my suggestion. Sheila gave me a faint smile and shook her head. If they noticed I was wearing a silk scarf around my neck, they tactfully ignored my new accessory.

Sheila said, "I'm going to go to bed for a week. Those two are powerhouses. I'm worn out."

Anya and Erik ran into the house, looking for Brawny and Ty. Sheila and Robbie exchanged looks. I waited for the bad news. My heart thumped so loudly I could hear it in my head.

"I bet you are exhausted," I said. "I can't ever thank you enough."

"No," said Sheila in a husky voice. "Thank you. Thank you for trusting me. Us. Thank you for raising such wonderful children. We are so lucky. I hope the children will never forget all the good times we had."

Robbie added, "They are terrific. So are you. Thanks for...everything."

My husband draped his arm over my shoulders. "Everything went okay?"

Sheila swallowed hard and nodded. "It was hard, but I'm now on my 67th day of sobriety. I plan to lick this thing."

And I knew she would

***

KIKI'S STORY CONTINUES WITH...

Law, Fully, Dead: Book #15 in the Kiki Lowenstein Mystery Series

A SPECIAL GIFT FOR YOU

I am deeply appreciative of all my readers, and so I have a special gift for you. It's a full-length digital book called *Bad, Memory, Album.* Just go here and tell me where to send your digital book https://dl.bookfunnel.com/jwu6iipe1g.

All best always,

Joanna

For any book to succeed, reviews are essential. If you enjoyed this book please leave a review on Amazon. A sentence or two can make all the difference! Please leave a review of *Grand, Death, Auto* here – here http://www.Amazon.com/review/create-review?&asin=B07V49VY82

THE KIKI LOWENSTEIN MYSTERY SERIES
BY JOANNA CAMPBELL SLAN

Every scrapbook tells a story. Memories of friends, family and ... murder? You'll want to read the Kiki Lowenstein books in order: Kiki Lowenstein Mystery Series - https://amzn.to/38VkBjW

Looking for more enjoyable reads? Joanna has a series just for you!

Cara Mia Delgatto Mystery Series, a traditional cozy mystery series with witty heroines, and former flames reconnecting, set in Florida's beautiful Treasure Coast - https://amzn.to/30z9urN

The Jane Eyre Chronicles, Charlotte Bronte's Classic Strong-Willed Heroine Lives On. – **https://amzn.to/3r3Ybmd**

The Confidential Files of John H. Watson, a new series featuring Sherlock Holmes and John Watson. - https://amzn.to/3bDnSWo

About the author...
Joanna Campbell Slan

Joanna is a *New York Times* and a *USA Today* bestselling author who has written more than 40 books, including both fiction and non-fiction works. She was one of the early Chicken Soup for the Soul authors, and her stories appear in five of those *New York Times* bestselling books. Her first non-fiction book, *Using Stories and Humor: Grab Your Audience* (Simon & Schuster/Pearson), was endorsed by Toastmasters International, and lauded by Benjamin Netanyahu's speechwriter. She's the author of four mystery series. Her first novel—*Paper, Scissors, Death: Book #1 in the Kiki Lowenstein Mystery Series*—was shortlisted for the Agatha Award. Her first historical mystery—*Death of a School-girl: Book #1 in the Jane Eyre Chronicles*—won the Daphne du Maurier Award of Excellence. Her contemporary series set in Florida continues this year with *Ruff Justice Book #5 in the Cara Mia Delgatto Mystery Series*. Her fantasy thriller series starts with *Sherlock Holmes and the Giant Sumatran Rat*.

In addition to writing fiction, Joanna edits the Happy Homicides Anthologies and has begun the Dollhouse Décor & More series of "how to" books for dollhouse miniaturists.

Joanna independently published *I'm Too Blessed to be Depressed* back in 2004 when she was working as a motivational speaker. She sold more than 34,000 copies of that title. Since then she's gone on to independently publish a full-color book, *The Best of British Scrapbooking,* numerous digital books, and coloring books. Her book *Scrapbook Storytelling* sold 120,000 copies.

She's been an Amazon Bestselling Author too many times to count and has been included in the ranks of Amazon's Top 100 Mystery Authors.

A former talk show host and sought-after motivational speaker, Joanna has spoken to small and large (1000+) groups on four continents. *Sharing Ideas Magazines* named her "one of the top 25 speakers in the world."

When she isn't banging away at the keyboard, Joanna keeps busy walking her Havanese puppy Jax. An award-winning miniaturist, Joanna builds dollhouses, dolls, and furniture from scratch. She's also an accredited teacher of Zentangle®. Her husband, David, owns Steinway Piano Gallery-DC and five other Steinway piano showrooms.

Contact Joanna at JCSlan@JoannaSlan.com.

~

Follow her on social media by going here
https://www.linktr.ee/JCSlan

Made in the USA
Monee, IL
19 May 2021

69047195R00173